Prelude to Darkness

Michael R. Ault

© 2015 by Michael R. Ault

© 2013 by Black Rose Writing (www.blackrosewriting.com)

All rights reserved. No part of this book may be reproduced, stored in a retrieval system or transmitted in any form or by any means without the prior written permission of the publishers, except by a reviewer who may quote brief passages in a review to be printed in a newspaper, magazine or journal.

The final approval for this literary material is granted by the author.

Second Edition

All characters appearing in this work are fictitious. Any resemblance to real persons, living or dead, is purely coincidental.

Printed in the United States of America

I would like to dedicate this book to my grandchildren Mikie, Hannah, Lillian and Isiah Thomas Bojczuk. I hope the events in this book never happen in their lifetime. I would also like to thank my father, Thomas Ault, an author in his own right, for his valuable feedback and reviews of the work in progress. I would also like to thank my wonderful wife of 40 years, Susan, for all her support and love. My only regret is that my mother isn't alive to see this book published, god rest her soul. I would also like to thank Chuck Clark for his hard work on editing this manuscript.

Prelude to Darkness

July 4, 2014

One hundred miles off the Texas coast, Gulf of Mexico, 05:00 Zulu

The tug towing oil barges was making good speed at ten knots, heading for the oil refineries near Galveston. The Gulf was calm, reflecting the summer moon and stars. Everyone was asleep except the engineer and the captain, Manuel Ortega, who was in the pilothouse monitoring the various readouts and radar screens that showed the Gulf's empty surface for a fifty-mile radius around the tug and its five-barge train. The pilothouse was lit by the eerie red glow of nighttime lights, used to keep sailors' eyes from losing their night vision.

Captain Ortega took a long pull on his Belmont cigarette, its tip glowing balefully in the dim light. He was thinking about how he would spend the money from this oil run, plus the extra bribe money for turning his head when a barge—he assumed full of smuggled goods or drugs—was added to the train at the last minute. He hoped to retire and move his wife and two children to America with the money. He glanced at their picture under the glass of the chart table as he took the cigarette butt from his mouth and, dropping it, crushed it with the heel of his seaman's boot.

Glancing at his watch, he hoped the first mate would not be late relieving him at midnight. He looked forward to hitting the rack after a shot or two of chicha, to settle his mind for sleeping, and a cold helping of mid-rats from the galley. When he awoke, it would be time to prepare for tie-up at Houston's oil docks and offload the cargo. The captain assumed another tug would meet him before then to take the extra barge off the train.

In the engine room, Miguel Jesus Rodriquez, the engineer,

was nursing the twin Fairbanks-Morse Model 38 8-1/8 opposed-piston diesels, supposedly bought from an American salvage yard after being retired from submarines. All he really knew about the massive engines was that they were over thirty years old and well overdue for an overhaul. He wiped sweat from his face with a grimy rag; temperature in the engine room was over 110 degrees. One of the turbochargers was whining and he hoped it wouldn't come apart before they reached Houston. Unlike the captain, he had no relief and therefore catnapped when not nursing the engines. He took a long pull from a water bottle; wishing it was an ice-cold Cerveza Polar, but the captain had threatened to personally throw him overboard if he caught him drinking again. Cursing, he rushed to engine number two as he noticed diesel spurting from the fuel line to number-three injector. With a brass wrench he tightened the fitting, praying it wouldn't rupture and spray fuel over the hot engine, causing an instant, fatal fire.

In the bowels of the contraband barge a digital timer finished its countdown; well-oiled hatches opened along the barge's full length, revealing shadowed cylindrical forms that nestled in the modified interior. Hydraulic pumps whined loudly as the four cylinders slowly rose to an upright position, looking like midnight-black sewer pipes pointing at the night sky. Inside a control computer also secreted in the barge a program read the precise GPS location and loaded that data into computations whose results uploaded into the contents of the cylinders. As soon as the onboard computers registered that the transfer of information was complete, the moonlit night's peace was shattered as four missiles launched simultaneously.

It wasn't until the missiles actually launched, lighting the night with exhaust fire and filling the air with the cacophonous burning of solid-fuel motors, did the captain realize something had happened. Rushing out of the pilothouse, he watched four missiles streak high overhead, arching toward the invisible coast of Texas and America one hundred miles away. He barely was able to utter "Mio Dios!" before the first barge detonated with a fuel-air blast, eliminating the ocean-going tug, the remaining barges and nearly all other evidence of their existence, a burning oil slick the only reminder.

Peterson Air Force Base, Colorado Springs, Colorado, 05:01 Zulu

The NORAD computer barked warnings as the missiles cleared the ten-to-fifteen-mile altitude mark. "Holy shit," the duty officer yelled as he stilled the blaring alarms. "Mark those bogeys; where're they heading? Get the General on the horn, now!"

"We have four contacts — repeat, four contacts — apparently incoming missiles from the Gulf of Mexico," the radar operator reported.

"Do we have a trajectory?" The duty officer balanced the red-alert phone on his shoulder as he flipped though the SOP manual.

"One seems headed for the West Coast, ultimate target unknown, two are heading toward the Midwest and the other toward the East Coast, and all four continue to rise."

"Sir, we have four incoming missiles, this is not a drill," the duty officer reported over the secure line. "Yes sir, one headed for the West Coast, one for the East, and two for the Midwest, no final targets, all missiles continuing to rise."

"Engage THAAD, take them out!" the duty officer bellowed.

"Yes sir." The missile defense officer loaded coordinates from one computer to another and, after releasing the cover over the fire switch, engaged the anti-missile shield, modeled after that used by Israel and by the USA in Iraq. The room was silent as they watched the tracks of incoming missiles converge on their defense missiles. "Come on . . . come on!" someone muttered, encouraging the defense missiles. As the multiple plots of defense missiles were about to meet their targets, blossoms of light replaced the incoming bogies.

"Sir, altitude one hundred miles, we have detonation of all four missiles!" The radar operator yelled as the flared points of light faded from his screen.

The duty officer frowned as his phone squealed and went dead.

Northern outskirts of New York, New York, 11:00 Zulu

Frank Lowman awoke to silence.

The usual drone of the hotel room's air conditioner was missing; the room temperature was easily over eighty degrees. Throwing sweaty sheets off his body, Frank rolled over and looked at the clock. It was dead, not even blinking to show it had lost and regained power. The window, covered by heavy drapes that blocked out the parking lot lights, showed a bright line of light around them, indicating it was past sunrise.

"Damn it." Frank jumped out of bed. If it were past 07:00 he wouldn't make his flight. It appeared the hotel had not made his wakeup call.

Grabbing the bedside phone, Frank noted no dial tone; he slammed it angrily into the cradle. Stumbling over the cheap cocktail table in front of the sofa, he opened the curtains. The sky was clear blue, other than at the horizon where the sun had begun to rise. Usually on a Friday the hotel's parking lot would have been partially empty. Frank could see some cars had their trunks open, but no one near. The lot was as full as it had been the night before when he closed the drapes.

With the light from the window, Frank was able to get into the bathroom and take a quick shower. The water was cold so he showered enough to soap up, rinse, and wash his hair.

Shivering even in the eighty-degree temperature, he dried off, shaved, dressed and packed away his toiletry. Making a final check of the room, he grabbed his suitcase and laptop bag and headed for the main desk, glad his room was on the ground floor and not up on fourteen.

As soon as he opened his door he heard angry voices echoing down the hall. Coming around the corner into the lobby, Frank saw irate guests surrounding the desk.

"Somebody screwed with my car!" a red-faced man yelled. "It won't start! I need to get to the airport!"

"Your shitty power killed my iBook!" yelled a petite blond.

The young desk clerk was overwhelmed. "Please, please, the manager is on his way. I'm sure there's an explanation; please, calm down."

Looking out the large plate-glass windows, Frank saw that stoplights at the major intersection in front of the hotel were out, and no lights were visible at any of the nearby buildings. Frank pulled out his cell phone—its screen was blank. He assumed the charge had depleted; it had happened before.

"Has anyone got a working cell phone?" asked the petite blond, looking at a state-of-the-art cell phone in her French-nail–manicured hand.

"Wait a minute," said a man nearby, fishing his out of his briefcase. "Nope, looks like mine is out too."

"So is mine."

"And mine!"

Frank peered at his watch—it had frozen at 12:03 in the morning. "Anyone got the time?"

Everyone's watch was either blank or stopped at nearly the same time, 12:03 a.m. Finally, a retired gentleman in a Navy Veteran ball cap said, "It's 7:05." His watch was a self-winding Timex.

A nagging thought bloomed in Frank's mind. Before he voiced it, he had to check something out. He exited the lobby and walked to the parking garage stairs. Setting his suitcase at the top, he went down two levels to his car. The night before, he'd been pissed he'd had to park down two levels; now he wasn't so sure that was a bad thing. Reaching the rental car, he pulled out the remote and pushed open. Nothing happened. Examining the fob, he pressed a small button and a hard key ejected like a switchblade knife, with which he opened the door. Frank gave thanks that the dome light came on. Sitting in the driver's seat, Frank inserted the key and prayed . . . the engine turned over and then started. He turned off the engine and thanked God.

In the lobby, things appeared to be getting rough. The manager obviously wasn't going to show up anytime soon and the clerk was looking intimidated.

"Whose car isn't working?" Franked yelled over the sound of angry voices. He had to yell twice to get their attention.

"Mine."

"Me too."

"Piece of shit won't start!"

"OK, where are you parked?" Frank asked over the rising clamor.

They looked askance at him, but answered. All were on the top deck or second level; none were from the third level where Frank had parked.

"Anyone parked on the third level?" A couple of hands went up in back. "Could you please check your cars? See if they start."

Looking oddly at Frank, only one, a middle-aged woman, would go. She was back soon. "The remote won't work but I could start it with the key."

"OK everyone, listen up." Frank called out. It took a while for people to quiet. "I think we're in the middle of an EMP event."

Most looked puzzled; a couple looked like the light dawned as soon as he said EMP.

"What the hell is that?"

"Electromagnetic pulse. It could be deliberate, as in a nuke, or natural, like a solar flare. From the range of things affected, I would say a nuke." It was dead quiet. Finally the blonde said, "Oh! My! God! Are we going to die?"

"I don't think so. To get an EMP from a nuke it has to explode at least thirty miles in the air."

She looked relieved but skeptical.

Roswell, Georgia, 13:00 Zulu

Katie Lowman stretched like a cat waking from a nap. Her brunette hair was tousled from sleep and she missed Frank telling her how sexy she looked when she woke. Dressed in a short, pale-blue baby-doll nightgown over silk pajama bottoms, she eased out of bed and into the bath. She flipped on the lights only to be greeted with no such thing—no flicker, nothing. With a frown, she eyed the switch and noted that the switch's on and off telltales weren't lit. Glancing at the bed, she noticed the clock not only wasn't displaying the time, it wasn't even blinking.

Since the windows were unshaded—faux stained glass for privacy—she had plenty of light, and turned on the water in the sink to brush her teeth. The initial surge slowed and then stopped. "Glad I didn't try a shower," she said aloud, and brushed her teeth without rinsing. She brushed her hair, applied makeup, put on clean undergarments, then jeans and a tee shirt. Passing the three-drawer dresser, she grabbed her iPhone and tapped its screen; it didn't respond. Frowning, she returned to the bathroom and the walk-through closet wrapping the double sinks. She opened an emergency duffel bag, unbundled the shield blanket protecting the interior, and extracted an emergency radio and batteries. She smiled to herself, remembering that the blanket had been designed to protect a mother's unborn baby from stray EMF radiation.

A few seconds cranking on the built-in generator restored charge to the batteries and the emergency radio crackled to life. With a prayer of thanks, Katie ran the dials on the FM and AM bands—nothing but static. On one of the short-wave bands, she heard someone frantically trying to reach anyone. Turning off the radio, she carried it into the kitchen.

None of the utilities or the house phone, which was VOIP on a major Internet provider, was working. The phone didn't click, or indicate charge condition of the hand unit's battery. Charge indicators were dysfunctional on anything with rechargeable batteries. Katie noticed in the air an ozone tang and a shorted-insulation smell. Turning on the front burner, she heard the gas hiss, but not the piezo-electric click-click-click. She turned off the burner and pulled out a book of matches. Striking one, she held flame to burner and got it going. From the oven cupboard she took a European-style coffee maker, loaded it with bottled water and fresh grounds, and set it on the burner.

She opened the double-door refrigerator and grabbed eggs, bacon, peppers, mushrooms and a jar of chopped garlic. After chopping peppers and mushrooms, she lit a second burner, PAM-ed a fry pan, and sautéed vegetables. She poured dark, strong coffee from the aluminum pot into a cup and then slid veggies onto a plate. She whipped two eggs into a smooth yellow, poured the liquid into the now-empty fry pan and swirled it, coating the bottom with egg. When it was almost done, she added the veggies and folded the egg onto itself to make an omelet.

She restored the unused veggies and eggs to the fridge, removing a yogurt as she closed the door. She knew to keep the doors shut to maintain coolness until power came back—if it came back, a little voice said. She carried her breakfast to the back deck, where the sun was barely up and a light breeze kissed her skin. After last night's storm the sky was clear and blue. Thunder, lightning and the patter on the roof of a steady downpour had soothed her asleep. In cool morning light she ate, thankful that the sun hadn't yet raised the humidity.

Still no power. She placed her dishes in the sink and, not thinking, tried to run a little water and then immediately shut the tap. She went downstairs and took the WaterBOB bladder out of its box and rolled it into the downstairs tub. Holding the BOB's large mouth under the faucet, she filled the bladder with as much cold water the pipes would give, then closed its seal — a couple of gallons. In the storage room she grabbed the flashlight from its holder near the door and found the scenario guide that she and Frank had put together over four years of preparation and gathering emergency and disaster supplies. Turning off the flashlight, she returned it to its place and took the heavy three-ring binder upstairs.

"Oh crap, it must be an EMP . . . ," she said, matching symptoms to conditions she'd discovered so far, when her reading was interrupted by an agitated knocking at the front door. Closing the binder, she ran to the door and peered through the peephole to see her ditzy neighbor and good friend Marlene. Turning the deadlock and unfastening the chain, she opened the solid-core metal door to find Marlene in a rare state.

Usually Marlene was to the nines before she left the house, primping at least two hours before the mirror, doing hair and makeup. The Marlene in front of her had no makeup, unbrushed hair and clothes obviously yanked from the closet on a first-come, first-serve basis.

Marlene rushed in, terrified that someone else would see her, and, with her Irish brogue, asked, "Kaitie, is your power oot?"

Closing the door to preserve cool air, Katie studied her neighbor, wondering how much truth to tell. "Not a watt, Marlene."

"Shet. How'm I going to get ready today?" Marlene's accent made the swear word sound proper.

"Plenty of light in my bathroom. No hot water though."

Marlene followed Katie into the breakfast nook. "Is that food I smell?" Marlene had an all-electric kitchen.

"Yep. You want an omelet?"

"If you wouldn't mind, you are such a dear."

As Katie fixed another omelet and more coffee, Marlene glanced in the binder Katie left on the table. "What's this book?" Marlene asked as Katie served the omelet, yogurt and a cup of coffee.

"Oh, just something Frank and I put together," Katie breezed.

"This isn't just a power outage, is it?" Marlene had found the page on EMP attacks.

Katie sipped from her now cold coffee. "No, I don't believe it is, Marlene. "Look at these." Katie passed the cell phone and house phone receiver to Marlene. "Try them."

"Hmmm," said Marlene after unsuccessfully trying the phones. "Mine don't work either. Nothing electrical works at all."

"Flashlights and simple things work. Nothing more complex than that, from what I've seen."

"When I came out through our garage I tried the car. It wouldn't even turn over," said Marlene around mouthfuls of omelet.

"I have a working radio. No stations on the air, either." Katie watched Marlene for signs of panic.

"Oh, well, as a child in Éire I lived on a farm. Power was dicey and we did most things the old ways." Marlene put down her fork. "This is serious, isn't it?"

Marlene rarely talked about her childhood. With the admission of farm experience, Katie's opinion of her friend's abilities went up a notch. "Yes Marlene, I think we've been attacked with what is called an EMP bomb or bombs." Katie gestured to the binder. "Frank and I've been assembling various disaster scenarios and making plans."

Marlene read the first page of the section describing EMP effects and her expression grew more serious than Katie had ever seen. "Earl is visiting his Da."

Katie's heart fell to her feet. Earl was English and his "Da" lived in the London outskirts. Marlene had tears in her eyes. "It's not likely he'll be comin' home Friday."

"I don't know, Marlene. If they — whoever they are — only attacked the USA, then the rest of the world may not be affected. But I doubt any flights will be coming in, other than military and aid, for a long time." She looked closely at her friend. "Listen, let's go over to your house, we'll get some of your stuff and you can move in here." Katie paused. "You see, Frank is in New York. I doubt he'll be getting home anytime soon, either." In her mind she was checking her inventory of bottled water and other necessities, wondering how they'd get out of town if they had to.

Northern outskirts of New York, New York, 14:00 Zulu

"Alright everybody, find a seat," Frank yelled over the crowd milling nervously in the hotel's lobby. It took a while, but eventually everyone who could, did, and looked at Frank, who wondered how the hell he'd been elected leader.

"Here's what we know: no electronics are working, including car ignitions and computers. This indicates an EMP has occurred."

A nervous elderly lady, who had barely made it down from the twelfth floor, raised her hand; Frank acknowledged her. "Young man, what is an EMP?" She was worried and curious.

Frank pondered the other, similar faces he was seeing, sighed, and explained. "When a nuclear weapon—" There was a collective inhale. He started over. "When a nuclear weapon is detonated thirty to one hundred miles above the ground, it causes a massive electromagnetic pulse when its radiation interacts with the earth's magnetic field. This pulse generates eddy currents in anything that conducts electricity. These eddy currents can harm the small chips used in electronics. They short out. This appears to be what has happened."

"Could it've been an accident?" asked a surly young man in gym-suit bottoms and an NYU sweatshirt.

"Doubtful. I think we've been deliberately attacked." Frank

paused to let this sink in. "Who's parked on the third level down in the garage?"

Six people raised their hands.

"OK. So far, two of us" — Frank caught the eye of the woman who'd checked her car earlier — "have working vehicles. Let's see how many we have." Those who hadn't yet checked their cars shuffled out. Frank used the time to get a glass of lemonade from the lobby cooler, now at room temperature. Soon, four people returned; two were angry.

"What happened? Where're the other two?"

"Took their cars and ran."

"Predictable" was all Frank said, wondering at some peoples' mindset. "So we have six working cars."

Frank grabbed a pad of paper and a pen from the desk clerk fidgeting beside him. "Everyone write down your town. We'll group together folks who live near each other."

It took several minutes to sort things out. Several were from upstate New York, down for a teacher's convention; a few were from Tennessee and Georgia; one poor fellow was from Washington State. The rest were scattered along the routes of the terminal destinations.

"Here's what I propose. There won't be any public transportation if this is indeed an EMP. If we want to get home we'll have to do it ourselves, or hunker down here at the hotel and wait for the authorities. Show of hands — who wants to wait it out?" Five people from the northeast raised their hands. "Good, not a problem. Do any of you have weapons?"

"This is New York," a voice in the back said. "They don't trust citizens with weapons." General snickering greeted the comment.

"I know, I had to leave mine at home." Frank turned to the clerk. "Is there an actual kitchen here?"

"A small one, nothing fancy," the clerk said. "All electric save for the portable omelet stove, which uses propane, but we're low on propane tanks."

"OK. For those who are staying, you'll need supplies right away. These snacks won't last long." Frank looked to the clerk for confirmation.

"They deliver once a week, and today was it. We've a day's worth for normal use; it won't last beyond today with everyone using it."

"I suggest that in all the unused ground-floor rooms, we fill the tubs with water and cover them. We need to do it now so we lose as little as possible to leaks." The clerk took volunteers and was soon back, looking worried.

"We got only about two to three tub's worth before we lost pressure."

"So our priorities are food and water, stuff that doesn't need cooking, or camping stoves and food that does, propane for the omelet stove—these are priority for you who are staying." Frank turned to the clerk. "Where's the nearest store?"

"Call me Buddy," the clerk said. "A map behind the counter shows the major stores." He held one up. "Nearest are a block or two away."

"OK, unless I missed the mark on the EMP, credit cards are useless. We need to pool our cash for supplies, both for those who'll be leaving, and those who are staying. Cash won't be worth much in a few days so don't hoard. Here—" Frank reached into his wallet, took out two hundred dollars of traveling money and tossed it into a decorative bowl liberated from a display on the fireplace hearth. "I put in two hundred. Divvy in as much as you can. Once store owners realize what's happening, prices'll sky-rocket."

When the bowl returned, it held nearly a thousand dollars in loose bills and change. Frank doubted the change would do much good, but accepted it in the spirit given. Buddy added three hundred or so from the till.

"We have two basic groups: those leaving and those staying. We need shopping teams for each. People who are staying, you know what's needed. Road people need simple food, like beef jerky, Clif Bars, bottled water and sports drinks. Divide up and head out. My fellow road people—who has a small backpack?" About a third of those planning to leave raised their hands. "Be on the lookout for small backpacks; we need eight more." Frank took out one hundred dollars and split the remainder between the two teams. "Spend as little as possible, but get what's needed."

"Eh . . . Frank?" One of the ladies in the hotel group touched his sleeve.

"Yes, ma'am?"

"How many days should we plan on waiting here?"

"Well, I don't know if any infrastructure is still working. It'll take a minimum of three days to get relief organized. If there isn't any support by then, I'd leave for home, because after that all hell is going to break loose."

ROSWELL, GEORGIA, 16:00 ZULU

"We have to get everything from your house that you'll need, here." Katie handed Marlene a flashlight. "Are you ready to go?"

"Well, now that I look half decent, I guess so!" Marlene smiled. She brushed her red hair in the multi-colored light from the faux stained glass windows that pictured mermaids, sea turtles and dolphins.

Grabbing a second flashlight, Katie followed Marlene out of the bathroom and through the breakfast nook to the front door. Marlene waited as Katie locked the door behind them.

"Afraid of the neighbors?" Marlene teased.

"As the old Arabic saying goes: 'At the narrow passage there is no brother and no friend'," Katie answered. Marlene stared as Katie scampered down the stairs from the wooden porch to the landing. She hurried to keep up.

"You can't really believe—" Marlene started.

"Maybe not now, but how about in a day or two, when what little food people have starts to rot and the pantries and stores are empty?"

"Surely the government will have fixed this by then," Marlene gestured at the intact power lines. Katie said, "Marlene, the main substations contain huge transformers that are no longer manufactured in the USA. EMP destroys them. The lead time to get them from China is eighteen months, assuming China isn't the one responsible." She marched across the front lawn toward Marlene's. "Not to mention what it does to computer networks and transmission cables."

"Oh my God," Marlene put her hand to her mouth. "Eighteen months! How will we survive?" She was clearly horrified.

"Let's hope it's not that long, but it is best to be prepared."

They walked the rest of the way in silence, each lost in thought. Reaching Marlene's driveway, they found her side door standing open.

"Kaitie, I am sure I closed that door." Marlene squeezed Katie's arm hard.

"Marlene, let go. I have to get something," Katie said calmly.

Marlene did so reluctantly. Katie leaned, lifted the left leg of her jeans and pulled her Smith & Wesson Bodyguard .38 Special from her ankle holster and said, trying to sound calmer than she felt, "Wait here while I check this out."

"Holy shet, Kaitie, you had that the whole time and didn't tell." With wide emerald green eyes, Marlene studied Katie, who said dryly, "That is the concept of 'concealed carry,' Marlene."

"Maybe we should call the police." Marlene realized how silly that sounded as soon as she said it. "Shet, never mind."

Katie smiled at her friend. Looking back at the door she said, "If you hear shots, run." With that she entered the dark doorway.

"I am armed! Show yourself!" Katie called, holding the flashlight in her left hand over her head and the .38 slightly forward in her right. The revolver trembled slightly.

"Please, don't shoot! It's me, David," a voice cried. "Is

Mom OK?" Marlene's oldest son entered the beam from the 8-LED flashlight. Katie lowered the gun and moved the light to the floor so as not to blind David any more than she already had. "Sorry, David. We saw the door standing open and . . ."

"I completely understand. Is Mom OK?"

"Davie, is that you? Oh Davie!" Marlene fiercely hugged her son.

"Jeesh, Mom. It's just a power outage, not the end of the world. John brought me over on his Indian."

"On what?" Marlene was confused.

"An Indian motorcycle, 1952. It was the only thing that would run."

"Lucky," Katie commented. "David, I believe an EMP has occurred."

"An EMP?"

"An electromagnetic pulse from a high-altitude nuclear burst. Fries all electronics in its line of sight. From over a hundred miles up would include most of the USA."

"Crap, it fits. Nothing would work this morning. Oh my God, Father—he's in England!"

"David, let's get your mother's stuff together and any supplies we can, she's coming to stay with me."

"Got another room? My condo's all electric, and on the fifteenth floor of a twenty-story building. Not very hospitable."

"Sure. Spare room in the basement and a futon in Frank's office. Frank's in New York; be good to have a man around." Katie's voice cracked only a little.

"Marlene, do you still have that 9mm?"

"Of course. Follow me." Marlene led them to the master closet, left side top shelf, under some old gardening magazines, where a black plastic case held the weapon. David, at six feet the tallest of the trio, retrieved it.

All three sat on the bed as Marlene opened the case and removed the Glock 19 9x19mm pistol, which was cable-locked in the breach open position. She opened the nightstand drawer, removed a small key, placed it into the breach lock, removed it and, after inserting the empty magazine, handed it to Katie.

Katie snorted as she stifled a laugh, and then laughed out loud.

"And just what's so funny?" asked Marlene indignantly.

"I just had an image of someone breaking in and you and Earl in your night clothes getting the pistol, unlocking and loading it." She blushed slightly as she remembered her friend frequently slept in the nude. "By the time you finished, the house would be empty! You do have ammunition?"

"Of course, somewhere . . ." This admission by Marlene brought more laughter from Katie and a few stifled ones from David as well.

"I'm sorry Marlene, this is just so British . . ." Katie laughed a bit more as Marlene got more and more flustered searching for ammo, finally finding a box of 9mm shells in the top drawer of Earl's dresser.

Taking the box of ammo, Katie loaded the pistol's magazine—click, click, click—and then slammed it into the pistol butt. Racking the slide, she loaded a round and, after checking the loaded-chamber indicator, laid the pistol carefully on the bed. She removed the Kydex belt holster from the plastic case, said, "David, put this on your belt," and handed it to him. He did as instructed. "You have fired it, haven't you?"

"Oh, Dad and I went out a couple of times when they first got it." He smiled weakly.

"OK, here." She handed him the pistol, grip first.

David took the gun and, keeping his finger off the trigger, carefully pulled the slide back, checking its load status even though he had just seen her load it.

"Good. Looks like Earl trained you right." Katie smiled and he blushed.

The three made short work of Marlene's clothes and what little pantry goods she had—about three days' worth of various foods. Luckily it was market day and the refrigerator, except for Earl's stout, was basically empty.

Katie went into the garage to see what else they might need. Next to Marlene's gleaming Lexus loomed the large form of a tarp-covered vehicle.

"Marlene," Katie called to her friend, "Could you come out here?"

"Yes, dear?"

"What is that vehicle under the tarp?"

"Oh that," she said dismissively, "That's Earl's latest folly." Marlene remembered the fiasco with the Sunbeam convertible that Earl had spent several months trying to restore. Even with a replacement wiring harness he had never gotten the entire vehicle to function at the same time.

"Well, what is it?"

"He bought a classic Land Rover. Had to drive it off the boat from South Africa himself when it arrived in New York. About two hundred miles toward home, the dashboard caught fire. Mice chewed the insulation off the wires."

"Marlene, what year is it?"

"2015 of course. What a question."

Exasperated with Marlene's ditziness, Katie said, "No, the Land Rover, Marlene, the Land Rover." She strode to it and pulled away the tarp.

"1958 or so. What a wreck."

"Marlene, this wreck may just save our lives. Does it run?"

David, who had joined them, climbed in the driver's side— on the right— switched on the heaters for the diesel cylinders, and smiled as the heater indicator light came on. "Let's find out."

PETERSON AIR FORCE BASE, COLORADO SPRINGS, COLORADO, 15:00 ZULU

Several hours' work with Darpanet protocols restored communications. Lieutenant Colonel Bryant was finally able to reach his commanding officer, General Smith.

"No sir, we can't be sure where the missiles came from.

They just appeared, about a hundred miles out in the Gulf, off Texas."

"Contact the Coast Guard and Navy; see if they were tracking any ships out there." General Smith was nearly screaming. The joint chiefs were breathing down his neck, and the president, at Alert One in Air Force One, circling at 30,000 feet above an undisclosed location, was on theirs.

An airman dressed in fatigues handed Smith a sheet of computer printout. The old TTY units were about the only things operational and communicating with outside systems.

"General, according to the Navy, the only thing in that area was an oil barge train from Venezuela."

"Damn Chavez! Him and his Iranian buddies are due for a glassing!"

President Hugo Chavez of Venezuela had been dealing with Iran for their Shahab-3 medium-range ballistic missiles. Combined with nuclear warheads from North Korea, another of Iran's and Venezuela's allies, this might be the source for the unprovoked attack.

"But the Shahab-3 has a maximum range of only 2,000 kilometers, sir."

"Get the Navy checking whatever the hell they can check. Any chance of communicating with the high-altitude spy birds?"

"We don't know, sir. Combined gamma pulses of this magnitude probably fried everything on this side of the planet. We're waiting for the non-geostationary birds to get into position. We hope we can reach them."

"Shit, I hate being blind. Contact me soon as you know anything."

"Yes sir." The colonel was talking to a dead line.

Northern outskirts of New York, New York, 19:00 Zulu

Frank was getting desperate. In the two stores he'd been to so far, neither was willing to part with anything worthwhile as a weapon. He'd hoped that for a hundred-dollar cash bribe, a clerk would part with a hidden weapon, but so far, no go. He cursed inwardly that whoever had caused the EMP had done it when he was in New York, one of the most gun-unfriendly states in the union. Why couldn't they have waited until next week, when he'd be in Denver with his personal carry weapon, a Springfield 9mm XDSC with two extra sixteen-round magazines? As things stood, he had only his Zaplight, which also contained a million-volt Taser. He only used it as a flashlight, and hoped he never got close enough to violence to need it, or the three-inch folding knife he carried in his checked-baggage emergency kit.

At his fourth stop—a rundown electronics store whose owner, a man of Indian descent, was tossing fused laptops into a waste bin—he struck pay dirt.

"Excuse me, sir?" Frank said to get the man's attention.

"Yes? Nothing works, all is gone." The man waved his hands in a shooing motion. "My store is closed, go away, please!"

"I'm not interested in electronics." Frank held up the money. "If your store is closing, would you like to sell your protection?"

"Protection? Do I look like I have protection?"

"Come on, this is New York. Only two types of people have guns besides police: criminals and shop owners." Frank swished the money back and forth.

"Why should I sell it to you?" Frank gave a silent thanks; it was further than he'd gotten with any other shopkeeper.

"I'm traveling to Georgia, with no idea what I'll find on the way."

"How much?"

"I have a hundred dollars cash, and a Visa I can let you take an imprint for whatever extra is needed." Frank could see the wheels turning in the man's head as he considered the offer. He hoped the man didn't understand the depth of shit the USA had just fallen into.

"OK. I have pistol and shotgun. Give me two thousand for both."

"Fifteen hundred," countered Frank, knowing it was expected.

"Eighteen hundred."

"Seventeen hundred."

"OK. Seventeen hundred. But no cash; you keep that. I'll take the card scan, but two cards or no deal."

Frank breathed a sigh of relief. "Done." He pulled out his Visa and the company American Express card. After the shopkeeper imprinted both cards and had Frank sign the slips, he pulled out a .357 Magnum Ruger Blackhawk with a six-inch barrel and a Saiga 12-gauge pistol grip shotgun with folding stock and detachable twelve-round magazine. He also handed over a holster, a fifty-round box of .38 Specials and two six-round boxes of 12-gauge double-ought buckshot. With the Saiga's stock folded, it all fit into a duffle bag Frank had snagged from a deserted luggage store. Frank felt a momentary pang of guilt, knowing there was zero chance credit cards would be functional within the next two years at a minimum, if then. Especially cards from before the EMP event.

At a nearby camera store he scored a snubnose .38 and a partial box of ammo. And at a deserted, looted restaurant he found in a hidden compartment under the register a Colt .45 M1911 Automatic with an extra magazine. With the heavy bag slung over his shoulder, he made his way back to the hotel, hoping the others would appreciate his efforts. Amazingly, he still had the hundred dollars cash.

Frank was last to return. Heads turned as he entered.

"Frank, where you been?" Buddy came over.

"Getting some supplies." With a weighty thunk, Frank put the bag on the reception counter. He had everyone's attention.

"I need from each car one person who has firearms experience."

Frank watched as the people eyed each other, some shy, others guilty, as if having firearms experience was a sin. At last, including himself, several people admitted experience with weapons. Frank chose a former Marine, a retired policeman and a housewife who was an NRA-certified marksman. Keeping the shotgun for himself, he divvied out the other weapons, letting each choose what was comfortable. The former Marine took the M1911, the retired cop the .357, and the housewife the .38. Frank split the .38 ammo between the retired cop and the housewife because the .357 Magnum could also shoot .38 Special ammo as well as the .38 snubnose.

"Hopefully we won't need these, and with luck the EMP destroyed all credit card records and they won't ever be cashing in those chits I signed." Several folks laughed nervously. "Keep them concealed unless you need them."

"I don't think those are really needed," NYU-Jersey said.

"Not today, not tomorrow—but believe me, once the unsavory realize that police have no communications and rules are out the window, we'll need 'em."

"I won't travel with someone who has a gun," NYU said smugly.

"Fine, stay here. Frees a place in my car. Any takers?" Frank said harshly.

"I'll take it." One of the teachers from the convention group raised her hand. "Hell, I wish you had a gun for me."

"Wait a minute, I—" NYU stammered.

"Sorry, bud. But I wouldn't want to compromise your principles." Frank smiled. "I suggest we get maps and plot routes avoiding main highways."

"Who gave you the right to tell me I can't go?" NYU got into Frank's face. "Do you know who I am? Who my father is? I am Willie Wright, son of Senator Wright from the Great State of Alabama!"

"Back. Off." Frank tightly controlled his voice.

"Or what? You'll shoot me with your gun?" Willie Wright sneered. He hadn't seen Frank slide the Zap from his fanny pack.

Z-A-A-AA-P! The Taser cracked as it discharged. For a moment, people thought Frank had shot the senator's son, especially when he fell to the floor, twitching and crying.

Frank held up the Zap. "Don't leave home without it! Have to say I'm glad the EMP didn't fry it." A few actually clapped. Frank guessed that NYU had been throwing his weight around.

"OK, let's get down to some route planning."

ROSWELL, GEORGIA, 19:30 ZULU

With a cough of black smoke, the diesel rattled to life. David smiled. "Looks like it still runs." He reached through the open window and patted the Rover's hood. "Good girl!"

"Great, but the wiring?" Katie asked, remembering Marlene's story.

"Dad and I replaced the bad sections last weekend before he flew to England." David expression darkened. "We had planned to check out the rest of it this weekend."

"Hey, that's great!" Katie exclaimed, trying to lighten the heavy mood. "Do you think it can make an eighty-mile trip?"

"Well, it has over 200,000 kilometers on the odometer, but it can probably make it that far." David smiled again.

"OK, turn it off." Katie waved away the diesel exhaust in the closed garage.

"We can just load our stuff into the Rover and drive down to your place, Kaitie," Marlene said after the diesel engine shut down.

"No, I think we should keep her right here until we need her, don't want anyone to get any ideas."

"Do you really think it'll be that bad?" Marlene had a quizzical look.

"I don't know Marlene. I hope not, but let's be safe."

With that they finished packing Marlene's stuff and the useful kitchen items. Loading their spoils onto a yard wagon they walked the two blocks back to Katie's, waving at neighbors who stood outside now hot houses getting hotter as July sun beat down from a clear North Georgia sky. In spite of the heat, Katie felt more optimism than she had since she realized how screwed the country really was.

Back at Katie's, Marlene and David stashed their things in the spare rooms while Katie tried to plan their next moves. She knew they had to escape the Atlanta area before food in the stores ran out—three to four days at most. In their planning sessions Frank had been adamant that if she didn't hear from him in three days she was to get to their BOL—bug-out location—and wait for him there. She glanced at the freezer and knew they needed to process the food stored there. With the food she and Frank had stored in the downstairs office closet, they didn't need it, but she refused to waste anything.

After taking the various cuts of meat out to thaw, she started planning what to do with them. Still planning, she began packing Marlene's meager items into the pantry.

Downstairs, David put his bag next to the office desk. Moving some files and a camera bag off the futon, he unfolded and tested it, finding it hard, but acceptable. Besides, he couldn't beat the price. Noticing bi-fold doors to the closet, he opened the one not blocked by the futon and peered inside. The basement windows provided ample light to see floor-to-ceiling shelves stocked with both canned and dried foods, and supplies.

David whistled. "Wow, someone's been planning for apocalypse! Who knew that it was Frank and Katie?"

"David, you finished?" Marlene entered and saw the now open storage closet—her gape-mouthed, wide-eyed expression was almost comical.

"You'll catch flies like that, Marlene." Katie needled, startling both of them as she came up from behind. "Come on, there's work to do."

They followed her upstairs. As they sat around the casual table in the breakfast nook, Katie opened a bottle of water and poured three glasses. After taking a drink she set down her glass.

"OK, we need to process as much of the fresh food as we can."

"Heavens why? Look downstairs!" Marlene exclaimed.

"No reason to be wasteful. We have no idea how long we may need to rely on what we have."

"Of course, silly me. What can we do to help?"

"David, in the garage are a couple bags of charcoal, Could you get one of the twenty-five-pound bags and bring it up to the deck?" Katie took another drink. "Marlene, you and I need to cut the beef into strips to make jerky."

David finished his water and went to the garage for charcoal. Marlene and Katie sorted the cuts of meat for slicing. Katie stopped long enough to gather a couple of long pans into which she poured soy sauce and dry red wine, and added garlic salt and cracked pepper. As they cut the near-frozen beef into strips, they soaked the trimmed meat in the marinade.

"Katie, what's with the old Chevy Blazer?" David asked as he hefted the twenty-five-pound sack of charcoal toward the deck.

"Well, Frank was fixing it up. The engine is at the garage for a rebuild." Katie looked wistful. "Wish he was here." She wiped away a tear. "Well, come on, let's get moving."

As the day progressed the temperature in the house increased to over eighty degrees. Marlene and Katie opened the windows but the still, humid air gave no relief. The temperature continued to climb. Finally, after wiping sweat from her eyes for the third time in ten minutes, Katie had had enough.

"Enough! Geesh, it's hot." She paused to wipe away the

sweat with a dish towel. "Let's let this stuff marinate and go down to the pool." She looked up from the pans of cut beef to see chicken and pork sitting in pools of condensation on the counter. "Crap, I'll have to do something with those first."

Turning on the oven, she carefully lit it with a long fireplace match, causing a loud woosh of flame. Unwrapping two chickens and several pork chops, she placed them in pans, liberally seasoning them, slid them into the oven and closed the door. She set the oven on 275 degrees to slow cook the meat.

"Come on, I have a suit that should fit you, Marlene. David, Frank has some old trunks in the closet. Let's beat this heat!"

As they walked the three short blocks to the community pool, they could hear children yelling and adults talking. In a moment of panic, Katie searched the towel bag for the gate pass before she remembered it probably would never be needed again. The pool was packed with other neighborhood residents trying to escape the heat. They hadn't been chilling more than twenty minutes before someone blocked the sun.

"Katie! Marlene! Great to see you! How about this power outage?"

It was Hank Petrod, the homeowner's association president, his potbelly pushing his double-X tee shirt over his red Speedo.

"Hi, Hank." Katie had to keep from laughing every time she saw Hank in the ridiculous red Speedo. She wondered if he really thought he looked good.

"It's good you're here. We're about to have a meeting."

Katie and Marlene groaned; meetings were usually long and boring.

"What about?" Marlene asked.

"Sharing of resources. Many feel that we need to pull together as a neighborhood to get through this. Some people have a lot more than others. It's only fair that everyone shares."

Katie, Marlene, and David exchanged looks.

"I only have enough for a couple of days," Katie said. "In fact, Marlene, David and I are already sharing at my place."

Katie hoped Marlene and David wouldn't reveal Frank and her preparations.

"Kaitie's right, Hank, we only have enough for a couple o' days," Marlene chimed in, exchanging a wink with Katie. David kept mum.

"With all those boxes ya'll get? Don't think we haven't noticed." Hank smiled, but it didn't reach his eyes as he looked at Katie.

"You know Frank and his hobbies—first it was photography, then scuba, then, heaven forbid, hunting!" Katie gave a credible act as a wife nearing the edge. "Now, of all things, it's bird watching!"

Mollified, Hank smiled and went to greet another set of sweaty residents entering the open gate.

"He must be a Democrat," Katie said under her breath as they joined Katie's across-the-street neighbors, a young Jewish couple, under the remaining empty umbrella. After a few seconds of small talk, all three took off their covers and got in the pool.

The water was tepid, but cooler than the hot, humid, still air. They were getting comfortable when Hank started yelling for everyone to listen up.

"Everyone, listen. We don't know what has happened to power, phones and other electrical items. Heck, probably a solar flare." Everyone but Katie's group nodded as if this were the most likely possibility.

"Could it be?" Marlene asked Katie under her breath, not wanting to be overheard.

"Nope. A solar flare wouldn't hit small electronics, just large stuff like transmission line breakers."

"Marlene, Katie, do you have some input on this?" Hank made a point of singling them out.

"We were joost saying you're probably right, Hank, go on, please!" Marlene called out.

"I sent my son John up to the store; he says the shelves are nearly empty already." That got things buzzing. Hank shushed everyone.

"Since we don't know how long this emergency will last, the other HOA members and I decided we need to pull together and share resources."

Katie studied the other association officers grouped around Hank. They looked distinctly uncomfortable. "In a pig's eye," she said under her breath. Marlene giggled. Hank gave them a stern face and then went on.

"Starting tomorrow we will be coming around to inventory what everyone has, and then we will decide how it should be divided."

"Bullshit," Katie said, loud enough for others to hear.

"Katie, you have something to say?" Darkness filled Hank's expression.

"I said bullshit. You come into my house uninvited you'll leave in a body bag." She crossed her arms and stared back into his beady eyes.

"Katie, surely you don't mean that," Hank stared with hate in his eyes in spite of his smile.

"Try me. I'll help as I can, but you or your myrmidons set foot in my house, you'll get the business end of a shotgun at worst, a Taser at best." She turned her back and climbed out of the pool. "Come on Marlene, I think we've spoilt the meeting." She helped her friend out and, grabbing the towel bag, pushed through the crowd, followed closely by Marlene and David. Several other couples and families left as well.

"David, go and check out the Rover, make sure it has fuel for at least a hundred miles in case we have to use detours, and that everything vital works." She paused to make sure no one was nearby. "After dark, we'll move it to my garage and pack."

"It should be fine. Dad and I filled it before we put it in the garage."

"Good. We need to get out of here tomorrow morning. I don't like the way things are working out."

Northern outskirts of New York, New York, 21:00 Zulu

"OK. You drivers and navigators have your routes; remember that it's best to avoid main roads. If the government declares martial law, they'll blockade the main roads first." Frank paused to drink more tepid lemonade. "It's nearly four o'clock; we shouldn't leave until we've rested." Outside, a couple gunshots popped, not close, but near enough that people jumped.

"We should establish watches and block all doors but the main ones. Make sure drapes and shades are fully drawn. Let's all move onto the second floor to put a little buffer between the ground and us, so we've time to react. Block all stairs but the one furthest from the outer doors, and all outside doors."

"Uh, I don't think that's up with fire codes," Buddy said.

"Buddy, fire codes are the least of our worries." Frank turned to the rest of the group. "Firearm holders: we need to take turns on watch, four hours apiece. I'll take first watch until 8:00 p.m. Decide your schedule."

It didn't take long to set a simple watch. After everyone had settled in, with doors blocked and windows shaded, Frank eased into a stiff-backed chair to complete the rest of his duty. The lobby was warm, quiet... dark... Frank stood several times and roamed the ground floor, checking for signs of tampering. Toward the end of his time, he sat for a moment too long.

"Frank— Frank! Wake up!"

He felt someone shaking him. With each movement his head exploded in pain.

"OK, I'm awake. Holy shit, what happened?"

Frank realized he was on the floor; the side of his head was wet and sticky—blood. He sat up; it took a moment for the room to stop spinning.

"When you didn't fetch me for my watch, I thought I'd better check on you." Charles, the former Marine, was kneeling beside him, then helped Frank into the chair. "Do you know what happened?"

"It was warm and quiet. I must have dozed off." Frank gingerly touched the back of his head—a goose-egg-sized lump with an oozing gash. "I'm sorry, guess I should have stayed on my feet." He took a clean handkerchief from his pocket and held it to the back of his head. "Anyone missing?"

"I don't know. I just found you."

Frank patted his pants pocket and then looked desperately around the floor, forgetting the pain in his head. "The shotgun, my keys, they're gone."

Day Two

Roswell, Georgia, 00:10 Zulu

When the trio returned from the pool, the house smelled wonderfully of roasted meat and they realized they hadn't eaten since morning. Katie fixed a salad with the refrigerator vegetables and, along with a platter of bread, they made a feast of fresh-roasted chicken and pork.

While David went to Marlene's to check out the Rover and pack odds and ends, Marlene and Katie spread beef strips on drying racks. They turned the gas as low as possible and placed drying racks in the oven; with so many strips of meat they soon ran out of space. Katie loaded and lit the charcoal smoker on the deck. After the coals turned white, she stacked in the remaining beef strips, closed the dome, and then cracked the smoker door to keep the temperature low.

With the meat taken care of, Marlene and Katie started deciding what to take and what to leave in the kitchen. Once they finished there, they moved into the bedroom and packed sturdy clothes for both Katie and Frank. As they moved to the basement to pack the storage room, a knock came on the upstairs door.

"Kaitie, you stay here and keep packing. I'll go see who 'tis."

Katie heard low talk, steadily increasing in volume until she could tell Marlene was about to lose it. One time, Earl had angered her and she dumped a full bowl of hot pasta on his head. Now, she sounded madder than that evening. Katie grabbed her Taser flashlight—hoping it still worked—and ran up the stairs.

One of Hank's lackeys was at the door, saying, "You will let me in to inventory your supplies. For the good of the neighborhood!"

Katie recognized the woman—the one who, at every association meeting, had a list of people who didn't watch their dogs, needed their lawn mowed, or did California stops at the stop sign outside her house, a woman whose entire life was watching through her window or walking her rat-dog, a bark-happy Pekinese, noting who needed what done to their lawns.

"Is there a problem, Marlene?" asked Katie.

"Rosie here wants to inventory our supplies," Marlene said with a taste of venom.

"Rosie, why don't you come back tomorrow, it's getting late."

Katie smiled her best smile, trying not to get angry.

"No, Hank said that especially you folks had to be done tonight. After all, it is time for us to share in the sacrifice." Rosie smiled but her eyes were cold.

"Rosie, usually when someone like you says 'share the sacrifice' it's the hard-working ones who sacrifice while the worthless sons of bitches share it."

"Well I never!" Rosie said indignantly.

"Yep, that's your problem. Maybe if you had, you wouldn't have such a telephone pole up your butt," Katie said sweetly.

"I have to inventory you, now!" Rosie crossed her fat arms. The wattles wiggled.

"I don't think so." Katie brandished the Taser and, with a prayer it would work, triggered it with an ominous Z-A-A-A-P and electric flash on its terminals.

Screaming for help as she turned, Rosie stumbled down the front-porch steps and waddled rapidly across the front lawn toward the street. Katie slammed the door, turned around and burst out laughing.

"Hmm, that could a' gone better . . . ," Marlene said, joining the gaiety.

"Maybe if you could have demonstrated on that mutt of hers . . . ," Katie said between laughs. "We better hurry up. No doubt she went to get the other yard nazis."

Wiping tears of laughter from their eyes, they hurried into

the kitchen to finish prepping. Katie hoped to forestall the association hacks long enough for the jerky to dry. She hated the thought of leaving anything useful behind.

While Marlene and Katie moved various boxes and plastic totes to the garage, David was at Marlene's, finding the spare jerry cans of diesel fuel and the special tools needed to maintain the Rover. He strapped the jerries to the rear fender racks and then stored the toolkit in its special locker.

He pulled the outer-trolley release rope for the garage door opener chain. The drive-chain trolley disengaged with a snap. David manhandled the door up, started the Rover, then drove it into the driveway, parked, got out and returned to the garage. Pulling the door down, he re-engaged the opener to lock the door in place. David did a quick run through the house, locking doors. Finally, he drove the Rover down the deserted street to Katie's.

Hearing the Rover's rattling engine, Katie and Marlene lifted the garage door and let him in, David backing in to face outward, and then closed the door.

As David exited the Rover, Katie asked, "Did you see anyone? More importantly, did anyone see you?"

"Well, I didn't see anyone, but people would've seen me if they looked out their windows. Maybe heard me as well."

"Damn. We have to pack and get out as soon as possible." Katie wiped sweat from her brow.

"Why, has something happened?"

They told him about Rosie's visit. After he finished laughing—as a teenager he'd had run-ins with both her and her yappy dog—he sobered and agreed they needed to leave as soon as possible. They immediately began loading supplies into the Rover. It was obvious that even though it was the 108-inch version of the Land Rover, it was too small.

"Wait a minute." Katie smacked her forehead. "Quick! Over here." She gestured to the right side of the garage around the gutted Blazer where boxes were stacked. After a few minutes of searching, she triumphantly lifted a dusty black bag.

"What is that, Kaitie?" asked Marlene.

Laying the bag on the floor, they could see hold-down straps and buckles. "It's a car-top carrier. We can load stuff in it, and people won't be able to tell what we're carrying."

David attached the carrier to the rooftop rack and they filled it with items they wanted hidden. Leaving David and Marlene to keep loading, Katie went inside to Frank's reloading bench.

At the reloading bench she took a ratchet wrench that Frank had left out and undid the hold-down bolts for the four-place turret-style reloading press. She removed the heavy metal press and loaded it into a large plastic tub. She then grabbed all the sets of dies for their several calibers: .38 Special, 9mm, 8mm Mauser, as well as various ammo components such as cases, bullets and primers, all of Frank's various powders and the Lee Reloading Manual. Dragging the heavy tub over to the door, she yelled for David.

"Frank's reloading gear — it may come in handy."

David eyed the large tub dubiously. "Well, I'll try to load it, but it's getting a bit tight."

"I have faith in you, David," Katie said, turning toward the steps to upstairs. "I'm going to check the jerky."

Upstairs, she could smell the slow-cooking meat. She went to the oven, tested the consistency of the strips — not quite done, but she knew they didn't have time for the meat to completely cure. Grabbing a large Tupperware container and a pair of tongs, she quickly loaded the jerky into it. As she pulled the last tray out of the oven, she noticed something missing. The almost sub-audial hiss of the gas burner was gone. "Well, that's the last of the gas pressure," she muttered, carrying the container and tongs to the smoker, where she loaded the rest of the meat. As she was snapping the lid on, an angry knock came on the door.

"Katie! Marlene! Open this door immediately!"

Katie could tell by the bellow that it was Hank in all his rotund glory. He banged louder. Katie stifled a laugh as he swore over the pain it caused his soft, no-doubt-manicured hands.

In the bedroom she retrieved the gun-safe key from its hiding place and, after opening the gun safe, began loading a multi-gun canvas case. First, the .40 caliber and .22 LR pistols and their spare magazines went into inside pockets. She racked the long-barrel Remington 12-gauge slide and emptied its three-round magazine onto the bed. Unscrewing the slide-retaining nut, she removed the slide and disengaged the barrel. She put the slide and retaining nut back in place and packed the two pieces into the bag. In the case center, she packed the 9mm carbine and its three spare fifteen-round magazines. In the final compartment went the modified Marlin Model 60 .22 caliber rifle and its EZ-loader. Taking a second case, she loaded the 8mm customized hunting Mauser with its 3x9 scope, along with the spare hunting ammo. The military anti-personnel ammo was already loaded in the prep supplies. She could hear more yelling and pounding on the door as she slung the heavy rifle case over her shoulder. She pulled the last item from the safe, a short-barreled Mossberg 12-gauge home defense shotgun with a seven-place magazine. Katie knew it was already loaded with double-ought buckshot; she carried it in one hand and the case with the hunting rifle in the other, with the heavy multi-gun case strapped over one shoulder.

Grunting with the heavy load, she carefully made her way down two flights of steps and handed the two cases to David. She kept the Mossberg.

"OK, time's up. Hank is at the door — no doubt with his minions."

"So we figured," David said. "We heard the bluster. Everything's packed, although the person in the back seat is going to be crowded."

"David, you drive. Marlene, you're shortest; you get the back seat. Lock all doors except the passenger-side front. I'll raise the door; you drive out. I'll close the door, leap in and we'll be away before they realize we aren't inside."

Unfortunately, like most plans made by men and women, it didn't quite go the way they hoped.

Northern outskirts of
New York, New York, 00:30 Zulu

"Well, I don't see any difference in your pupils." Alex Barnes, a medical student, took the bright light out of Frank's eyes.

"Small blessings, I guess." Frank rubbed his eyes. "I feel so stupid for falling asleep."

"Nothing we can do about it now," Charles said matter-of-factly. Frank hoped the folks who were planning to ride home with him felt the same way.

"Uh . . . maybe we can," Buddy said, peering out the window toward the garage. "He's coming out of the garage, walking."

"What!" Frank rushed to the window. Sure enough, it was the senator's son, still gripping the shotgun, looking pissed. Frank closed the drapes before he glanced over at the others.

"Charles, go 'round to the north door and flank him. I'll exit the west door and try to intercept him."

"Are you sure, Frank? He still has the shotgun," Buddy was concerned.

"There isn't a round in the chamber, and the safety is on. I'll bet my life he's never fired a gun," Frank said in tightly controlled anger. "Let's go."

Frank hurried to the west door and unblocked it, trying to be as quiet as possible. Depressing the release, he cracked the door and peered out. Willie had just walked past, very close to the building, moving quickly. Frank pushed open the door and smacked him in the back, making him stumble.

While Willie tried to catch his balance, Frank rushed up behind him and, grabbing the butt of the shotgun, roughly ripped it from Willie's startled hands, nearly tearing away Willie's trigger finger.

"—Ouch! —Shit! What the hell?" As Willie shook the blood-spraying injured finger and spun, Frank worked the cocking lever of the Saiga—modeled after the AK-47, the Saiga uses a cocking lever rather than a slide—and flipped off the safety lever, pointing the muzzle directly into Willie's face.

"I should remove your head, butt wipe," Frank said through clenched teeth, his finger tightening on the trigger. He could feel the slackness tighten as the sear started to release.

"Frank, don't! He isn't worth it!" Charles ran up.

Reluctantly, Frank took his finger off the trigger. "I know, but what do we do with him?" Frank noticed the smell of urine and a dark stain spreading down the right leg of Willie's jogging suit. "Where's my keys?" Frank gestured with the shotgun muzzle.

"You're a damn liar," Willie babbled. "The car doesn't start. I tried and tried with these damn things. The ignition switch wouldn't work. Take 'em!" He reached in his pocket and threw the keys on the ground at Frank's feet.

"Charles, would you be so kind?" asked Frank, keeping his eyes on Willie.

Charles picked up the keys.

"Press the small button near the loop," Frank instructed.

After a glance, Charles found the button on the keys of the Lincoln Town Car that had been the only vehicle available at the rental center. Charles pushed the tiny button on the key fob and the top popped out. Attached was the emergency key; should the fob battery discharge, it was the only way to start the car—a standard feature for keyless ignitions. Frank was glad now, even though he hadn't wanted the huge car. Charles displayed the key and smiled.

"Shit." Willie looked totally defeated.

"I sure am glad you're as smart as you look. You should have realized the fob wouldn't work anymore. I guess you never learned about emergency keys for keyless ignitions." Frank smiled.

"What do we do with him, Frank?"

"Nothing." Frank gestured at Willie with the shotgun. "Go.

You aren't welcome here, especially after we tell everyone what you tried to do." The sound of a distant automatic weapon sounded, followed by the loud bang of a shotgun. Both were too close for comfort.

"You can't do this. My father is—"

"Probably cowering in a shelter, glad you aren't with him," Frank finished for him. It seemed to trigger something in Willie as he foolishly lunged at Frank, rage in his face.

With a quick upward movement, Frank caught Willie across the side of the face with the edge of the shotgun butt, opening a gash and dropping him to the concrete of the parking lot. Willie smacked his head sharply as he collapsed and lay moaning.

"When you can, I suggest you get the hell away from here. The next time I'll use the other end." Frank wiped the blood off the butt of the stock onto the back of Willie's shirt. "Come on, Charles, something smells around here."

"Right behind you."

They re-entered the hotel, blocking the door behind them.

"You sure you weren't too hard on him, Frank?" asked Charles.

"Would you want him in your car? You want him watching your back?" Frank flipped the Saiga's safety back on.

"I see your point, but it's a hell of a thing, Frank, leaving a man behind."

Charles shook his head.

"Yep."

ROSWELL GEORGIA, 00:20 ZULU

"You ready, David?" Katie said over the sound of the diesel. She clutched the Mossberg under her left arm as she reached for the ridge that ran along the door at the edge of one of the panels. David gave her a thumb's-up. She pulled the door open as quickly as she could and stepped aside to let David race past. Out of the corner of her eye she caught a quick movement to her right.

As the Rover slid past, Hank rushed her, too close for her to bring the shotgun to bear; he was able to grab it. As they fought over possession of the weapon, Katie remembered her target-focused training and, as Hank pulled up on the shotgun, she shoved it at him, throwing him off balance. As Hank flailed backward, she kicked her size-8 lady's hiking boot into his groin. Dropping the shotgun, Hank doubled over, reaching for his ruptured balls. Katie grabbed the back of his head and slammed his face hard into her rising knee. She felt his nose crack under the impact and Hank collapsed to the concrete driveway. A shout from the front of the house showed someone had seen the fight.

With a quick look around, Katie retrieved the Mossberg, racked the slide and chambered a round. Firing a shot into the air and then holding the shotgun on the advancing association members, she reached behind and opened the passenger-side door to the Rover. Climbing in rapidly, she slammed the door behind her. "Go! Get us the hell out of here!"

The aging Rover roared and the clutch squealed as David slammed it into gear and took off. After a few jerks it began accelerating, leaving the association lackeys staring in shock. But when the trio thought they were clear, they turned onto the collector road to find two cars blocking the subdivision entrance.

"Well, haven't they been busy. This thing has a cowcatcher on the front, right?"

David, wide-eyed like his mom, looked over at Katie. "Yes."

"Ram them."

Thinking of all the old war movies he had watched as a kid, David said, "Ramming speed, aye!" smiling as he shifted into second and mashed the accelerator to the floor.

Eyeing the ancient behemoth bearing down on them, the

men manning the barricade frantically attempted to push the blockade cars aside then, at the last minute, jumped back. The Rover flashed past, knocking the dead cars aside and nearly rising onto two wheels as it rounded the corner onto the highway. The last thing the association members saw was Marlene in the rear passenger-side window, blowing them a kiss with a raised middle finger.

"Well, that was fun!" Marlene said from the back seat, fairly glowing with excitement.

"Fun?" Katie said, glowering.

"You should a' seen his face when you kicked him in the boolls!"

Katie tried to hold the glower, but as she replayed the scene, she found herself smiling, then laughing outloud. "All I could think of was that stupid red Speedo," she said between laughs, tears running down her face.

David alternately looked as his mom in the rearview mirror and Katie sitting beside him. "Great. Stuck with a couple of whackos." It only made them laugh harder. "When you two are finished, I need to know where we're going."

"To Frank's and my BOL," Katie said, recovering her breath. "Use back roads and try to get to Highway 41 North."

"Your bole?" asked Marlene.

"No, our B-O-L — short for bug-out location."

"Well that's clear as mud, dear." Marlene sounded confused.

"Property we own over in Alabama, about thirty acres. We have a cabin and some supplies."

"Property? You never told me about any property, Kaitie," Marlene sounded hurt.

"Marlene, you didn't need to know. It's part of what's called operational security — the more people know about something, the less chance of keeping it secure." Katie looked back at her friend. "I'm taking you with me, aren't I?"

"Well, all right, but keeping such a thing a secret," Marlene sounded indignant.

"It worked didn't it?" Katie smiled as Marlene stuck out

her tongue.

"Hey, guys . . . better look at this," David said, slowing the Rover by downshifting.

About a hundred yards down the main road, at the next major intersection, was a roadblock—police cars this time. Men with black flak vests with DHS on the back were inspecting several cars. An officer facing their way was waving them over.

"Crap, turn around!" Katie was almost frantic.

"What, why?" David asked, making a U-turn across the grass median.

"Department of Homeland Security has the authority to seize operating vehicles during an emergency. They'd love this one and everything in it."

"Shit! They're pursuing!" David looked frantically in his rearview mirror.

Katie studied the situation and then smiled. "Go cross-country."

It took a moment for David to realize what she meant, and then he smiled, saying, "Hold on ladies, this might get rough!"

As they braced, he turned off the highway and bounced over the curb into the nearest backyard. After smashing over several fences and trespassing into several other backyards, he finally lost the pursuit after it tore out its rear tires on a ragged bit of chain-link fence. Sticking to back roads, the trio rejoined Ga. 120 several miles beyond the roadblock.

"Thank God they don't seem to have working radios," David said.

"We hope," Katie said ominously.

Outside a Hotel, Northern Outskirts of New York, New York, 01:00 Zulu

William Wright, Jr.—Willie to his few friends and NYU to Frank Lowman—came to his senses slowly. Hot pavement was pressing into his cheek, and his jogging suit was uncomfortably wet. The events of the last few minutes rushed back and he groaned loudly.

"Need a hand, friend?" The voice was rich, melodious, and soothing.

Willie opened his eyes, turned his head, and painfully looked up. Framed by the late afternoon sun, a man offering his hand was hard to see.

"No, I can do it myself." Willie pushed to his knees, then, a little unsteady, stood. Blood streaked his cheek and NYU sweatshirt.

"Suit yourself, my friend."

Willie examined his would-be benefactor—a nondescript, vaguely Middle Eastern man of medium height, with olive skin, dark hair, and black eyes. The amazing thing about him was his voice: "Listen," the man intoned, "I need a hand myself. You know how to ride a motorcycle?"

Willie had ridden a dirt bike as teenager. "Yes, a little. Why?"

"I found one, but I can't ride it."

As the man led the way toward the garage, Willie noticed he had a serious limp in his left leg

"The EMP probably fried it," Willie said derisively.

"No. This one is an old one. Should still work."

Willie recalled seeing a bike in the garage, but hadn't paid much attention because he wanted to show that asshole Frank a thing or two by stealing his car.

"Here it is: an early Yamaha." The man stood beside a vintage 650 overhead cam two-cylinder bike, painted midnight black, flat.

"Whose is it?" Willie asked, feeling a hint of remorse.

"Does it matter? We need it worse." The man smiled.

"What's your name?" asked Willie as he looked the bike over.

"Just call me Nick. And you?"

"Willie . . . uh . . . William—Bill."

"Bill, great. Let's see if it starts."

Willie found a spare key under the seat in a magnetic case. Straddling the bike, he rolled it back and pointed it toward the garage exit. Turning the key, he saw the ignition switch light activate—a good sign. Willie checked the gas tank valve—it was in the main position—and then depressed the clutch and turned the switch to start. The resulting silence was deafening.

"Damn. Told you." Willie started to dismount.

"Whoa, try the kick starter."

After a couple of false starts, the roar of a powerful engine drowned out Willie's breathlessness from the unaccustomed exercise. Willie'd never heard a sweeter sound as when he rolled the handlebar accelerator.

"Get on," he shouted to Nick, who did so. As he put the large bike in gear and headed toward the evening street, the bike handled so well that Willie would have almost sworn that no one else was aboard.

Leaning into the turn out of the hotel lot, Willie cranked the throttle and nearly lost the bike in a sideways slide. "Slow down, Hoss, we have all day," Nick's voice was easy to hear over the bike's roar, and they prowled the back streets until forced onto a main drag. Nearing an intersection, Willie spotted a lone 1972 Impala, topped with a red flashing light, partially blocking the way. A man in a sheriff's uniform stood in the road.

"Crap," Willie said outloud, slowing down.

"Only one," Willie heard Nick say, and Willie knew what he had to do.

When they were almost at the officer, Willie gunned the bike, bringing the front into a half-wheelie and ramming him in the sternum as he drew his weapon. They rode him over with a sickening thud. Willie, fish-tailing the bike to a stop, nearly laid it on its side trying to get the kickstand down. He jumped off the idling bike and ran back to the struggling officer. Willie picked up the Glock 37 chambered in .45 GAP that had been knocked from the dying officer's grasp. He then undid the duty belt with its extra magazines, nightstick, mace and other police items. Finally, he frisked the officer and took his backup piece, a Springfield XD 9mm Sub-Compact Willie found in an ankle holster strapped to the officer's right leg. A couple of spare magazines, a riot gun and more spare ammo were in the car. By the time Willie finished, the officer was dead.

Willie eyed the Impala, but decided he preferred the bike. For the fun of it, he discharged the riot shotgun — after puzzling out how to rack in a round and undo the safety — into the Impala's radiator. The fourteen-inch-barrel shotgun felt good. Opening one of the Viking side-pocket saddlebags, Willie stowed the shotgun and other supplies from the police car. The butt hung out a bit, but with the lid closed, the gun seemed secure, and besides, he could grab and use it in a hurry. Willie looked rather stupid with the duty belt over the top of his piss-damp jogging suit — until you saw his eyes.

He examined the .45 pistol, noting a button near the trigger guard. Assuming it was a safety, he pushed it, causing the magazine to pop out. Almost dropping the pistol, he caught the magazine in midair and, after a bout of fumbling, locked the magazine back in position. Grabbing the slide, he grunted and tugged it backward, ejecting a round onto the ground. He knelt and picked it up. With the confidence of a sophomore, he ejected the magazine, restored the ejected round and replaced the magazine. Putting the pistol in the duty-belt holster, he felt sure he could work the pistol if needed.

"Well done," Nick said, walking up from behind.

Willie spun around, drawing the gun. With the .45 ready to fire, he discovered he faced Nick and relaxed. "Where the hell did you go?" he said, holstering the weapon, feeling ten feet tall.

"Had to piss. You seemed to have things handled," Nick said approvingly.

"Yeah, I did, didn't I?" Willie smiled, feeling validation for almost the first time in his young life. Willie offered the XD to Nick.

"No, I don't use guns. You keep it." Nick smiled as Willie strapped the pistol on his right ankle. "Good choice. It won't rub against the bike. Say, let's go find a clothing store. I could use some new duds."

Willie grinned. He could get to like Ol' Nick.

Highway 41, Adams Park, Kennesaw, Georgia, 01:30 Zulu

"Hold up a second, David. Pull over, please. I am such a ditz sometimes." Katie smacked her forehead with her palm.

David pulled to the roadside, watching for police or other signs of authority. "Should we be stopping?" he asked nervously.

"Just a quick minute. I have to get something." Katie studied the gear tightly packed in the Rover's rear. "Marlene, hand me that small black duffle bag."

"The one we took from your closet?"

Marlene tugged free the bag, nearly causing a landslide of miscellaneous packages and bags.

"Yep, that's the one."

Katie laid the bag in her lap and unzipped it. Rummaging inside, she extracted a Grecom PSR-700 handheld police scanner from inside its shielded bag, inserted fresh batteries, and switched it on. The Grecom squawked.

"All units proceed to Roadblock Seven, Blue Springs and

Cobb Parkway, Code 11-99 — officer needs assistance."

David smiled. "I guess we want to go around."

"Good idea. Left on Giles and take Old 41 until we get past."

They stayed on Old 41 to Nance Road, then turned left, rejoining Highway 41 beyond the problem spot. Using the scanner and keeping a good watch, they avoided other roadblocks. Reaching Cartersville, they turned onto 411/20 and headed west. Marlene asked, "Isn't your youngest 'round here somewhere?"

"Lizzie and her husband Jim live right up the road. We'll stop and check on them," Katie said. "They plan on going to Jim's parents in case of emergency."

They soon reached Lizzie's place. Katie jumped from the Rover before it stopped and ran to the back of the house. She soon returned.

"Their BOV is gone. Jim and Frank fixed up an old pickup about a year ago. I need to check one more thing." From beneath a front-porch frog statue she retrieved a key, unlocked the front door and entered. In moments, she came out clutching a paper, locked the door and replaced the key in its amphibian hideaway.

"They got out last night. Should now be at Jim's parents, past Barnsley Gardens near Adairsville. They'll be listening on our frequency."

"Your 'frequency'?" Marlene was perplexed.

"We have a designated ham radio frequency and a personal communications code in case of a bug-out."

"You're a qualified ham operator?" asked David.

"No, but I don't think anyone will be checking licenses."

Katie smiled at him. "OK, one less worry. On to Rome. Let's get back on 41 for a while, but we better bypass Rome itself. Marlene, in the backpack by your left foot should be a map case. Hand me the Georgia map, will you?"

Using side roads they bypassed Rome and rejoined Highway 20 at the west end of Benton. As they approached the Alabama line and a massive roadblock, they turned onto

Fosters Bend Road, then Old River Road to cross the state line. They continued on Highway 9 until they reached Highway 35, where they turned north. A few miles farther they reached Gaylesville and turned west on Highway 68, then north onto County Road 107.

"Watch for a gate on the left," Katie said as they traveled the old asphalt road.

"There! Hold up while I get the gate."

Katie jumped from the Rover, ran to the gate, used a key from her necklace to open it, signaled David to pull through, then closed and locked the gate behind them. She climbed in the passenger door on the left side of the British-specs Rover.

"Follow this a ways . . . at the fork, go right; the left goes to hunting . . ."

They soon pulled in front of a nine-by-thirty-four-foot travel trailer with a deck and awning out front. A shed, converted from a cargo container, sat half-embedded in a hillside behind the trailer.

"Well, welcome to Safe Haven," Katie exclaimed.

"I thought you said a cabin," Marlene replied.

"Well, in another year or so, it would have been. A second trailer is over the next rise, by the pond."

The trailer door banged and a tall, blond, pretty woman in her late thirties stormed out holding a short-barreled riot gun, which she leveled on the Rover. "Hold it right there! You have no right to be here! This is private property!"

Katie lowered her window and showed empty hands. "Max, it's Mom and friends."

With a cry of relief, Maxine — Frank and Katie's oldest daughter, known as Max to friends and family — lowered the 12-gauge, ran to the open window and hugged her mother. "I've been so scared. When the power went out I thought something bad had happened. I checked with the Becketts, but they're all on vacation in Florida."

"Well, it'll be OK now. You remember Marlene and David, don't you?"

"Sure. Where's Dad?" Max looked eagerly for her father.

"New York. I imagine it'll be a while before we see him again. And Earl is stuck in London," Katie explained, holding back tears, showing a strong front for her daughter. They hugged fiercely for a quiet moment, and then Katie pulled away, wiped her eyes and said, "Come on, let's get unloaded."

It didn't take long for four to empty the Rover and put away things in the shed and first trailer. Afterward, they crowded into the trailer and Max made breakfast as the new arrivals recounted their adventures. Max, laughing, almost dropped the pan of scrambled eggs when she heard how Katie had gotten the best of Hank.

"Get the spare PVs up?" Katie asked around bites of egg and bacon.

"Not yet. This is still battery reserves. I wanted to wait for help; those panels are heavy."

"Spare PVs?" This from David.

"Photovoltaic panels. We've got spares in case this happened; we figured any EMP would fry the ones in use."

After breakfast, David, Katie and Marlene uninstalled the fused panels from their tracking bracket and, after unwrapping the protective blankets from the spares, installed the new panels. After rewiring a fused inverter, the system showed full power and the batteries indicated they were being charged.

"Load up the other spare panels and a spare inverter; we'll need it on the other trailer, where you all will be staying."

Katie took a drink from her bottled water. It wasn't even 9:00 a.m. and it was already in the low eighties. In another hour, they had both trailers' power systems operable. Next, they replaced the panel that provided power for the well pump, which, since it was an in-well type, hadn't been damaged by the pulse. They soon had water pressure to both trailers.

"Let's get unpacked and settled in. After lunch we take inventory and check out the garden and pond."

Katie was giving orders like a general.

Marlene and David exchanged looks, wondering what they had gotten themselves into.

North of New York, New York, 02:00 Zulu

Frank wished the pain behind his eyes would go away. He appraised the meager supplies divided amongst the traveling groups. Stretched thin, it might last two to three days; after that they would have to scrounge. In his backpack he had a change of clothes, his toiletry and his survival kit, which he carried whenever he traveled — a 32-oz Nalgene bottle wrapped with twenty-five feet of paracord, fire starter, water purification tablets, space blanket and a folding multi-tool. He felt at his neck for the large silver-wire-wrapped arrowhead that, in a pinch, could be converted into an emergency knife.

"Alright, let's get moving. Last minute thoughts: police, National Guard, you name it — if they're associated with a government agency they probably won't be there to help you. Government agencies will be looking for working vehicles and supplies, and to confiscate weapons. If they stop you, more than likely you'll lose your ride home and end up in a relocation camp."

"You can't mean that," Terri Andrews, the blonde with the busted iPad, burst out.

"Whatever. I'm just warning you. Make up your own minds. Stay off the main roads; avoid normal state-line crossings. Let's get rolling."

The groups gathered at their respective vehicles. Frank walked down the line, feeling like an inspecting general. Approaching the last vehicle, he felt he needed to talk to a middle-aged woman who looked lost and confused.

"Ma'am? Do you need something?"

"Oh Frank, I don't know what to do. My husband, Leonard, was supposed to meet me here. He inherited a cabin upstate and we were going to go see it."

"Where's he coming from?"

"Springfield, Massachusetts. He was up there on business, going to fly in here to meet me." Frank could see her eyes start to cloud and tears begin to trickle down her cheeks. Frank got a feeling he should tell her to stay.

"You stay here and wait then. This isn't that far from Springfield."

"You really think so?" She looked at him beseechingly.

"Yes, I do. If I knew you were waiting, I would get here." He smiled; she smiled bravely back.

"OK, I will."

The other riders in her car removed her backpack.

"What's your name?" Frank asked.

"Linda, Linda Rhodes." She held out her hand; Frank shook it.

"Frank Lowman. You're doing the right thing, I feel it." Frank couldn't explain, but he knew in his heart it was right that she stayed. He returned to the lead car and got in the passenger side. With his headache and lack of proper sleep, he didn't trust himself to drive. Putting the shotgun beside him by the door, Frank nodded to Pete, the first-shift driver, and they were off, first stop Monroeville, Pennsylvania.

On the main road, Frank saw a lone figure approaching.

"Slow down, Pete, I want to see who this is."

Frank sat up and rubbed his eyes. As they neared, Frank saw it was a middle-aged man who looked road-worn and tired.

"Pull over. I want to talk to this guy," Frank said. Pete looked at him as if he were crazy, but did it anyway.

Lowering the Town Car window, Frank called out, "Your name Leonard?"

"Yes, do I know you?"

Leonard shielded his face and peered at Frank with bloodshot eyes.

"No, but I know Linda; she's waiting for you back at the hotel."

The effect of Frank's words was striking: a defeated man

straightened in posture, and his eyes, though still bloodshot, had new purpose.

"You wouldn't kid me, would you, stranger?"

"Nope. She's there. Just talked to her. Look, if I were you, I'd find a way to get to that cabin you inherited. Have any supplies?"

"It was my Uncle Mike's. He turned into one of those survivalists, and it's supposed to be supplied for years. I wondered what I was going to do with the accumulated junk. I guess I know, now."

"Well, good luck and God's speed," Frank reached through the window and shook Leonard's hand.

As they pulled away, he realized his headache was gone, settled into the seat and fell into a deep sleep.

North of New York, New York, 02:30 Zulu

Willie was almost lulled into road hypnosis by the bike's constant rumble and the warm breeze blowing by his body when he remembered Nick had wanted some new clothes. Paying more attention to the various shops that flew past, he spotted one that advertised clothes and leather goods, backed off the throttle and downshifted.

"Good choice," Nick said into his ear.

As the bike came to a stop in front of the store, Willie put down both legs then leaned to the left, kicked down the stand and settled the bike. Climbing off, he noticed Nick must have already gone in the store. He followed.

The light from outside showed rack after rack of leather goods such as trousers, jackets and accessories as well as shirts, regular pants and other stuff. A clerk, a young attractive brunette, looked startled as the small metal bell over the door tinkled.

"Sorry sir, we aren't open. I'm here just to check on things and close up until power returns." As she looked at Willie she couldn't help but feel a laugh coming on, dressed as he was in a dirt-stained gym-suit bottom and an equally grubby NYU sweatshirt. The desire to laugh caught in her throat as she saw the duty belt and gun, and died completely when she saw his eyes.

"I think you'll be waiting a long time," Willie said lightly.

"Sir?" She said, wondering what he meant.

"Power—it isn't coming back on."

Not sure what to make of his comment, she stared at him.

"I want new clothes. Frankly, these stink." He smiled, but the gesture fell far short of his eyes.

"But I have no way to take a payment. Registers and card swipers won't work without electricity."

"Who said I was going to pay?" answered Willie, drawing the .45.

The clerk held her small hands toward Willie, palms out. "Please, don't hurt me! Take anything you want!"

"I will," Willie said simply, and with those two words, the clerk knew he meant more than clothes. She turned to run but with one hand Willie grabbed her and with the other hand holstered the gun. Ripping the power cord from the register, he used it to bind her hands. Pulling a silk scarf from a display, he gagged her, then used more scarves to bind her legs. "We wouldn't want you to go anywhere."

"Good work," Nick said, coming from the changing room, where he had dressed in tight black-leather pants, a black tee shirt and black half-boots. Willie hadn't noticed it before, but in this light Nick resembled an Arabian James Dean.

"Watch her while I find a few things," Willie said.

The clerk watched Willie in growing horror.

Grabbing packages of underwear and tee shirts, Willie looked in the back of the store for a place to clean up and found a washroom. Stripping off the gym-suit bottoms, underwear and bloodstained tee shirt, he tossed them disdainfully in the trash. Willie bathed using paper towels. Rummaging through employee lockers, he found deodorant and a hairbrush. In the deep sink he rinsed the blood from his hair, using liquid hand soap as shampoo. He dried his hair as best he could and brushed it, trying to imitate Nick's style. The clean underwear was almost as good as sex. Feeling more in control, he pulled on a clean white tee shirt, grabbed the duty belt and headed back into the store, where he noticed that the clerk had moved toward the door.

"Nick, I thought you were going to watch her!" he admonished.

Nick smiled. "She isn't going anywhere; she can't open the door."

The clerk sobbed quietly into the gagging scarf, clearly terrified for her life. Ignoring her, Willie strode to the leather pants, found some in his size and length, draped the duty belt over the display rack, and tried them on. They fit as if they'd been made for him; he'd always had good luck with clothes. He chose a black silk shirt, liking the suppleness and knowing it would look cool. Even though it was hot, he wanted to complete the look, so he chose a light-weight, unlined black-leather jacket that just reached his waist. Re-donning the duty belt, Willie felt ready for the road.

"Let's roll," said Nick.

"What about her?"

"Leave her. There are better women out there, waiting."

"Right." Willie grabbed extra pants and shirts, and more underwear, and then left the store without a backward glance or thought.

As the clerk heard the motorcycle's rumble fade, she relaxed and tried to figure out how to escape her bonds. Then the doorbell tinkled and a gruff male voice said, "Well, well, well . . . what do we have here?"

North of Lake Weiss, Alabama, 06:30 Zulu

"OK, David, let's go check out the Beckett's place, make sure they're locked up and all's well." Reaching into a box sitting on the table, Katie pulled out a small battery-powered video camera. "We'll also install this to watch his driveway; we'll put a second one for our drive."

David took the camera and studied it. "Neat. How far can it transmit?"

"About nine hundred feet or so. Should be enough to reach here."

She pulled two nine-volt Eneloop batteries out of a charger. "This should power it for about a week."

Katie went to the weapons bag they'd brought from the house, removed the Ruger Mark II .22 caliber pistol and a holster, clipped it to her belt, and pocketed an extra magazine. "Here," she said, handing David a shoulder rig. "This should be easier to use."

She helped him adjust the holster and move the 9mm and spare magazine into it.

"Do we really need all this firepower?" David asked as he got the feel of the shoulder rig. He checked that the pistol was still loaded, placed it in the holster under his left arm, and the spare magazine in the pouch under the right. Katie watched approvingly.

"Hope not, but I'd rather have it and not need it than need it and not have it."

"Right."

"What do you want oos to do?" Marlene asked, indicating Max and herself.

"Max, could you show Marlene around and check that the level controls on the ponds are working OK?"

" 'Ponds'? You have more than one?"

"It was Frank's idea. We have one on top of the hill back there, with about a twenty-foot elevation difference from the one you see out here. The solar cells and wind generator, when they aren't charging batteries, run a couple of high-volume, low-pressure pumps that move water to the upper pond until it fills, then it overflows to this one."

"So?"

"So if we need to, we can run a micro-hydro-turbine generator off a pipe on the bottom of the upper pond. It'll provide three or more days of power should there not be enough wind or solar."

"A mini-pumped storage setup? Cool," David piped in.

"Exactly. Come on, let's get moving. Max, don't forget the shotgun."

"Mom, I'm not a kid anymore," Max smiled as she took the Mossberg and a shoulder sling. "Besides, it makes me feel like Alice in Resident Evil!"

"Sometimes I wonder about you, child," Katie said, pocketing a ratchet driver, a bit set and a couple of woodscrews from a tool chest.

"And sometimes, you know!"

They both laughed; it was obviously a running gag between them.

"We'll take the GRS with us; if we get delayed, we'll call." Katie gestured to David to follow, and on her way out grabbed a small radio transceiver from a wall charger and a mini-binocular set hanging on a nail by the door.

A short walk through hardwoods brought the pair to the edge of a pasture leading down to the Beckett's. From her neck, Katie picked up the small but powerful binoculars and gazed through them, scanning the barn at the far edge of the field; they couldn't see the house yet. "Looks normal. Let's go."

Even though it was only nearing noon, the day was turning brutally hot. The temperature was nearly ninety-three degrees and humidity 90 percent. By the time they reached the red two-story barn, both were sweating. At the barn, Katie scanned the house and visible grounds.

"Nothing odd. Let's check out the barn first."

The barn was completely locked and secure. Afterward, they walked the driveway from the road to the house, and then out again to the barn, Katie watching carefully to make sure no one was around. At a large oak tree that had a clear view of the driveway, she stopped.

"Give me a boost." She pointed to a limb about seven feet off the ground.

David formed his hands into a stirrup and lifted Katie to where she could reach the branch. "No need to be shy. Grab a hold and push," she grunted. With a charming blush, David, using her buttocks, pushed her higher, where she could get a good grip. She scrambled the rest of the way, straddled the branch and, using ratchet and bits, attached the camera to view the house and drive.

"OK, catch me," she called out, sliding off the branch.

David was barely able to prevent her falling on her face.

"Well, that was graceful," she said, brushing her disheveled hair into place. "Let's check the house."

A quick check showed everything was secure. Katie and David crossed the driveway and a small stand of trees; the driveway to the trailer was clearly visible. Katie mounted the second camera on a medium-sized tree, then grabbed the radio from her pocket.

"Base, this is Ranger-1."

"Ranger-1, go ahead."

Even over the small radio, Max's voice was recognizable.

"All clear, cameras planted. How are ponds? Over."

"Cleared overflow grates; pumps fine; generator test OK. Over."

"OK, we are on the way back; will gander the garden. Over."

"Roger that, Ranger-1. I'll start lunch."

"Roger Base, over and out." Katie stowed the radio.

David was staring open-mouthed. "Wow, you have this stuff down pat."

Katie was slightly embarrassed. "It's operational security. Someone could be listening."

"So what all do you have in the garden?"

"Jerusalem artichokes, some corn, tomatoes, peppers — the usual." She pointed toward the driveway. "It's right over there."

They walked in the heat over to the garden. Turning on a hose valve, Katie and David watched as sprinklers fired up, shooting sparkling lines of water through the air; the irrigation system, tens of feet lower in elevation than the ponds, worked by gravity feed.

"We'll let it run through lunch, then see what's to harvest."

"I am famished," David said as they headed back toward the trailers.

When they arrived, Max met them at the door, looking worried. "Mom, you better have a look."

"What?"

"Our driveway camera — someone's at the gate."

They entered the trailer where Max and Katie slept. Marline sat at a table, looking at an open laptop to which was attached a small box with an antenna.

"Let me see, Marlene."

Marlene turned the laptop. On the screen was a full-color image of the gate and a tall black man, looking directly up the driveway.

"It's Eli, the UPS man." Katie was puzzled. "What the hell is he doing here? David, get the shotgun from Max. We'll take the four-wheeler."

"Four-wheeler?" David looked confused.

"An ATV. It's in the all-metal storage container, so it should have been protected from the EMP."

Outside, Katie opened the container and touched a battery-powered dome light, revealing a Kawasaki Prairie 360. Straddling the ATV, Katie turned its ignition key, pressed the starter button and it roared to life. She shifted into reverse, backed the machine into the outdoors and said, "Well, get on! You are literally riding shotgun." David got on behind her and, kicking the ATV into gear, she headed down the long gravel driveway.

EASTERN PENNSYLVANIA, 07:30 ZULU

Frank's eyes popped open. For a moment he wasn't sure what was happening, then he remembered.

"Where are we?" he asked through a dry mouth. "Whoa, any water?"

Someone in the back handed him a bottle of Avian, as if it weren't already surreal to awaken in a stranger-filled car on a rural highway in the middle of what looked to be Amish farm country.

"We just crossed into Pennsylvania. You've been out for a couple hours."

Looking at the posh brand of water, Frank said, "Great, all I need is some Grey Poupon. No roadblocks?"

"A few on the main roads, but we've avoided them pretty easily. Had to go way north to find a bridge."

Their road was lined with small farms nestled between hills, and barns painted with hex symbols. All in all, things looked pretty rustic until they rounded a blind corner on Federal Road outside of Bushkill and an ancient police cruiser worthy of Mayberry, R.F.D. was barring the road.

"Oh shit," Pete stomped on the brakes, screeching to a halt just short of T-boning the old cruiser.

A tall, middle-aged man wearing a police uniform and a Smoky-the-Bear hat climbed out of the cruiser and, after straightening his uniform and checking his gun, strolled to the driver-side window and tapped on the glass with a ball point pen. Pete nervously rolled down the window.

"You folks in a hurry?"

The policeman had a badge and a nameplate reading

Taylor, which only added to the surrealism.

"Sorry officer. Is there a problem?"

The officer let off a big laugh. "Shit, son, you tell me! Hell, here we are on the backside of nowhere, the world's going to hell and they tell me to man a damn roadblock when I should be taking care of my family." He wiped the sweat off his brow with a red-checkered handkerchief. "You all armed?"

Frank sensed it was best to tell the truth. "Yes sir, we have a 12-gauge."

"Step out of the car."

The officer suddenly turned serious as he stepped back from the door.

Pete started to get out.

"Not you, him." He pointed his pen at Frank.

Frank clambered out, making sure to keep his hands as visible as possible. He left the shotgun in the car.

"Come over here."

Officer Taylor gestured toward the back of the patrol car. Frank didn't know if he should assume the position, or what the officer wanted. "So, that shotgun, it take two and three-quarter or three-inch shells?" He smiled as he opened the trunk. "And here, you should have a side arm," he said as he handed Frank a holstered .45 Automatic Colt Pistol. "I figured folks could use 'em a lot more'n we needed 'em for evidence, anymore." He handed Frank a box of buckshot and a fifty-round box of .45 caliber ammo.

"Getting many travelers?" Frank asked as they walked back to the passenger side of the car.

"Nope, you're the first. Why is your car working?"

"It was on the bottom floor of an underground parking deck in New York City."

"I guess that would do it, alright. They told me to confiscate all working vehicles, but hell, I figure you folks are just trying to get home. Stay off the main roads and you should be fine. How far are you going?"

"Shooting for Monroeville."

"Steer clear of Pittsburg itself, from what we hear it's all burning."

"Thanks, Officer Taylor." Frank transferred the box of .45 ammo to his pants pocket and shook the officer's hand.

"Stay safe." He returned to the cruiser and backed it off the road.

"That went well." Frank showed the others the pistol and ammo.

"Could today get any stranger?" Pete asked, waving to Officer Taylor as he drove past the roadblock and they passed a couple riding in the opposite direction on a bicycle built for two. "Sorry I asked!"

The entire car broke into laughter.

"Anyone else hungry? How about some food?" Frank looked into the back seat.

"We have lots of these" A woman named Delicia handed him a Moon Pie.

"Avian and Moon Pie," Frank said with a laugh. "What else does the distinguished post-apocalypse traveler need?"

NORTH OF LAKE WEISS, ALABAMA, 07:45 ZULU

The cool breeze felt good as the four-wheeler sped down the gravel drive, kicking up a plume of dust and gravel as its tires spun against the rough surface. David, hanging on for dear life, had to keep a hand on the rear rack. He was glad the shotgun had a sling or he wouldn't have been able to both hold it and keep from falling off.

Katie slowed the ATV as they approached the gate, and David was able to get a better grip, hoping he looked at least a little threatening as they skidded to a stop. Katie switched off the engine and dismounted.

"Stay here and cover me discreetly," she said, making sure her .22 Ruger Mark II was clearly visible as she marched to the gate.

"Eli! What are you doing clear out here on such a day?" she asked over the gate, hips akimbo and one hand on her pistol.

"Miz Lowman, there no need for a pistol, I have no weapons." Eli raised his hands and turned around to show he was unarmed. "I have nowhere to go. I am alone here and they made it clear I was not wanted back in Fort Payne."

"Don't worry Eli, I'm not going to shoot you. Why do they not want you?"

"I am a Muslim. Since no one knows who did this, we are easy to blame."

He shrugged.

"Eli, what do you want here?" Katie asked, getting to the point.

"In my country, before I came here, I was a farmer. I am good with my hands, and I can fix just about anything. I guess I am asking if you might let me park my pickup on your property. I can live out of it and help you out." He gestured to the garden. "I figure you need as many hands as possible to keep things going, and as many eyes as possible to help keep things safe."

"Eli, why us?"

"You was always nice to me. You gave me a present at Christmas, and remembered my birthday. Most people on my route don't even say hi."

"It isn't my decision alone, Eli. Hold on, and let me check with the others."

"Whatever you decide is OK by me, ma'am. I will abide by your decision."

Katie walked back to the ATV.

"He wants to join us, or at least stay with us and help out," Katie said quietly to David.

David studied Eli. "He looks strong; able to do good work. Do you feel he's being honest?"

"Never had a reason to doubt him. He's been our delivery driver for as long as we have been coming here, about five years. He always brought the packages to us, never just dropped and ran like the other delivery guys."

"Well, with only four of us, it may be difficult to keep things secure. Maybe you better call the others on the radio." He handed her the radio that was attached to his belt.

"Base, this is Ranger-1, over."

"Ranger-1 go ahead." Max's voice was clear over the small radio.

"Base, he needs a place to stay and has offered to help us for a place to park his pickup. Appears he has one of those large camper backs on it."

"Roger that; hold while I discuss with Red Rover." David choked back a laugh at the code name for his mom.

"Roger Base-1, Ranger-1 out."

It wasn't long until the radio crackled back to life. "Ranger-1, Base, Red Rover and I agree Brownie would be a good addition, over."

"Roger that. I will tell him he is a provisional addition to the team, over."

"Have him park in the shade at the top of the meadow, over."

"Roger that. Good choice, over."

Smiling, Katie went to tell Eli the good news.

Outside Philadelphia, Pennsylvania, 08:00 Zulu

When you aren't really going anywhere, any place is fine.

Willie was cruising, trending south and west, taking back roads and avoiding roadblocks. It is said God watches over fools and drunks, but whether it was God or some darker entity, Willie and Nick succeeded dodging authorities. Seeing a roadside diner that didn't look derelict, Willie parked in the lot and killed the bike's engine.

"Looks good. I'm hungry," Nick's melodious voice said

from behind him.

Willie put the bike on its center stand; in the day's heat the kickstand would have sank into the parking lot's softening asphalt and dumped their ride on its side. "Let's eat."

The sign on the door said closed but a quick strike with the butt of the .45 broke the glass and, releasing the door latches, they gained entrance.

"Check for matches; I'll check the gas pressure." Willie said, heading behind the counter. He turned the dial on the stove and heard the hiss of gas. "Find any?" He called out to Nick, but Nick was nowhere to be seen. "Damn, that guy can make himself scarce quicker than anyone I've ever met," Willie said to himself. On the counter, he found a bowl with paper matchbooks with the diner's name embossed on the front and an ad for a truck-driving school on the back. Appropriately, the diner was called Nick's.

A glance in the walk-in refrigerator revealed some hamburger that hadn't gone bad yet, and other condiments were easily found on a side table. Willie was handy with a backyard grill, so he cooked a couple of burgers and had them on plates by the time Nick returned.

"Where you been?" Willie asked with annoyance.

"Just looking around. Didn't find anything."

"Well, eat up." Willie indicated the hamburgers.

"Sorry man, I found some fruit and stuff, and ate. I'm more of a vegetarian anyway." Nick smiled. "Go ahead and eat mine. Thanks, though."

Willie was hungry and soon finished both hamburgers, as well as a couple packs of potato chips. Afterward, he let out a rumbling belch and grinned. "Shoot, the end of the world ain't so bad." Nick smiled in reply.

Finding an empty backpack in a storeroom, Willie took as much food as they could easily carry and packed it in the other saddlebag. With an evil smirk, Willie extinguished the gas flame at the stove, then turned the gas on full and walked out of the diner.

Stopping the bike about a hundred yards down the road,

Willie turned and pulled the .45 from its holster. Taking careful aim, he fired once, then twice, at the diner. With the second shot the building exploded in flame, the heat so intense they could feel it even from a hundred yards away.

"Nice shooting," Nick said in his ear as they fled the flaming ruins of the dinner, heading toward the Philadelphia city limits.

OUTSIDE MONROEVILLE, PENNSYLVANIA, 09:00 ZULU

"Frank, we may have a problem."

Pete's voice was tinged with concern and just loud enough to wake Frank from a light catnap.

"What'sa matter?" Frank asked, rubbing his eyes and stretching the kinks out of his back.

"We're on empty."

Frank looked at the gauge, it was on E and the low-fuel light glowed yellow. "Start looking for a gas station."

"But won't they not have power?" Pete sounded puzzled.

"There will still be gas in the tanks. Look for one with an attached garage or service center."

It wasn't long until they came upon a full-service gas station, which appeared to have already been looted — one window was cracked, the door lay half-open, and establishment's name, a small sign beside the door, was obscured by spray-canned graffiti. Pete pulled in and turned off the key.

"All right, everyone, time to stretch and take a bathroom break." Frank opened the car door. "Stay close and sing out if there are any problems."

Frank jacked the shotgun to be sure it was loaded; a red-cased shell bounced on the concrete. He retrieved it, pulled the magazine loose, pushed the shell in and reseated it.

"Who's comfortable with a handgun?"

Jane, a passenger in the back, spoke up. "I've done some shooting."

"OK, take this." Frank handed her the .45 and holster and watched, pleasantly surprised, as Jane checked if the weapon were loaded, checked the magazine for round count, slapped the magazine back in and said, "Carolina girls know their way around a pistol." Frank clipped the OTW holster onto the belt of her admirably sensible denim jeans, slipped the pistol into it and replied, "You'd get along well with my wife, Katie."

While Jane and Delicia and their other passenger, Allen, headed around back toward the bathrooms, Frank and Pete entered the garage wreckage. A quick search revealed a hand pump, used to draw oil from fifty-gallon drums, and some Tygon plastic hose. With duct tape they attached lengths of hose to the hand pump. With a bit more searching, Frank found a steel pry bar.

The fill-valve hatches were sturdily locked. But after a few good whacks with the bar and a bit of prying, the lock on the regular unleaded tank popped loose. Opening the hatch, Frank spun the cover off the valve, opened it, and snaked down the hose from the hand pump. Using a plastic jug, Frank pumped a gallon of gas from the tank through the mechanism to clear out any residual oil. "OK, Pete, bring the car over." Pete did so and hit the fuel door release; the driver's-side fuel door popped open. Frank removed the fill cap, threaded the pump outlet hose in and began pumping. After ten minutes, the tank overflowed. Frank was asking Pete to find a carry bag for the fuel rig when they heard the unmistakable boom of the .45 caliber pistol.

Dropping the fuel rig, Frank grabbed the shotgun and he and Pete ran to the back. As they cleared the last corner of the building, a frightening tableau presented itself: Delicia and Allen standing near the bathroom, cowering behind Jane, who was pointing a gun toward a group of five young, black-and-gold-clad Latinos. The Latinos were jeering and shouting.

Nobody had noticed Pete and Frank yet.

"Hey hombres, whachoo goffo uus?" taunted one of the Latinos, a stocky Hispanic with a pockmarked face. He pointed to gang tags, similar to the one in front, beginning to sprout on the back wall. "This is Latin Kings land, now."

Frank pointed the shotgun in the air and discharged a round.

"What do you want from us?" he barked after the ringing of the 12-gauge blast echoed away, then pointed the barrel at the speaker.

"Just our due."

Frank had to give the guy credit—he didn't flinch at the sight of a shotgun pointed at his stomach.

"Would a hundred dollars give us a pass?"

The guy, apparently the leader, exchanged glances with his gang. "Si."

"Pete, reach in my front left pocket and get the money out," Frank said, continuing to cover the gang with the shotgun as Pete pulled out the wad of money Frank had taken from the hotel weapons-cash bowl.

"Hand it to him, but don't get in the way of a shot."

Nervously, Pete offered the money to the stocky leader. With a sneer the scarred Hispanic took the cash and quickly counted it. He signaled his members and, with weary glances at Frank's shotgun and Jane's .45, they disappeared into a nearby alley, kicking depleted spray cans in Frank's direction.

"OK. Bathroom break is over, let's get the hell out of here." Frank lowered the shotgun, hoping they could soon find another respite. With all the excitement, he and Pete hadn't had a chance to use the restrooms.

The group piled in the car while Frank stowed the makeshift fuel pump in a plastic bag, which he tied shut in the trunk. Turning over the shotgun to Pete, he took a turn as driver and, after half an hour, they dropped Allen at his home in Monroeville, where Frank finally got a restroom break.

Though Allen offered shelter for the night, everyone wanted to continue heading south on the long road to Georgia via West Virginia and Tennessee.

Royal Air Force Station Brize Norton
North of London, England, 09:30 Zulu

Earl Tolliday rearranged his position on the uncomfortable bench for what seemed like the hundredth time since he had first tried to lie down and rest. After the shocking news about the EMP strike on the USA, he had been attempting to return to his wife, Marlene, in Roswell, Georgia. Since all commercial flight to the States were cancelled, his search had led him to the military base where the Brits were assembling relief missions to fly electronics, transformers and other infrastructure to the USA.

The RAF allowed American citizens to fly as supercargo on relief flights on a first-come, first-serve basis. Earl's father Brian, a retired RAF commander, had pulled strings to get Earl priority seating. Of course, "priority" meant he might get out in two to four days instead of ten. In the meantime, he waited.

"Earl Tolliday! Report to flight control," called a sharply English-accented voice over the PA system. Earl grabbed his reduced kit—limited by RAF policy to twenty kilograms—and moved quickly to the flight control counter.

"Passport."

Earl handed his passport to the officer.

"Mr. Tolliday, we have a flight leaving in twenty minutes that can take you to the Lockheed Martin factory field in Marietta, Georgia. Will that do?" The officer returned Earl's passport.

"Yes, sir, that would be brilliant! I can almost walk home from there."

"You may have to, from what we're hearing. Good luck, sir, and Godspeed."

Earl shook the officer's hand and then, hefting his kit bag, ran to Embarkation. After a quick check of his papers, the embarkation officer opened a door and the engine roar from the huge Lockheed C-5 Galaxy transport washed over them. Earl followed guide lines to the rear cargo hatch and was soon inside a cavernous cargo hold filled with row after row of electrical transformers. He was directed to a fold-down jump seat and handed a heavy military parka and ear protection. Placing his bag under his seat, he fumbled a bit with the flight harness until a young airman in the adjacent seat offered assistance.

With a high-pitched whine, the rear cargo door slowly closed and sealed. The noise level reduced but it was still a deep, chest-rattling throb. Earl closed his eyes as the pitch of the engines changed and the behemoth started to move. After a brief time the nose pitched sharply up and Earl was pushed sideways and down into his seat as the Galaxy morphed from a slowly accelerating ground machine to a miracle of modern flight technology.

The airman pointed at the side of Earl's headgear. Earl felt with his right hand and noticed a small switch and a dial. He flicked the switch.

"Can you hear me now, Mr. Tolliday?"

"Yes, quite well actually."

"Good. Once we reach cruise altitude I'll break out a couple of MREs—meals ready to eat. Care for a few hands of poker?"

"Sounds brilliant. Any idea of how long the flight?"

"Fully loaded, we'll have to refuel halfway to make it in one hop. Should arrive by 23:00 hours." The pilot's voice took precedence in the headgear: "Airman Peters, we have reached flight altitude."

Earl watched as Peters unbuckled his harness and moved to a set of cabinets. Opening the latched doors, he pulled out two MREs and two MRE heaters, then re-latched the cabinet and returned to his seat next to Earl.

"Here is how you warm it up."

He demonstrated how to open the MRE heater and trigger

the chemical reaction that heated the food. Earl followed directions and soon his MRE was warming nicely. Peters went to a small ice chest.

"Do you mind having a stout? It's all that's left."

"Nope, not at all!"

On his way home, a meal heating in front of him, and a cold stout—what else could he possibly need.

North of Philadelphia International Airport, Pennsylvania, 10:00 Zulu

Avoiding Philadelphia, whose skyline was marked by tall columns of black smoke, Willie traveled down PA291, marveling at how the Philadelphia International Airport was nearly engulfed in two-story flames. When the EMP disabled cockpit navigation and control computers, several planes had crashed into the facility and nearby aviation fuel storage tanks. Since large jetliners are fly-by-wire, the EMP had wiped out the possibility of safe landing for any airliner even a few dozen feet off the ground.

"Looks like a nice wiener roast," Nick whispered in his ear. Even several hundred yards from the conflagration, heat was pouring off the flames in waves almost visible in the hot July air. Just then the motorcycle sputtered and coughed beneath him. "What the hell—" Willie said loudly.

"Flip the reserve switch on the tank," he heard Nick say.

Reaching down the tank's side he felt a small lever, flipped it and the engine revs smoothed out. "We better find some gas!" He yelled back to Nick. Up ahead he saw a woman standing by the side of her stalled car. From the look of things, she had spent the night in the vehicle, waiting for help.

"We can get gas from her car," Nick whispered, adding, "And she is fine!"

Willie pulled the bike behind the car and set it back on its center stand. He dismounted quickly, but once again Nick had beat him off the bike and was obviously scouting around to be sure they were alone with the woman.

"Can I help you?" Willie asked, still wearing his sun glasses.

"My car has stalled, I don't know what has happened, and I'm terrified for those poor people over at the airport. Is anyone helping them?"

She had a pleasant voice, but looked to be a bit of a spoiled princess.

"Nope, I think they're beyond help. Everyone is," Willie said hollowly.

"Well I 'm glad you stopped. Can you get my engine going?" she asked haughtily, looking closely at Willie for the first time.

"I'll try," he said, grabbing her wrist and twisting it roughly behind her. "I'll try real hard!" He jerked the rear car door open and, shoving her face onto the back seat, got in behind her.

Later, as he climbed out of the car, Nick returned.

"You want some?" Willie asked, grinning. He had some scratches on the his face and a few bruises, but after he had smacked her around a bit she had calmed down. In his self-centered mind he thought she ended up enjoying it—she hadn't complained when he got started. Actually, when he shoved her very hard after she tried to backhand him, he had broken her neck, but in his "passion" he failed to recognize that he had forced himself on a corpse.

"Nope. Looks like you used it all up, my friend. Pop the trunk. Let's see if there is anything to siphon gas with."

As Willie fumbled with the controls on the front dash, the dead woman's body relaxed its anal sphincter muscle and let loose a disgusting stream of gas and waste. Willie realized she was dead.

Stumbling from the front seat, he barely made it to the ditch before he vomited, just missing his shiny new boots.

"Like I said, looks like you used it all up," Nick said, grinning.

Willie wiped vomit from his mouth, stumbled back to the bike, opened the saddlebag, grabbed a bottle of tepid water, wrenched off the top and rinsed out his mouth. He set the bottle on the pavement and returned to the now open trunk, where he searched a well-provisioned tool kit with a shaker siphon hose. However, the trunk did not offer a gas can.

"Great! How do we get the gas into the tank?" He asked Nick, who had been looking into the back seat of the car with a smile on his face.

"Disconnect the gas line and the tank should pop off the frame."

Willie examined the bike and sure enough, the gas hose was a pressure-fit coupling; two rubber mounts with metal snap clamps held on the tank. Willie soon had the tank on the ground next to the car's fill pipe and was filling it with the siphon hose. When the tank was full, Willie tore a piece of cloth from the woman's blouse, then twisted and stuffed it into the car's gas tank fill line. He then removed it, squeezed it — soaking its lower quarter with gasoline — and restuffed it into the pipe until a third of its length protruded.

Remounting the bike, Willie asked, "Well, where to?"

"After here, anything is up. Let's keep heading south."

Willie cranked the bike, eased to the car, reached and lit the rag with a Bic lighter. It caught with a whoosh. Willie and Nick roared off, and they were only a few dozen yards down the road when the car's gas tank exploded and the concussion wave reached them with a large thud. With a rebel yell, Willie gunned the bike down Pa. Hwy. 291 toward the small town of Chester.

North of Lake Weiss, Alabama, 12:45 Zulu

Eli parked his truck as directed, then everyone went to the main trailer.

Katie spoke first. "Eli, I'm afraid you will need to stay in your truck until we get other shelter built." She handed him a canned turkey sandwich.

"Many thanks." His smile lit up his face. "That will be fine. I am afraid I have no arms or means of defense." He hungrily consumed the sandwich.

"We have plenty. Have you ever used a shotgun?" Katie handed him a glass of cold well water.

His face darkened from whatever memory the question raised. "A long time ago, before I came to the States."

"OK then. It's settled. You can eat your meals here with us if you like, or take supplies to your truck. Do you have means to warm things up?"

"A Coleman stove, but not much fuel."

"We can fix that."

After Eli finished his sandwich and water, Katie led him to the storage container, making him wait outside as she disappeared into its dark recesses. Soon she was back pushing a wheelbarrow containing a Grab & Go Meal Bucket, a gallon can of white gas, a pump-action short-barreled 12-gauge shotgun and spare ammo, a five-gallon container of water, and a five-gallon bucket with attached toilet seat, liners and chemical packs.

"Do you need a cook set? Plates? Silverware?"

"No ma'am, this will be fine." He gave another blinding smile as he admired the barrow's contents.

"David can take you back to your truck."

"No ma'am. If I can just use this wheelbarrow, I can walk

back."

"OK. Get settled in. Tonight, come up about six p.m. and we'll all eat together and decide on duties."

"Yes ma'am!"

"Eli."

"Yes'm?"

"Call me Katie."

"Yes ma'am. Er, I mean, Katiee." He drew out the last syllable of her name in an almost Jamaican accent.

Katie returned to the main trailer, where Marlene was still watching the monitor.

"Any new visitors?"

"A fella on a motorbike, but he just watched a bit, then drove back toward town."

"Odd."

"Yes, indeed."

"Do you think he was watching Eli, or just checking us out?"

"I really couldn't tell, love."

"David, get the quad runner and go get Eli. We need a watch point in the woods by the southeast corner of the property. There's plywood and other materials in the storage container."

"Eh, how do I carry all that?"

"What? Oh damn, I forgot, in the back of the pole barn is an ATV trailer, get it and I'll help you hook it up."

After hooking up the trailer and loading supplies, David went to fetch Eli while Katie got a second, smaller quad-runner from the shed. Soon the sound of the first quad-runner could be heard laboring up the hill from Eli's camp.

"Marlene and Max, I'm going to show the men where to build the watch post. Keep an eye on the monitor. If you see anyone else, give a yell on the radio."

"Will do, be careful," Marlene answered with a worried tone in her voice.

With a squeal of brakes and a cloud of dust, the larger quad-runner came to a halt.

"Follow me," Katie shouted over the engine noise, signaling to David. She shifted her quad-runner into gear and headed toward the far edge of the property. At the southeast corner she called a halt, parked her quad and began searching for a suitable site for a watch post. Finding a small hollow under a large fallen oak she signaled the men.

"This is a good spot. We need to build a shelter from which we can observe the road from town without being seen."

Eli looked over her choice.

"Katie, if I may be so bold, over there would be easier to conceal and give better cover." He indicated a spot further back but with a better view of the road.

She looked over his suggestion. "Sounds like you have done this before."

"A long time ago, but yes." Darkness returned to his normally happy face. "A time long ago, a place far from here, but it seems the times are returning."

"David, follow Eli's instructions." She handed David the radio. "If we see anything on the monitors, we'll give a yell. If you need anything, call and we'll run it down to you."

Eli looked over the supplies. "Do you have any plastic sheet? We can use it to waterproof the roof and shield the watch from the damp ground."

"Yes, we have heavy-duty plastic tarps; I'll bring a few down."

"Wonderful! We will get started." Eli slapped David on the shoulder and started unloading supplies.

Aboard Air Force One, Circling above the USA, 13:00 Zulu

"Are you sure Jack? We have to be sure." President Paul looked directly into the dark green eyes of his security advisor, Jack

Arnold.

"The scientists at Oak Ridge confirmed the source signature of the fissionable based on the fallout we are seeing. Our sources in the Mid-East confirmed the agreements between Chavez and Iran."

"It was Chavez then? No doubts?" The president looked down and rubbed his hands across his eyes. He had hardly slept in the two days since being rushed aboard Air Force One.

"No doubts. Oil barges known to have departed Maracaibo would have been at the coordinates of the reported oil slick. We sent down a ROV and confirmed the wreckage contained parts that appear to be launch tubes."

"God forgive me. You say we can do the same to him?"

"Yes sir."

"What about Iran?"

"Yes sir."

"Make it happen."

"We have the submarine USS Henry M. Jackson within launch range of Venezuela; we have several that can target Iran and North Korea. We've already sent target coordinates for a salvo of high-altitude bursts. Guidance system modifications should be complete by the time we send launch orders."

"Modifications?" The president looked puzzled.

"The missiles weren't designed to be atmospheric weapons. The guidance computers had to be manually recalibrated," Jack explained.

"No one will die from the detonations?"

"No sir, it will, however, destroy anything with microcircuitry and unprotected transformers."

"If it must be done, let's get it done," the president said, resignation in his voice. "It won't get any easier."

"Yes sir. Should we also target North Korea and Iran?"

"Venezuela first, then have the subs target the others, but hold off the strikes for a day or so and see what develops."

"Yes sir." Jack Arnold signaled the naval officer who had "the football," the case with the nuclear arming codes, and stood by grimly as the protocols were enacted.

Presidential Palace, Caracas, Venezuela, 14:00 Zulu

Hugo Chavez was an old man. He felt proud that he had lived and ruled long enough to see the USA humbled. He had been warned about retaliation but felt the USA had grown weak. His Iranian advisors and North Korean contacts assured him the USA couldn't respond because of the weakness of their leaders. He hoped they were correct.

He glanced at his security chief's report. His ability to control the populace had been eroding for years. Only his security forces' advanced technology kept him ahead of rebel forces. If he lost the edge he would be dead within the week, and none too pleasantly. The rebels had adopted the Mexican drug cartels' use of machetes and beheadings. Lost in thought, it took him a few seconds to realize the alert phone was buzzing.

With a weary hand he picked up the line. A voice on the other end was speaking in frantic Spanish.

"Señor! Tenemos tres lanzamiento indicaciones 170 kilómetros de la costa!"

"¿Está seguro?"

"Si, Si señor! Deberíamos sonido las advertencias?"

"No, no importa." Chavez hung up the alert line.

From the top left drawer of his desk he removed an ancient military version of the .38 Special revolver and laid it on the desk. Ironically, it had been manufactured in the USA. Standing, he moved toward the large window overlooking Caracas. At that moment, it seemed as if a second sun were sharing the sky. If he'd had a 360-degree panorama, he would have seen two more suns. His phone chirped but didn't ring, and a sudden smell of hot circuitry filled the air as the various electronics in his office emitted small popping sounds.

Walking back to his presidential desk, he calmly put the pistol to his head and, with a sad smile, filled the air with thunder.

MONROEVILLE, PENNSYLVANIA, 13:15 ZULU

The Lincoln had just passed Monroeville Mall on Monroeville Road when the tire inflation light started blinking.

"Crap, what now," Frank said to himself as he pulled over to the side of the road, glancing around for potential problems.

"What's the matter, Frank?" Delicia asked.

"Tire inflation alarm. Front right tire is indicating low pressure. I'll check it," Frank said.

The tire looked flatter than the others. A visual check showed the head of a roofing nail embedded in the tread. "Just when things were moving along," Frank muttered. He hoped the Lincoln, a high-end car, would have a full-size spare. He didn't recall seeing one in the trunk, but it was perhaps under a mat.

"Pull the trunk release, will you?" He shouted to Pete, who was riding shotgun. The trunk lid hissed open.

After nearly emptying the trunk, Frank was visibly upset. "No spare? No damn spare at all?" He angrily stomped to the passenger-side door and jerked it open. "Get me the manual from the glove box, will you, Pete?" The other riders eyed each other nervously. Pete handed the manual to Frank.

"Great, just great. Pete, cover me, will you?" Frank returned the manual to Pete, who then joined Frank at the rear of the car.

"What's up?" Pete cradled the shotgun anxiously.

"No damn spare. Just a flat-fix and inflator kit."

"You're kidding!" Pete was incredulous.

"I guess they figure with the tire inflation monitor you'll catch it before it gives out. Heaven help you if you rip a hole in a side wall or tear up a tire." As he talked he opened a small compartment and pulled out a black device with an inflation hose and a car-plug power cord. The date on the tire sealer canister mounted on the device was only six months out of date. "Great," he said.

"Let's see if this works."

Frank went to the offending tire and noted that the valve was positioned at the top. "Pete, hand me the shotgun, then roll the car forward. We need the valve at the bottom."

"Don't we need to pull out the nail, first?"

"Not according to the instructions."

As Pete walked to the driver's side, Frank opened the passenger door and plugged in the cord, then switched the control to inflate and seal. Lowering the window, he passed the inflator through the opening and closed the door.

"Ready," Pete called.

"OK, roll it slowly."

The car inched forward . . . as the valve neared the bottom, Frank signaled stop and the car ceased moving at the correct valve position. Frank removed the valve stem cap, attached the hose, pushed start and watched as the tire initially over-inflated, then deflated slightly, then increased to normal pressure. He turned off and disconnected the inflator, replaced the valve stem cap, and passed the inflator in through the window, laying it on the passenger seat. He opened the door, took the inflator into his lap and sat down.

"In three miles we recheck pressure." He indicated that Pete should drive.

After three miles, the pressure had dropped about eight PSI and Frank breathed a sigh of relief. According to the manual if the drop had been more than ten pounds per square inch, the repair was a bust and the tire needed immediate replacement. Reconnecting the device, he set the control to inflate, ran it to full, detached the thing and stuck it in the trunk.

"We should be good for seventy to a hundred miles. Watch the inflation alarm, and watch for a Lincoln dealership."

"Can't we just watch for another Lincoln?"

"Well, Pete, they didn't include a jack or a tire iron, either," Frank said testily. "Just pray."

"Pray we find a dealer?"

"Pray we don't have another flat. The fixer cartridge is a one-timer."

Smyrna, Delaware, 14:15 Zulu

Willie was sore in places he didn't know he had. He and Nick had ridden most of the night, stopping only for the occasional call of nature. The Yamaha's constant vibration, nice at first, had grown annoying; he was chaffed and his back ached.

"Bill, I like the bike, but man is my butt sore," Nick said in his ear. "Let's find a different ride."

"Sounds good. Let's get off Highway 1 here in Smyrna and find what we can," Willie answered into the sixty miles an hour slipstream.

"You are driving, my man."

They exited onto Commerce, and after a few blocks spotted a Jeep dealer.

"How about a Jeep?" Willie had always wanted one, but his father had said with his driving record it was out of the question.

"Good choice. Let's look at older models, less likely to be EMP-ed."

They pulled in to the used lot and Willie parked the bike, feeling his muscles ache as he swung his leg over the seat. Nick was already walking toward the used vehicles. At 9:15 a.m., the place appeared deserted.

"What about that CJ with the canvas top?" Willie pointed

to a bright red Jeep with lots of chrome.

"Pretty, but we want something inconspicuous, like this." Nick stood beside a lifted 1980 CJ with a flat, camo-green paintjob. The tires looked new, including the spare. On the back it sported a jerry can in a rack, and inside it was spotless, had a toolkit, and, mounted on the back of the front seats, a gun rack.

"Looks perfect," Willie sat in the driver's seat and checked the manual transmission. "I don't have much experience with sticks, though."

"You can learn. Come on, let's find the keys." Nick headed toward the trailer that was the used-car office.

At the trailer, Willie made short work of the door glass and soon they were rifling keys for the proper set until they were startled by a deep voice.

"Can I do something for you?"

They turned to see the biggest guy they'd ever seen — six four and three hundred pounds.

"I'm Big Jake, and this is my lot." He gestured with a Kimber .45. "I wouldn't touch those if I were you."

Willie glanced at Nick, but Nick was no help, staring straight ahead. "We didn't mean any harm. We wanted to swap the bike for a Jeep."

"That piece-of-shit bike is worth about five hundred bucks; my least expensive Jeep is five thousand." Big Jake didn't lower the gun. "And now, if a vehicle runs, it's worth its weight in gold."

"Well, we'll just leave," Willie said, fidgeting.

"We? You got a mouse in your pocket?" Big Jake eyed him suspiciously.

Willie looked and Nick was gone. How he managed it was beyond Willie's imagination, but if he'd snuck out, maybe they'd get out with their skins intact. And there was Nick, standing behind Big Jake.

But Big Jake, seeing Willie's eyes look past his shoulder, turned in that direction to assess the threat, and Willie, seizing the opportunity, grabbed the pistol from his duty belt, aimed it at Big Jake and pulled the trigger.

The first shot went high and wide right as Willie jerked the trigger; the second caught Big Jake in the shoulder, and the third in the center of his chest. Flailing, knocked backward by the impacts, Big Jake fell backward over the trailer entry handrail and somersaulted to the ground below.

Willie rushed to the rail, looked down at Big Jake's moaning form and aimed the pistol at Big Jake's head, only to realize the action was stove-piped with a spent shell casing. Willie fruitlessly tried to pull the stuck shell from the action until he finally he racked the slide, dropping the shell to the ground. Willie reloaded. Re-aiming, he fired one steady shot, which entered Big Jake's left eye and exited the back of his head. Big Jake stopped moaning.

"Good job," Nick said from behind him.

"I couldn't have done it without you distracting him! How'd you get behind him like that?"

"I have my ways."

They quickly found keys to the camo-green Jeep. Being pre-electronic ignition, the CJ started. Willie and Nick transferred supplies from the overloaded saddlebags to their new vehicle and cradled the shotgun into the rifle holder on the seat backs. Without a backward glance they drove off, Willie stalling and grating gears.

Over the Atlantic, 17:15 Zulu

Earl Tolliday, lulled by the constant engine drone and airframe vibration, was sleeping after a few hands of poker until a sudden jostling of the plane startled him awake. He was disoriented, and unsure where he was.

"You all right, sir?" A disembodied voice said through his earphones.

After a bit of fumbling Earl managed to turn on his microphone.

"Brilliant! Where's the loo?"

"Unplug your head phone and I'll show you."

Earl stood unsteadily on the up-pitched deck and followed Peters toward the front of the compartment. Putting his head close to Peter's, Earl asked, "Why so much vibration now?"

"Getting ready for a mid-air refueling. It's like a mid-air collision without the flames." Peters enjoyed gallows humor.

"Great," was all Earl could think to say as he closed the bathroom hatch.

After stumbling twice due to the maneuvers of the plane, Earl decided to sit instead of stand to do his business, then washed his hands and dried them on the rough brown paper towels that seemed to be in infinite supply in military facilities. He opened the hatch, extinguished the light and returned to his jump seat. Peters indicated he should plug in.

"That's better, Mr. Tolliday. If you'd like, the pilot invites you to watch the refueling."

"Thank you. That's not something you see every day, I'm sure."

Earl unplugged and followed Peters to the cockpit door. Peters knocked, a flight officer appeared, signaled Tolliday to enter, and Peters waved goodbye. The flight officer indicated an unoccupied seat from which Earl could watch over the pilot's shoulder, and helped him plug in to the cockpit chatter.

The tanker took up position in front and at a slightly higher altitude. When both planes had reached the proper positions, a long refueling boom with a small set of wings trailed out of the tanker, which was on autopilot. The boom moved up and overhead, toward a refueling port above and behind the cockpit. Earl spotted the refueling operators lying on their stomachs in the tanker's control area, and watched as status lights turned yellow on the tanker's underside, indicating fore and aft and down and up alignment. The refueling boom locked into place. The planes synchronized, and minor misalignments were handled by the boom's capability to telescope. Earl let out the breath he hadn't been aware he was holding.

"You blokes make it look easy," Earl shouted above the din.

"Thanks, Mr. Tolliday. Would you like stay up here awhile?" The captain asked.

"If it wouldn't be a bother, I would love to."

Earl watched, fascinated as the crew completed refueling and the boom disengaged. As the tanker banked away, Earl swore he saw the refueling operator wave to him.

"Mr. Tolliday, I believe Airman Peters has another MRE and more stout if you're hungry." The navigator indicated that Peters was at the cockpit door. Reluctantly, Earl unplugged and followed Peters back to their jump seats.

"Quite a show, eh, Mr. Tolliday?" Peters handed Earl a roast beef MRE.

"Well worth the price of admission." Earl opened the warmer and keyed the reaction to heat his MRE.

"Yes sir, we hardly ever collide in mid-air anymore and die in huge fireballs."

Earl studied Peters to see how much of what he said was a joke, but with helmet and flight visor in place it was difficult to tell. Earl was halfway home. Somehow he knew the easy part of the journey was coming to a close.

Border of Pennsylvania and West Virginia, 18:00 Zulu

Frank slowed as he crested a hill a mile or so from the Pennsylvania–West Virginia border. Ahead were several plumes of black smoke.

"I'm going to scout on foot," Frank said as he pulled onto the shoulder of US119 and parked. "Time to check the tire, anyway."

The tire they'd fixed with the contraption that replaces the spare in a Lincoln still showed full pressure. Frank thanked God for their luck, and hoped they would soon find a Lincoln dealership, or at least a jack they could use to replace the bad tire. Frank took the .45 1911, and handed the shotgun to Pete. "You hear shots, you wait ten minutes. If I don't come running over that hill by then, get out of here."

"I don't intend on leaving you behind, Frank," Pete stated unequivocally.

"Look, you have two other people to watch out for. Don't be a hero. I can take care of myself." Frank held up his hand as Pete protested further, then turned and walked toward the pillars of black smoke over the hill.

Rather than tackle whatever was ahead head-on, Frank left the road and made his way to the timberline on the highway's left side. Using trees for cover, he soon came within sight of the source of the smoke.

At the rest area that straddled the state line, the Pennsylvania State Police had set up a roadblock—at least it had been a roadblock. Someone had set fire to the patrol cars and Frank, from his vantage point, could see several bodies lying in and around the wrecks. Some of the bodies wore State Patrol uniforms, others camouflage. Frank wished he had binoculars so he could see more details; he made a mental note to find some as soon as possible. He watched for any motion, but other than the crackling fires and the smoke in the light breeze, he saw no signs of life in the grisly tableau. Nervously, he checked that the .45 was cocked and locked, then made his way to the burning cars.

It appeared that a militia or paramilitary group had ambushed the roadblock crew: Frank found .40, 7.62x39, and .223 caliber cases lying all over the road. The .223 and .40 rounds could have come from the police, but the 7.62x39, the usual round for AK-47s, was popular with both radical and non-radical survivalists due to its availability and low cost. Those bodies not in the burning vehicles had been stripped of useful articles, and the patrol car trunks gaped open, showing that they had also been searched. As the sickly sweet smell of roasting flesh and burning oil and gas made Frank sick to his stomach, he noticed shards of broken glass bottles near the burning vehicles. He searched a bit more, then jogged back to Pete and the waiting car.

"What's going on?" Pete asked.

Out of breath from the jog, Frank took a moment to answer. "It was an ambush. A group took out a roadblock up ahead, using assault rifles and maybe Molotov cocktails. As far as I can tell, no survivors. Must have happened within the last couple of hours so whoever did it is ahead of us."

"Should we go on?" asked Delicia.

"Well, we'd probably catch up to them. If they have scouts out, they'd see us before we saw them." Frank spoke truthfully, not pulling his punches. "I say we take an alternate. Let's stop here, eat something, and study the maps."

Over a quick lunch of energy bars, water and assorted hard candies, they planned a route that would necessitate backtracking to SR3002, also known as Gans Road, which led east to SR857 heading south. With luck, they could use back roads paralleling US119 all the way to Interstate 68 at Cheat Lake. The general plan was to follow I-68 to I-79 at Charleston, where Pete lived, but if I-68 proved troublesome, they'd have to resort to secondary highways or worse.

"Frank," asked Jane, "do you think there'll be more roadblocks?"

"I don't really know. As local police realize the extent of the disaster, many will desert and flee with their families. It's probably too early to expect military in any great numbers, but opportunistic people may try it," Frank answered around a mouthful of crumbly snack bar.

" 'Opportunistic'?" She looked puzzled.

Frank reached into a bag of beef jerky and extracted a few chunks. "Yep. People out to rob, or towns trying to keep out looters and such."

"It doesn't look good for me to reach Charlotte, does it?"

She had a tear in her eye as she asked.

"I will do my best to get you there, Jane. I intend on getting to Roswell, where I live, and Charlotte is on the way." He smiled, trying to encourage her.

After lunch they backtracked to SR3002, and soon they were headed south on SR857, occasionally observing people in their yards or staring out their windows. Over all, things were eerily deserted, people crouching in their homes, uncertain, lacking the siren songs of radio, TV, and familiar jobs—sheep trapped by a perceived lack of mobility.

A few miles before the outskirts of Cheat Lake and the merge with I-68, Frank kept an eye out for signs of smoke or other destruction. Approaching the I-68 interchange, he again parked the car and scouted ahead. Other than several abandoned cars, there was no mayhem or even traffic. They merged easily onto I-68, and after only a mile or two, Frank saw something that put a smile on his face. "Look," he said, pointing at a roadside sign. "A Lincoln dealer in Fairmont. Here's hoping we can get a replacement tire."

The Fairmont dealership was easy to find. As with most businesses, it was closed. Frank pulled up to the entrance, parked, exited, tried the doors and knocked on several other doors in buildings that were part of the facility. Finally, at a small trailer in back, a frightened voice called out: "Go away! We're closed."

"My name is Frank. We aren't here to hurt you. We need a tire."

The door rattled as it was unlocked and a chain undone. "Are you under warranty?" An older man, carrying an old .38 Special revolver, peered out suspiciously.

"It's a rental. Here . . ." Frank handed the papers for the man's scrutiny.

"Well, normally I'd tell you to call the rental folks and get them to send a car out, but that isn't an option now, is it?" He returned the papers to Frank. "Let's have a look." Frank followed him toward the front of the facility.

"You from around here?"

"Afraid not. I'm trying to get these folks home; we left New York yesterday." Frank indicated the Lincoln and its three hopeful riders.

"Figures. One o' them newer models without a spare. Been a real pain in the ass to us. We keep some on rims in the shop, ready to swap out." He pulled a large ring of keys from his pants pocket and unlocked the shop door.

The shop was dark. Cars in various states of dismantlement filled all but one repair bay. "Pull your car up to that door," he said, indicating the bay with no vehicle. "My name is George, by the way. Night watchman. They let me keep my trailer on the back lot."

"Good to meet you, George. Heard anything about what's going on?"

"Not a word."

Frank drove the car to the indicated bay, as yet unopened. He left the car running and went inside to offer assistance.

"Dang motor ain't working, of course . . . need the crank for the manual operator," George said as he came in. "Check those cabinets and I'll look here." He indicated some toolboxes.

They soon found the crank and opened the door. Frank drove the Lincoln in and then helped George position the hydraulic jack under the side with the flat. Frank noted it was still holding pressure.

"That stuff seems to work pretty well," Frank said.

George gave him a disgusted look.

"Half the time, it goops up the inside and makes proper fixing a pain in the ass. You were lucky." He pumped the jack handle and raised the car. "Get the nut key, will you?"

"The what?"

"The nut key. These hubs lock onto the studs via one locknut that takes a special key," George explained. "Keeps people from stealing when they get a flat; each set of lug nuts has a different key."

"Good to know. We'd considered finding another Lincoln and grabbing a tire, but without a jack, that was an iffy option. Guess it wouldn't have worked."

"Nope. Not a chance. The key should be in the compressor kit."

Frank retrieved the key; it looked like a regular socket but with an odd-shaped hole obviously fitting a specific lug nut. George mounted the socket on a long-handled wrench, removed the special locknut, then returned the key to Frank. "Put that back in case you need it."

Stronger than he appeared, George grabbed a regular lug wrench, removed the damaged tire, rolled it to a section of the shop where several other tires awaited repair. He then fetched a good tire and mounted it.

"Why don't you go get another in case you have another flat?" George told Frank as he tightened the lug nuts. "And get that key again; I should've realized I'd need it to put the damn thing back on."

Frank got him the key, then rolled over another good tire. "Trunk's full, George, where're we going to put it?"

"Tie it on the roof."

George fetched an old woolen blanket, folded it to the right size, and placed it on the roof. Frank helped lift the tire and secure it with tie-downs.

"Oh, you might need a set of these . . ." George indicated a small hydraulic jack, handle, wrench, and a lug socket.

"We don't have any money, George." Frank said honestly.

"I get the feeling money isn't worth much anymore. So I'll trade you; I need to get to Marietta, Georgia, where my son lives. They don't need me here, and the trailer's all-electric."

"I think we have a deal, George. I'm heading to Roswell." Frank and George shook hands. As Frank backed the car out of the repair bay and cranked down the door, George went to pack a small bag.

"Everyone, meet George."

Frank introduced George to the group. "This is Pete, who gets dropped in Charleston, West Virginia. Back on the left is Jane, bound for Charlotte, North Carolina, and beside her is Delicia, on her way to Spartanburg, South Carolina."

"Glad to meet you George," said Pete. Jane and Delicia

shook his hand.

"Where can I put my shotgun," George asked as he got in. Frank thought it amazing that no one flinched.

North of Lake Weiss, Alabama, 18:30 Zulu

Eli and David took a well-earned break. The labor of clearing the site for the lookout had drenched them both in sweat. David probed for information about Eli's past but hit a brick wall after all but the most general questions.

The radio beeped and David answered. "Rover-2, over."

"Rover-2 this is base. Why don't you two come up for some lunch, over."

"Base, Rover-2. You read our minds. Be right up, over." David smiled as he lowered the radio. "Unhitch the trailer and let's head for lunch."

They rode the four-wheeler by the lower pond to sluice off the grime and sweat. Feeling more presentable, they drove to the main trailer, where the women had set up a table under a small outdoor pavilion.

"Where'd this tent come from?" David asked, sitting down to a steaming bowl of beef stew.

"It's a folding one from our scuba diving days; it protected the gear from the sun," Katie explained, helping herself to stew. "Want some bread with that?" She held out a platter of slices from a fresh-baked loaf.

"Man, this is great," exclaimed David, attacking his food. "Better than I usually eat at home. Where'd you get fresh bread?"

"We put back several hundred pounds of wheat, and have an electric grinder. Luckily, it's low-tech enough it wasn't affected by the EMP. The rest was elbow work. Max did the hard part yesterday, getting the dough ready. All we had to do today was bake it."

"But doesn't that take milk and yeast and . . ." started David.

"We have all that, powdered or dried, at least enough until we set up trading with someone with cows or goats. Speaking of which, I'll have to show you the tilapia," Max said.

" 'Tilapia'?"

"A fast-growing, low-upkeep fish—just water and food," Eli answered. "I used to help raise them, where I came from."

"Well, well, well, Eli, you are becoming more valuable every second." Katie smiled at Eli, who looked away shyly.

"It is I who owe you and Mr. Frank, Katiee. By now I might be strung-up or worse, and if I escaped such a fate, I'd surely be without a place to stay."

"Is Fort Payne that bad already?" Marlene piped up.

"I am sorry, Miss Marlene, but sections are. One of the fundamentalist preachers got that big church toward the center of town all stirred up against Muslims. Said we were to blame. By the time I got home from work, they'd trashed my apartment, and mobs roamed the streets terrorizing anyone who looked Muslim. They beat and raped some Hindu women, and lynched a Sikh because they wore robes or turbans."

Eli looked embarrassed to have said so much. He drank from his water glass to cover it up. "I am afraid I may bring bad luck on you. I think the motorcycle man was one of them."

"Eli! You should have told us right away," Katie scolded.

"You are right, Miss Katiee, I will leave after lunch." He looked down.

"Nonsense! That isn't what I meant. Had we known, we could've started on the lookout and planned more defensive actions sooner." Katie patted Eli's shoulder. "Eat your lunch. The lookout needs to be completed, and we have planning to do," Katie said firmly.

Lunch was finished in relative silence. David and Eli headed back to the lookout. Katie gathered the women: "Max, could you and Marlene take care of the lunch cleanup? I need to get something from the emergency cache."

With a nod of approval from Marlene, Max said, "Sure, Mom. Whatever's needed. Do you want help?"

"Nope, I'll take the tractor. The front loader's still on,

right?"

"Yes. I haven't touched it since we did the cut on the upper pasture a couple of weeks ago." Max looked concerned. "It's pretty serious, isn't it?"

"If your father and Earl were here, maybe not, but I've had some run-ins with the Right Reverend Sanders. He's mean as a snake and hates other religions. I'll bet a dime to a dollar he's behind this."

"It's amazing anyone listens to him."

"People need someone to blame; looks like he provided it."

After fetching the tractor key, Katie left them to clean up. At the pole barn behind the trailer she found the John Deere 1630 tractor they'd bought at a farm auction. Climbing onto the large machine, Katie inserted the key and turned it until the gauges showed plenty of charge and fuel. She pulled out the choke, made sure the gear was in neutral and started the fifty-horsepower motor, which rumbled and belched burnt oil from its exhaust stack.

Katie let the tractor idle a bit, then pushed in the choke, allowing the engine to steady. When she was satisfied it was warmed up, she depressed the clutch and shifted the tractor into gear. As she eased up the clutch and nudged the gas pedal, the tractor hitched into motion, smoothing out as it sped up. Katie waved as she passed the trailer.

"Where's she going with that?" Marlene asked, watching out the window and passing a plate to Max to dry.

"To the emergency cache. We buried supplies out back on the property."

"You all have been busy as beavers," Marlene exclaimed. "And all this time Earl and I thought you came up here and laid about."

"Hardly."

Reaching a small clearing in the back corner of the property, Katie put the tractor into neutral, set the brakes, climbed down and paced off distances from a large boulder and distinctive, three-trunk oak. Remounting the tractor, she used the hydraulic controls to position the front-loader blade and began to dig.

Over northeastern USA, 19:00 Zulu

Earl gazed out his small porthole as his aerial chariot flew over cities small and large. Many looked peaceful, as if catnapping on this hot July day. Others were plumed with smoke from fires both deliberate and accidental. Over a seemingly deserted forest, Earl heard what sounded like hail hitting the plane, which suddenly veered.

"Taking a little ground fire, nothing we can't handle," the pilot said over the headphones.

"Are we getting shot at?" Earl was astounded.

"Surprised it hasn't happened sooner." The pilot said cryptically.

"Idiots, blooming idiots," Earl said to no one in particular.

"Affirmative that!" was his only answer. Earl couldn't tell if it were the pilot or one of the crew.

"How much longer till we reach Marietta?" Earl asked.

"Don't make me turn this plane around!" someone said, attempting humor. "ETA is 20:45, Mr. Tolliday," the navigator said. "We should be right on time."

To Earl, the next two hours seemed longer than the entire first leg of the flight. He dreaded the sight from their approach into the base in Marietta. Would the suburbs of Atlanta be peaceful or a war zone?

"Mind if I come up front for the landing?" Earl asked over his headset.

It was several minutes before he received an answer. Obviously they were discussing whether a civilian should see full on what was happening in Atlanta.

"On one condition, Mr. Tolliday," the pilot said finally.

"Name it!"

"You don't spit up MRE all over my clean cockpit."

Earl could tell the pilot was serious.

"Yes sir, I promise."

Earl waited patiently to be escorted to the cockpit and placed in the seat behind the pilot—175 miles out and Earl could already see smoke smudging the horizon.

As they neared, Earl could see many houses on fire, some in the better sections of the suburbs. Atlanta had numerous spires of smoke and at least two skyscrapers, the IBM and ATT towers, were burning. With only fire truck-based pump pressure, it was nearly impossible to effectively fight anything above the twentieth floor.

They didn't swing far enough south to see Hartsfield-Jackson airport, but the pilot said that bad weather before the EMP event had closed the airport, only a couple of small planes had crashed, and none had reached the tank farm and its hundreds of thousands of gallons of high-octane aviation fuel. However, with no flight control and only a few civilian planes able to fly, the airport had been shut down and evacuated.

With a surprisingly gentle touchdown, the huge transport landed at the Marietta facility and taxied to a large hanger. Earl thanked the flight crew and was preparing to leave the plane when Airman Peters pulled him aside.

"Look, the mates and I decided we need to give you this . . ." Airman Peters handed Earl a worn TT-33 Tokarev 7.62x25mm automatic pistol and an equally worn, leather shoulder holster.

"Do you know how to use a pistol?"

Earl took the pistol, ejected the clip, racked the slide and ejected the round from the chamber. He then picked up the round, put it back in the magazine and slammed it back into the pistol. He racked the slide again, reloading the pistol, and then thumbed on the safety.

"Guess that answers that, eh, mate!" He gave Earl a couple plain-cardboard boxes of cartridges. "You'll not find many additional rounds, so use them sparingly."

"I hope I don't have to use it at all," Earl said, putting on the shoulder holster and arranging a light jacket to cover it.

"Hope I don't stand out too much with a jacket in this hot weather."

"Mate, you'd be more conspicuous without cover for your pistol."

Shaking Airman Peters' hand, Earl felt a kinship. He knew the hardest part would be the last few miles to Roswell, and he dreaded it.

"Any way I can get to Roswell?" Earl asked the man behind the desk in Flight Operations, who looked like he had been up for several days. Without air conditioning, the office was hot as an oven.

"Does this look like a fucking taxi stand? There isn't any; it's shanks' mare from here on, buddy."

" 'Shanks' mare'?"

"You walk." The clerk turned dismissively to a field telephone warbling unpleasantly behind him. Earl grabbed his kit bag and quit the overheated building. Afternoon sun was cooler than inside. Earl spotted an ancient, single-speed bicycle with a number stenciled on its fenders. Glancing around, Earl looped his bag's strap over his head and mounted the old machine. After a shaky start, he regained his two-wheeler bearings and peddled for the gate and home.

VIRGINIA BEACH, VIRGINIA, 19:30 ZULU

Willie studied the Jeep's gas gauge; it was flirting with E.

"We need gas."

"Yep, running on fumes," Nick answered. "Over there looks good . . ." He indicated a Wawa Food Market and gas station on the far side of the road. It looked deserted. Willie drove over the median and across several empty lanes to the corner of Diamond Springs Road and Northhampton Boulevard. He parked next to one of square hatches covering the fuel refill stations for the underground tanks that serviced the huge pump island.

"Stay here and watch the Jeep. I'll find keys to the lock and something to pump the fuel."

"Nah. Get a gas can and we'll punch a few tanks on those cars..."

Nick pointed at some abandoned cars in the refueling bays. "All you need is a gas can and a screwdriver."

"Excellent! Sounds easy," Willie answered, not realizing that the fifteen gallons he'd need to fill the Jeep would take several trips. In addition, he'd need to use a small-capacity can to fit under the scavenged cars.

After smashing the glass on the Wawa's door, he found a hammer, a Phillips-head screwdriver, and a one-gallon gas can. Going to the car nearest the Jeep, he lay on the hot asphalt, positioned the can under the fuel tank and hammered the screwdriver into the tank. Yanking out the screwdriver, he held the can to catch the amber liquid. After the third run to the Jeep, Willie thought maybe his idea was better. Across the parking lot sat a warehouse with several semi-trucks parked around it, and there appeared to be a couple of service bays for the big rigs.

Abandoning a punctured gasoline tank spewing fuel, he walked to the service bays to find a pump. In the first bay, he saw a hand-crank pump inserted into a fifty-gallon oil drum. He removed the pump and cranked it a few turns to purge the oil. Nearby, he found a length of hose that could attach to the feeder pipe on the pump's bottom. He placed pump and hose in an empty five-gallon plastic bucket and lugged it to the Jeep. Nick was nowhere to be found.

Willie broke the glass on the door to the service building and unlocked the deadbolt. Opening the door, he strode to the fuel service desk and searched, soon finding a large ring of keys for the refill hatch locks. With his handful of keys he returned to the Jeep and found the one that fit the lock on the hatch he had parked next to. He lifted the hatch, identified the unleaded-regular fill valve, removed its cover, opened the valve and inserted the hose attached to the hand pump. Once he reached the tank bottom he cranked the pump until he got a stream of gasoline. The first flow from the hose was oily water from condensation that had settled in the bottom of the tank, followed by oil-contaminated gas, which cleaned the pump's internal mechanism. Once he was sure the fuel was clean, he stopped cranking. He moved the Jeep so he could pump directly into the vehicle and then cranked until the tank was full. He also filled the jerry can strapped in the back rack.

Satisfied with a full tank and a full jerry can, Willie pulled the hose, emptied what gas he could from the hose and pump, put the pump and hose coil back in the five-gallon bucket and placed it in the back of the Jeep. In the Wawa, he grabbed sacks of snacks, beef jerky and drinks. After several trips, the Jeep was loaded with non-perishables, including many six-packs of beer.

"Wow, have you been busy," Willie heard as he loaded the last of the provisions. Nick emerged from behind the building.

"Where the hell you been?" Willie said, angry at Nick's disappearing acts.

"Checking things out. Not much going on."

"I could've used some help with gas and provisions," Willie said sourly.

"Looks like you did fine. We need a place to crash; we've been driving for hours." Nick's yawn made him look feral.

"Good idea. I'm so wound-up I didn't realize." Willie couldn't help but yawn, too, as the fatigue of nearly twenty-four hours of activity hit him.

Back in the Jeep, they continued down Northampton and turned south onto I-64. A few miles out, at a thick copse of woods, Willie drove the Jeep in as far as he could, hiding it from the road. Inside the trees the temperature dropped by ten to fifteen degrees and a slight wind brought the scent of pine. After beef jerky and Twinkies washed down by warm beer, Willie fell into a deep sleep, lulled by the waving pines and the cool, gentle touch of breeze through open windows. His last thought: he was disappointed things had gone so easy; he had wanted to hurt someone.

Outside Charleston, West Virginia, 20:00 Zulu

After I-68, Frank switched to I-79 South toward Charleston. Because of an adrenalin shock— for him and his riders—from waking up nearly off the road, he realized that other than the short nap after leaving New York, he hadn't slept in almost two days. He turned the wheel over to Pete, swapped seats with George, nestled against the right passenger door, and fell into a deep sleep.

The sudden screech of tires startled Frank to full awareness. The sight that greeted his opening eyes would birth many nightmares. The Lincoln was skidding sideways down an embankment and then rolled over twice, coming to rest on its wheels in a dry streambed. The moans and a sharp, aborted scream told Frank that the others in the car had been taken equally by surprise. He undid his shoulder belt and studied the other passengers.

George was swearing and trying to get his belt undone; other than bruising from the deployed airbag, he appeared unhurt. Pete, on the other hand, was not. Apparently he had fallen asleep, head forward; during the wreck the driver's-side airbag had also deployed, knocking his head back and snapping his neck. Pete had died almost instantly. The two women were shaken and would probably have whiplash necks, but otherwise were unhurt. Incredibly, the engine was still running. George turned the ignition off; the resulting silence was deafening.

"Well, this sucks" was all Frank could think to say. He had to force the door open since the latch had sprung during the rollover. He went to the hood and signaled George to release the latch, which George did, and with a sharp snap the hood popped up an inch.

Frank hit the catch release and popped the hood. Inside the engine compartment, motor mounts were solid and no fluids leaked. Everything OK, he closed the hood. Now he had to deal with the hard part, the people.

He forced the driver's door and released Pete from the seat belt. Frank pulled Pete's limp body from the vehicle and laid it on the streambed. By this time, George had opened his door and helped him open the passenger door for the women. A survey of the Lincoln revealed no ruptured tires and intact axles and universals as well as struts, shocks and other gear.

"OK, get yourselves together. I'm going to scout upstream. George, you feel up to going downstream? Look for a way to get back onto the road."

"Sure, Frank, but what about Pete?" George asked.

"Nothing we can do for him. He was dead instantly. We'll bury him as best we can, and stop by his house in Charleston and tell his people where he is." With that, Frank headed upstream.

About a mile upstream, the bank tapered down to a small enough slope the car could climb out. To be certain, Frank climbed to the road and eyed things. The two-lane blacktop had no signs visible. Where the hell are we?, Frank thought as he returned to the creek bed and the car.

"Looks like we might not have to walk out of here. Do we take Pete's body to his people in Charleston, or bury it here?"

"How would we carry him? On the roof with the tire?" Jane asked.

In a black humor, Frank pictured the scene from the movie American Vacation, where they wrapped Grandmother's body in a rug and traveled cross-country. "We don't have anything to wrap him in, and a body strapped to a car would draw unwanted attention. It's the back seat or the trunk."

"I vote we bury him here and tell his folks—if we can find them—where to come get him." George made his preference clear.

"I think I speak for Jane: I agree with George," said Delicia, Jane nodded in the affirmative.

"OK then. We bury Pete, here."

George and Frank used the pry bar to dig a shallow grave for Pete's body. After burial, everyone gathered stones and piled them over the grave. Not knowing whether Pete was a Christian or not, Frank decided to say a few words anyway.

"Dear Lord, we commend into your hands Pete Gregor. Please give him a place in heaven and keep his soul. We didn't know Pete for long, but he was a good companion and we shall miss him. In Jesus' name, Amen. Dust to dust and ashes to ashes." Frank threw a handful of dirt onto the mound; the others did likewise.

After Frank cut away the airbag remains with the knife from his emergency bottle, everyone somberly got back into the car and George used paracord from Frank's emergency kit to tie the doors shut. They maneuvered the creek bed to where Frank had found the gentle slope to regain the road and, after a tense moment of spinning tires and side slipping, they made it.

Rather than the four-lane divided Interstate they expected, it appeared to be a two-lane country blacktop. With no road signs in sight, Frank again asked himself, Where they hell are we?

NORTH OF LAKE WEISS, ALABAMA, 21:00 ZULU

The manic screech of the front-loader blade against concrete told Katie she had removed enough dirt. She secured the tractor's hydraulic controls and then turned it off. Grabbing a small shovel from the toolbox behind the tractor seat, she walked to the freshly dug hole, which was about two feet deep. She could see the white streaks the blade's teeth had gouged in the old concrete at the bottom of the hole. She climbed into the hole and, using the shovel, completed clearing the top of the circular concrete cistern.

Frank had found the old cistern when they had checked out the land for possible house sites. One look at the old structure was enough to show it wouldn't hold water, and would be difficult to remove, so they concocted a different future for the thing.

It wasn't long before Katie had cleared the circular hatch with the crude U-shaped handle made of embedded rebar. She restarted the tractor and positioned the loader blade over the hatch. Again she climbed off the tractor, this time carrying a length of chain with tow-hooks on either end. Looping one chain end through the handle, she looped the other over a tooth on the loader blade.

Once the chain was secure, Katie clambered aboard the tractor and used the hydraulics to lift the cistern's hatch, which emitted a loud creak as the plug loosened and swung free. She moved the plug to one side and lowered it onto the cistern top. Grabbing a flashlight from the toolbox, she once more returned to the pit. Shining the flashlight into the dark hole, she could see a gleaming new aluminum ladder lag-bolted to the cistern side. Knowing how dangerous a broken bone or serious cut could be, now that medical services might be unavailable, she slowly climbed down the ladder.

At the base, she shined her light around the cistern, inspecting where she and Frank had patched and sealed cracks and holes. While it wouldn't hold tons of water as a cistern, it was now an air- and moisture-tight vault. In the flashlight's beam against the north wall she could see two large rectangular storage containers and many small, airtight boxes and plastic-wrapped packages. Leaning against the concrete wall was a folded tripod with a coil of rope and block and tackle. She wrapped her arms around the tripod and dragged it to the ladder. She tied one of the rope's loose ends to an eye on the tripod's top brace and then wrapped the rest around her waist, leaving enough to allow her to climb the ladder and get out of the cistern. Putting the block and tackle over one shoulder, she climbed the ladder and was soon on the top of the cistern.

Uncoiling the rope, she slowly pulled the heavy tripod up.

Once the tripod was out, she mounted it over the top of the hatch, attached the rope by the block and tackle, and then dropped the rope's working end through the hole. Climbing into the cistern, she dragged the first large rectangular storage box to the ladder. Wiping her sweat-dampened hands on her jeans, she caught the cargo hook on the heavy-duty handle of the military-surplus storage container and then climbed back up the ladder.

Using the mechanical advantage of the block and tackle, she hauled the heavy box out of the hatch. The careful sizing of the tripod allowed her to clear the cistern edge and swing the box so that she could slightly lower it and use leverage to lay it over on its side. Unlatching the cargo hook, she dragged the heavy box off to one side. She then repeated the effort with the second box.

Drenched with sweat, she opened a small cooler beside the toolbox and removed a water bottle, pouring some over her head and taking a long drink.

"That's better," she said out loud and sighed with pleasure as a slight breeze cooled her with evaporation from her sweat-saturated blouse.

She climbed into the hole and neatly coiled the rope and laid the tripod to one side. Then she used the tractor to reinstall the cistern hatch. After the hatch thumped into place, she removed the chain and re-stowed it. Then she lowered the loader until it rested beside the storage boxes. With her last strength, she leveraged the boxes into the loader, used cargo straps to secure them, and then elevated the blade.

Katie gingerly drove the tractor back to the trailer. Once there, she grounded the blade, shut down the tractor, wearily climbed the trailer steps and, without a second thought to the energy it would waste, switched on the air conditioner and reveled in the cool blast of air as she regained her strength.

Soon, she heard the buzz of the ATVs returning to the main camp and realized it was nearly dinnertime. She guiltily switched off the AC and changed into a clean blouse. As the ATVs pulled up, she opened the door and met them.

Max and Marlene carried bundles of fresh vegetables tied to the back of their ATV. David and Eli showed from their sweat-stained clothes that they had been working hard and were anticipating a shower and a good meal.

All four gathered around the two storage containers.

"What's in the boxes?" asked David, wiping sweat from his brow with a soiled handkerchief.

Eli remained stoic, although Katie could tell he was curious.

"Well, let's take a look," Katie said, snapping open the latches lining the containers' lids.

Once the containers were unsealed, Katie lifted the first one's lid, reached in with both hands and pulled out a crude but effective-looking rifle.

"This, ladies and gentlemen, is a Mosin-Nagant bolt-action rifle. In the other box are several thousand rounds of 7.62x54mm ammunition. In the next few days we'll all become proficient with the use of this rifle and associated stripper clips."

" 'Stripper clips'?" asked David as he took the rifle from Katie and cycled the bolt to check if it was loaded. "What the hell are stripper clips?"

Opening the other container, Katie removed what looked to be a large canned ham. Using a key taped to the can, she removed a strip around the can's top and opened it—it was packed with ammunition, all loaded onto clips that each held five rounds. She displayed one.

"This is a stripper clip on Polish 7.62x54 rounds. In the next few days, like I said, we'll learn to use them to reload the Mosin. We may need them, and soon," she said ominously, passing each a rifle and a 300-round can of ammo.

"Bloody hell!" was all Marlene managed to say as she took the heavy rifle.

Marietta, Georgia, 21:30 Zulu

Dear Earl,
 If you are reading this, thank God! It means you have made it home and for that David and I are grateful. We are sorry we aren't there to meet you, but I knew you would find this in our secret place. We wanted to stay but the yard nazis were getting restless and we have no way to cook. Katie is taking us in; hopefully you will find us there.
 All our Love,
 Marlene and David

Earl put down the quickly scrawled note that Marlene had stuffed behind a loose brick in the fireplace. He stood for a moment in the trashed living room of their dream house and felt a cold anger. The house had been ransacked and stripped of anything of use; the rest was destroyed as if by a vengeful child.

He had pedaled the back way into the neighborhood so he hadn't passed Frank and Katie's place. Seeing a barricade on the rear entrance, he had walked the bike in via a jogging trail, avoiding the watches. Of course, as he passed he noticed they were mostly asleep, so it wouldn't have mattered.

He checked the rest of the house. Destruction was complete. Someone had taken the Land Rover—he hoped it was Marlene and David. In the vandalized kitchen he managed to find an unbroken bottle of Guinness stout, which he was now drinking even though it was hot. After fruitlessly searching for anything worth saving, he slung his bag over his shoulder and rode the few blocks to Frank and Katie's.

If it were possible, Frank and Katie's house was even more wrecked than his own home had been. Holes had been kicked in some walls and on another someone had smeared Traitors! in feces. Surprisingly, the back deck was relatively undisturbed: the gas grill had been pushed over the rail into the back yard, and the smoker upended and its ashes spread across the deck boards. Earl could see where coals had burned into the wood. Frank once told him the deck had been treated with fire-retardant; Earl guessed it must have worked, or the entire house would have gone up.

"Earl?"

The voice caught him unaware and he spun, reaching under his coat for the Tokarev pistol.

"Oh, it's you, Fred." Earl dropped his hand as he recognized his neighbor and golfing buddy. "What happened?"

"Katie and Marlene left, against the will of Emperor Hank. He and his yard nazis 'searched' yours and Frank's houses." He gestured to the chaos.

"Hank. That asshole." Earl's simmering rage boiled over. "I'll kill the bastard!"

"Too late. Old Man Summers put a load of double-ought buck in him a hour after he did this; he died this morning."

"Summers? That old fellow at the top of the hill?" Earl felt cheated.

"Seems George wanted to confiscate the Summers' supplies they'd stockpiled for the good of the neighborhood. Mr. Summers objected." Fred shrugged. "I guess Summers' time on Hamburger Hill served him in good stead. Things calmed after Hank got shot, but it's still pretty creepy around here. Katie and Marlene were right to get the hell out; I wish I could."

"Do you know where they went?"

Earl righted a lawn chair and sat, feeling defeated.

"Nope, but you'll love this: Hank tried to take Katie's shotgun when he tried to stop them. She kicked him so hard in the nuts he couldn't walk for an hour, yanked back the gun and then, in a tank of a Land Rover, she and Marlene and David smashed through Hank's 'roadblock' and escaped."

The thought of Katie kicking Hank in the balls lightened Earl's mood a bit, but how was he going to find his wife and son?

"They left a message, but no one has deciphered it," Fred offered.

"Where?" Earl asked, coming to his feet.

"Downstairs on the garage door. Follow me." Fred retreated through the broken sliding-glass doors. Earl rose and followed.

They navigated the debris-strewn basement stairs. Earl noticed that Frank's reloading equipment was missing; Frank had once demonstrated it, and twice, when Frank was loading 9 millimeters, invited Earl to help.

The garage mayhem was worse: boxes that had neatly lined the walls had been torn; the contents scattered and defiled. Fred pulled the door down into the closed position, revealing the white-chalk message: gone to bol.

"I'm guessing Hank didn't see it. He'd have erased it if he had."

"Glad he didn't," Earl responded.

"Mean anything to you?"

"Not a damn thing. What the hell is a B-O-L?" Earl felt darkness return.

SOUTH OF VIRGINIA BEACH, VIRGINIA, 22:30 ZULU

Willie woke suddenly, as if from a dream of falling. He wiped his hand across his mouth and came away with drool.

"Teach me to fall asleep sitting up," he said, yawning.

Willie didn't see Nick; perhaps Nick went to take a leak. The Jeep door creaked as he stepped into hot afternoon air, nonchalantly took out his pecker and let loose a rush of dark yellow urine. It felt good to empty his bladder and he signed with contentment. He put his penis back in his pants and zipped up.

"All finished, eh?"

Willie jerked, startled as Nick spoke behind him.

"Nick, Jesus Christ! A moment sooner and you'd have been wet!"

"Not hardly. Anyway, why don't you get something to eat and drink, and we'll get on our way."

"You in a hurry?" Willie asked, rummaging through supplies for a bag of beef jerky, Twinkies and a warm beer. Walking to a convenient stump, he sat, tore open the jerky and offered Nick a piece of the dried, spicy beef.

"I already ate, but thanks" was all Nick said.

After a couple pieces of jerky washed down with warm beer, and wolfing the Twinkies, Willie belched, then turned to Nick.

"So where you in such a hurry to get to?"

"Your dad was a senator for Alabama, wasn't he?"

"Yep. We moved there just so he could run. Democratic machine promised him he'd get elected, and he did. What a lousy state—fifty years out of date." Willie finished his beer and tossed the bottle in the bushes.

"Let's go there. Raise some hell. Show Dad you're your own man." Nick looked at him expectantly, his dark eyes flashing.

"Alabama? I was thinking Florida."

"Florida with no air-conditioning? Snowbirds with sweaty Hawaiian shirts and weird shorts? Sandals with socks? That Florida?" ribbed Nick.

"So why Alabama? As I recall, it's hot and humid there, too."

"North Alabama is tolerable this time of year, I hear. Nice lakes, small towns. Shoot, I'll bet we can find one to run if we try."

"When you're going nowhere, one place is as good as another, I guess. Alabama it is. Maybe we'll run over my old man." Willie stood, brushed off Twinkies crumbs and walked to the driver's-side door.

"Don't you mean run into?" asked Nick, getting into the Jeep.

Willie smiled, climbed in, started the car, drove out of the copse of woods to the road and headed south.

NORTH OF LAKE WEISS, ALABAMA, 23:00 ZULU

Drying dishes after their dinner of reconstituted freeze-dried beef stew and fresh garden vegetables, Katie reflected on the hours she and Frank had spent, cleaning cosmoline from the Mosins, soaking rifle parts in mineral spirits and wire brushing the hardened anti-corrosion treatment—at least the others wouldn't have to endure that—then reassembling and checking functionality. She was glad Frank had made her repeatedly disassemble and reassemble one of the Mosins until she could do it outdoors in the dark. They had both practiced loading rifles from stripper clips until they were proficient.

"Penny for your thoughts, dear," said Marlene, handing Katie the last plate.

"Just remembering everything Frank put me through. I'm glad he did, now." She undid her apron and hung it on a hook by the sink.

"Alright everyone. It's Mosin time!"

"Good heavens, dear, these must have cost a fortune," Marlene said, admiring the rifles in the storage case and all the ammunition.

"Not really. Rifles were less than eighty-nine bucks each in bulk; ammo about seventy dollars a spam can."

"But why so many?"

"It takes about eight adults to properly watch a place, 24-7, and get anything else done. Frank and I intended on a few couples coming with us, if we'd been able to complete our plans." She paused for a breath. "We decided to standardize on an easy-to-use and inexpensive defensive weapon."

They carried their rifles to the large picnic table and, under Katie's guidance, disassembled and reassembled rifles, and practiced cleaning them.

"It's critical to clean a rifle after every shooting session," she explained as she used the cleaning rod attached to her rifle to ram a cleaning patch down the barrel. "All we have is surplus ammo, which has corrosive primers, which leave behind corrosive salts," she added, using Windex to clean the chamber and bore.

Once everyone was proficient—Eli, Katie noted, seemed to already know the rifle very well, but he worked right alongside everyone else—she hiked them to the makeshift shooting range, each carrying a rifle and boxes of ammo. It wasn't far, but even so, Marlene was panting when they reached the section of the pasture set aside for target practice.

"My God, these bloody things are heavy," Marlene said as she set down the ammo and rifle. Katie and the others smiled at her.

From a plastic, water-resistant deck box, Katie removed targets, earplugs and shooting glasses and handed them out. Setting their targets against an earthen berm about fifty yards downrange, they donned glasses and earplugs on the way back to the rifles. From the box, Katie pulled out bamboo mats and rolled them onto the short grass.

"First, some basic rules. You've probably heard these before, but since we'll be living with these rifles until we determine we don't have to anymore, everyone must commit them to memory.

"Rule One: always keep the gun pointed in a safe direction.

"This is the primary rule of gun safety. Safe direction means that the gun is pointed so that even if it were to go off it would not cause injury or damage. The key is to control where the muzzle—front end of the barrel—is pointed at all times. Common sense.

"Rule Two: always keep your finger off the trigger until

ready to shoot.

"When holding a gun, rest your finger on the trigger guard or along the gun's side. Do not touch the trigger until you are ready to fire.

"Rule Three: always keep the gun unloaded until ready to use.

"Whenever you pick up a gun, immediately engage the safety device, if possible, and, if the gun has a magazine, remove it before opening the action and looking into the chamber, which should be clear of ammunition. If you don't know how to open the action or inspect the chamber, leave the gun alone and get help." Katie paused, pleased that she remembered the NRA safety rules nearly verbatim.

"Now with that out of the way, let's do some shooting.

"Eli, help Marlene, will you?"

Katie helped David snuggle the rifle into his shoulder while in the prone position so the kick wouldn't overly bruise him, then showed how to determine the proper sight picture. She also taught him the proper way to breathe: a couple of deep breaths, slowly exhale the last one and hold it halfway, then slowly squeeze the heavy military two-stage trigger until the rifle barked and spit the bullet downrange. Looking at Marlene and Eli, she could tell Marlene was getting the hang of using the heavy Russian rifle.

After shooting a couple of clips of ammo, everyone was getting reasonable accuracy, their bullet holes within a pie-plate diameter, or, in the case of Katie and Eli, a three-inch or less grouping.

"OK, great work. Now we do it standing."

Marlene was incredulous. "With this heavy thing? You must be kidding."

"Oh, come on, Marlene, it isn't as heavy as a bag of potatoes," Katie chided. "Eli, can you show her how to use the sling to help steady the rifle?"

"Yes Katie," he answered with a smile.

Eli showed Marlene how to wrap the sling around her supporting arm for additional support. David watched and emulated what Marlene was shown; soon they were both shooting the rifle reasonably well. After a couple more clips, Katie noticed Marlene trembling, unable to hold on target between shots.

"Let's break for today. Don't forget, we need to clean these things before we put them away."

Marlene lowered her rifle and unwrapped the sling. Sweat beaded her forehead and perspiration saturated her blouse from the effort of holding the heavy Mosin. She dreaded even the short walk back to the trailers hauling the rifle and ammo can.

"So, is everyone having fun?" Katie said with artificial cheerfulness as she picked up ammo and rifle and started for the trailers. Marlene, ears ringing in spite of earplugs and right shoulder beginning to ache, was too tired to answer.

Back at the main camp, Katie sent David and Marlene back to their trailer to shower, and Max went into the one she now shared with her mother, but with the admonishment to return and clean rifles. Once they were gone, Katie pulled Eli aside and spoke bluntly.

"Eli, do you think Marlene can handle it?"

"She'll do fine if she builds up arm strength over the next few days . . ." He hesitated.

"But . . ." Katie prodded.

"But we may not have a couple of days before that group from town comes looking for me." His eyes were guarded.

"Is there something else I need to know, Eli?"

"Yes ma'am. I had to fight my way out; someone may have gotten hurt."

"Tell me."

She sat at the picnic table and indicated Eli should sit across from her.

He sat down.

"It was right after they recognized what had happened. Reverend was getting them all fired up on the steps of his church when I came around the corner. Two men grabbed me, and when I saw what was up, I fought back. I may have

seriously hurt one with a punch to the throat."
Katie was quiet for a moment.
"You were just defending yourself."
"Yes, ma'am, but that isn't all."
Eli looked down, then back up at her, hardness in his eyes reflecting every bit of his fifty-five years.
"It was Reverend's son."

Day Three

Outside Charleston, West Virginia, 00:00 Zulu

Frank sighed relief when a County Route 27 sign appeared around the next bend. George quickly located it on the map. "Looks like Pete took a side road; must've been a roadblock or something up on the highway."

"How soon can we get back on the Interstate?"

"Well, unless we want to backtrack, looks like we have to get on I-77 and head south. About a mile up."

"OK. Pete's place is five miles down 79 past the 77-79 interchange."

Frank stepped on the gas. At about thirty-five miles an hour the front end began shaking; any faster threatened to make controlling the vehicle difficult. "Wonderful, just wonderful," Frank said, frustration at the pace apparent in his voice as the scenery creeped by.

They hit the I-77 interchange a couple of minutes later. Charleston showed some smoke from fires, but looked relatively normal. It was fortunate the EMP happened at midnight Eastern Standard Time, when most people were at home and roads relatively clear. They pulled up in front of Pete's home about ten minutes later. Frank parked in the driveway and walked to the door, dreading giving the news to Pete's family that he had died less than ten miles from home.

Repeated knocking gained nothing. Frank tried rear and side doors without answer. Everything was locked tight and appeared deserted.

"Hey, anyone got paper and a pen or pencil?" Frank hollered at the car.

Jane pulled from her purse a small notebook and pink ink pen and handed it to Frank, who wrote a detailed note explaining what had happened and where Pete was buried. He slid the note under the front door.

"Nothing else we can do," he said as he got back into the car and retied his door.

"Don't worry, Frank, you've done more than was required." Jane touched his shoulder from the backseat by way of reassurance.

"Well, it's getting toward evening. Shall we try to find a place to stay tonight? We need to find a new car tomorrow; this one won't go much further."

"I agree," George said. "That front-end wobble is probably a damaged universal. If it separated even at thirty-five miles an hour, it'd be dangerous."

"What would happen?" Jane asked.

"The front wheel would fly away off," George answered matter-of-factly.

"Yep. We might roll over or something," Frank said dryly, backing out of the driveway and steering toward the Interstate. Stifled laughter was his answer.

Near the Interstate was a Red Roof Inn. The office was deserted so they took two room keys and left a note. They offloaded everything they couldn't lock in the trunk; amazingly, the latch hadn't sprung in the rollover.

Sharing a room with George worried Frank. If George snored, Frank, normally a light sleeper, couldn't sleep, but the fatigue and stress of the last two days proved a potent narcoleptic. He was out as soon as his head hit the pillow.

State Road 58, west of Virginia Beach, Virginia, 00:30 Zulu

After consulting a map, Willie and Nick decided that State Road 58 westbound to I-85 would be best. I-85 ran all the way to Atlanta, where they'd pick up I-20 to Birmingham, Alabama, where Willie hoped to track down his father.

The road was mostly deserted save for an occasional stranded car, forlorn at the shoulder. Now and then, Willie would try the radio, usually getting nothing but static on the AM dial and not even that on FM. But when he was ready to give up, the emergency broadcast tone sounded on frequency 1670.

"This is the Emergency Broadcast Network with an announcement from the president of the United States of America. Please stand by."

Willie and Nick looked at each other as the silence ticked by. Finally the president's voice rang out.

"My fellow Americans, this is a dark time for the United States of America. The cowardly dictator of Venezuela, Hugo Chavez, launched a devastating electro-magnetic pulse attack—EMP, for short—against the continental USA and managed to bring down the entire electrical grid and most electronic devices. Let me assure you he has not escaped unscathed. At 8 a.m. yesterday morning, Venezuela was treated to a similar EMP attack from our nuclear submarine the USS Henry M. Jackson. Venezuela is not as dependent on technology as the US, so the general population will not suffer severely. However, it has been confirmed that Chavez's body, after an apparent suicide, was hanged by rebel forces outside the presidential palace just after noon, yesterday, and the country has erupted in civil war.

"I ask that all of you please be patient and help each other during this emergency. The government of the USA will be doing everything we can to re-establish electrical power, however, this will be a long road. Many countries including England and Germany are flying replacement parts such as transformers and electrical cable to the USA. With the help of our many allies, we hope to have limited electricity established in many cities within weeks.

On a darker note, already there are reports of looting and gangs of armed marauders taking advantage of the reduced state of readiness of our law enforcement personnel. To remedy this, I am declaring immediate nation-wide martial law, with the exceptions of Alaska and Hawaii. Travel will be restricted starting immediately and all National Guard units are activated.

"Please, stay in your homes except to secure food and water. The armed forces and National Guard will maintain order and distribute supplies. Pick-up points will be established within walking distance of population centers. Those needing additional care will be evacuated to centralized facilities. In order to speed recovery, I have activated the ten FEMA regions; state and local governments will report to them. Pamphlets describing the limits of martial law, the pick-up points for food and water, and the locations of FEMA operational headquarters will be distributed soon.

"For the duration of this emergency, please follow orders given by your local FEMA governor in accordance with and as authorized by Executive Order 13528. These are perilous times. If we are to survive as a nation, some personal freedoms must be temporarily suspended or limited. Stand by on this channel for further announcements. As your president I will do everything in my power to protect and preserve the United States of America. May God bless you and keep you safe."

After the initial shock, both Willie and Nick broke out in laughter. Once the sheep followed the president's directives, the pickings should be easier and easier. With a new sense of purpose, they sped down State Road 58.

MARIETTA, GEORGIA, 00:45 ZULU

Earl looked at Fred with disbelief.
"Did the president just bleeping say what I think he said?"
"Well, if you mean did he just declare martial law and

essentially suspend the Constitution? Yes, he did." Fred looked troubled.

"But what exactly does it all mean?"

"Well, I'd say that if you have to go anywhere, it better be within the next day or so or you're going to be stuck." Fred looked pensive. "I plan on heading for my cabin at Big Canoe. You're welcome to come along."

Earl looked thoughtful. "You said that Katie, Marlene and David bugged out. What about Frank?"

"Well the neighborhood scuttlebutt is that he was on a trip to New York."

"New York! He'd need several days and a lot of luck to get back here." Earl spotted an atlas on the bookcase lining one wall of Fred's living room.

"Mind if I have a look?" Earl pointed to the atlas.

"Sure, go ahead."

Earl took down the atlas, returned to his seat, opened the book to a map of the eastern USA, and studied the roads between New York and Georgia. "Assuming he can't make top speed, it's about four days of driving."

"That sounds about right."

"I'll tell you what, Fred, if he isn't back by dinnertime tomorrow, I'll take you up on your offer." Earl knew if he stayed in metro Atlanta after they locked in martial law, he wouldn't have a prayer of finding his family. Only Frank would know what the women meant by gone to bol, so he'd wait as long as he could.

"Well, that's cutting it a bit close, but OK. I'd rather have someone along than go it alone. After all, 'two is one and one is none,' as they say."

Earl got down to brass tacks.

"Do you have much in the way of supplies, and what about weapons?"

"Follow me." Fred looked almost cheerful as he led Earl to his garage.

With the dim light of the garage door's ornamental windows, Earl could see two vehicles. Looking closely at the far wall, covered in pegboard from which hung a multitude of tools, he judged that the dimensions weren't quite right for the way the house appeared when they'd walked up the driveway.

"Figure it out?" asked Fred. "Hank and his goons didn't."

"It's a false wall isn't it?"

"Give the man a cigar!"

Fred walked to his workbench, pulled a rusted pipe wrench and—clack—a hidden door popped open. Inside the false wall was a five-foot-wide, eighteen-foot-long room. Along one wall, shelves held #10 cans of freeze-dried food, sealed five-gallon pails of beans, rice and wheat, and many more canned vegetables, meats and instant meals. At the end, next to a stack of ammo cans, was an impressive gun safe.

"By the Queen's teats! Do all you Americans prepare for doomsday?" Earl admired the extensive store of goods.

"Nope, not by a long shot. It was odd, I knew Frank did reloading and liked guns and hunting, but his OPSEC was great. I never figured him for a prepper." Fred started working the combination on the safe.

" 'OPSEC'? 'Prepper'? What do you mean?"

"OPSEC means operational security. By not telling anyone, Katie and Frank kept their preps a secret. If Hank and his minions had suspected I had all this, I might've had to fill his gut with buckshot instead of Old Man Summers." With a flourish he opened the safe, showing off several short-barrel shotguns, two scoped hunting rifles, a rack of handguns—automatics and revolvers—and a couple of AR-15s. " 'Prepper' means someone who prepares for emergencies."

Earl whistled at the amassed firepower.

"How can one person use all this?"

"Well, before my Annie passed away two years ago, this was for us and our kids. Now, the kids have moved to California and Alaska, so it's doubtful they'll make it back. I know you, and I like you and Marlene. I like Frank even more, now I know he's a prepper." He grabbed a Maverick 88, short-barrel shotgun, and passed it to Earl. "We better keep a couple of these, upstairs."

"I already have this."

Earl opened his jacket and showed off the Tokarev.

"Oh, those's fine, but remember that the purpose of a handgun is to fight your way to a rifle." With that, Fred pulled out a second shotgun, a Remington 870, and the two AR-15s. "You carry one of the ARs and the Maverick, and grab that ammo can marked .223."

As Earl put the rifle strap around his neck and took the Maverick, he grabbed the surprisingly heavy ammo can containing the .223 ammo. Fred did the same, grabbing an ammo can marked buck shot.

As they struggled past the two vehicles and into the house, Earl muttered, "The bloody Yanks are all crazy," adding after a moment, "Thank God."

CHARLESTON, WEST VIRGINIA, 07:30 ZULU

A particularly loud snore from George woke Frank. His sheets were wet with sweat in the room's warm, still air. The windows couldn't be raised and they'd been afraid to leave the door ajar, so they'd taken to bed locked in a motel room with almost no ventilation. Claustrophobic, Frank got out of the hard, uncomfortable hotel bed and stretched his back and neck. His mouth tasted like aliens with athlete's foot had been marching around in it wearing dirt-crusted socks. Looking around the room in near-absolute dark, he realized that the water and other drinks were next door in the women's room. Frank pulled on jeans and a clean tee shirt picturing a bear holding a rifle and saying "I uphold the right to arm bears," given to him by his daughter. He unlocked the door and went outside.

It was cooler outside the room than it was inside. Frank took a lungful of cooler air and thought how stuffy it was in there. After a few more deep breaths, he noticed Jane sitting outside the door to her and Delicia's room. She had the .45 in her lap.

"You doing OK?" Frank asked as he propped open the door to his room.

"Define OK. Hundreds of miles from home, not knowing what I'll find when I get there, with a car that may not make it ten miles. If OK, then we're doing just great." She smiled bravely. "And you?"

"At least we aren't in Philadelphia."

She was quiet a moment, then broke out in laughter. "W. C. Fields, right?" she said, wiping a tear from her eye.

"Yep. Of course that's an urban legend."

He sat beside her and gestured at her bottle of water.

"You mind? I don't have anything catching."

"Well, that's reassuring." She smiled again and passed the liter bottle. "We wouldn't want to do anything hazardous."

The warm water felt good as it washed the dryness out of his throat. He hoped it was imagination but he swore he heard his throat tissues crackling as they rehydrated.

"We have to find more supplies today," he said, returning the now half-empty bottle to Jane. She set it beside her.

"What do you think we'll find, you know, back at our homes?"

In the new-moon light, he saw that she had been crying for a while, if the pile of crumpled tissues beside her were any indication. "I don't know. My wife and I are preppers. It was all kind of a game, playing 'what if' and coming up with solutions. I hope she remembers everything we learned. If so, she should be safe, and at our BOL."

"BOL?" Jane was puzzled.

"A bug-out location. We have about thirty acres in Alabama with a couple of travel trailers, a garden and a stocked lake."

"Sounds pretty good. I have a one-bedroom apartment in Charlotte, North Carolina, and a cat that's at my mother's while I attended a conference—oh, and a refrigerator full of spoiled food."

"No one special, waiting?" Frank hoped he wasn't prying. Even though Jane was in her thirties, she was attractive, even when depressed and scared. It would be a shame if she were alone.

"I did. We broke up. He wanted to get married right away, wanted me to quit teaching, start a family, be a housewife."

"And you didn't?"

"Not yet, not as quick as he did. He didn't understand." She wiped her eyes on another tissue.

"He was a fool, then."

Frank stood up. "Let's check out the office for any supplies we can liberate." He offered his hand and she accepted it.

Jane stood, a bit stiffly, taking her hand from his to smooth her blouse. "Why don't you take this?" With her other hand she gave him the .45.

Frank took the weapon and checked it—the magazine was still full, the chamber now empty—and put it in his jeans waistband at the back. Side-by-side, they walked through pools of dark shadow and moonlight along the walkway to the office, where they saw that whatever had been useful had already been taken. They gave up after a few fruitless minutes of searching when the low grumble of a diesel semi engine brought them both to the front of the office to gaze anxiously out the broken picture window.

Across the parking lot, a Peterbilt semi-tractor pulling a forty-foot container squealed to an obnoxious stop that only the brakes of a big rig seem able to do. They watched as a tall, broad-shouldered trucker—they could make out little more in the shadows where he had parked—climbed down from the cab, relieved himself, and starting walking toward their car.

"Wait here," Frank ordered Jane, taking the pistol from his waistband into his right fist and cautiously stepping over the window's low threshold onto the sidewalk. Frank was pleased that the window had been broken inward so that little broken glass outside could crunch under his shoes. Hugging the darkened pools of shadow, he crept up on the trucker, within a couple yards as he reached their car. Frank racked the slide of the .45 and stepped into the moonlight.

"Can I help you?" Frank said with his best voice of quiet menace.

"Holy Shit! Pardner, I jus' 'bout swallowed my toothpick! You scared me out o' ten years o' life," the man said with a Texas drawl, turning toward Frank, his hands empty. "No need for that hog leg. I was wondering how this wreck got here."

"Put your hands up while I check you out."

Frank motioned with the gun.

The trucker stood passively, hands high. Frank approached and did a one- handed frisk, finding no obvious weapons. He stepped back. "OK, you can put your hands down."

Standing out of reach, Frank put the gun in his waistband, in front.

"Geesh pardner, like I said, I didn't mean nothing."

Frank could detect no malice in the stranger.

"My name's Frank, this is my car."

Frank thought the stranger didn't need to know about Jane and the others.

"I'm Bobby Allen, but friends call me Tex. I was stoppin' for the night when I saw this here wreck and wanted a look-see. What the heck happened?"

"I rolled it on the other side of town. Landed on its wheels, barely drivable, so after nursing it this far, I decided to stop for the night."

"You were darn lucky, pardner. A rollover can kill ya quick." Tex leaned and shined a small penlight under the front of the car; Frank wondered what else he'd missed in his frisk. "Left universal's all messed up; I'd be surprised if this goes another thirty miles." Tex stood, turned off the penlight, put it away and dusted his palms on his jeans.

"You're right. And after that, I don't know what'll happen."

Frank, deciding Tex was trustworthy, at least for the moment, held out his hand. "Sorry about the pistol, I've found you can't be too careful."

"Oh heck, that din't bother me," Tex smiled and shook Frank's hand soundly. "In south Texas, that's jus' saying hello!" He let out a laugh. "Tell your lady friend she can come out; I'm harmless."

Surprised that Tex had seen Jane, Frank gestured for her to join them. "This is Jane; we've been traveling together since New York."

"Miss Jane, I am happy to make your acquaintance."

Tex gave a sweeping bow.

"Where you heading, Tex?" Jane asked, shaking his large hand with her tiny one.

"Charlotte, ma'am, to the FEMA center there. Got a load of MREs, blankets, fuel pellets . . . shoot, just about everything you can imagine, then it's on to Atlanta to drop off the rest of the load."

Jane and Frank exchanged glances.

"You need someone to ride shotgun, Tex? How about four someones?"

"Tell you what. I've got a case of MREs in the cab and a hankering for dinner. Join me, and we'll talk about it." Tex shifted his toothpick to the other corner of his mouth and grinned.

Near Lake Weiss, Alabama, 10:45 Zulu

After yesterday's shooting session and rifle cleaning, Katie fired up the old tube-powered shortwave and spoke to her youngest daughter. She hadn't realized how worried she'd been, wondering if Lizzie and Jim had made it to safety with the children. They had. After exchanging stories and setting up communication schedules, she shut down the radio, climbed into bed and fell into a deep sleep. She awoke to a knock on her trailer door. Perplexed, she pulled on blue jean shorts and a tee shirt.

"Who is it?" she asked before unlocking the flimsy door.

"It is me, ma'am, Eli."

"Hold on a second." She unlocked the door and slid the retainer bar that Frank had installed to improve security.

"What is it, Eli? It's pretty early." She stood back and, with a glance at Max, sound asleep in the pullout, said, "I'll bring the coffee pot out."

Grabbing the European-style coffee maker and a bag of fine-ground coffee, she joined Eli outside.

"Get the stove going while I get this ready," she said.

Katie sat at the table and unscrewed the coffee maker top. Inside was the inverted funnel coffee holder that mated to the top's underside and the fine grate. She loaded the coffee holder with grounds, filled the lower chamber to the mark, replaced the holder and screwed the halves together. Meanwhile, Eli pumped up the pressure on the white-gas tank and lit a burner. Katie put on the coffee pot and adjusted the flame.

"Now, what can I do for you this early in the morning, Eli?" She eyed the sun coming up between the trees as the two sat across from each other.

"I am sorry to be so early, Miss Katiee, but I wanted to ask if I could scout the town." He looked at her through narrowed eyes. "We need to know what they are doing. The earlier the better; I hope to catch them sleeping."

Katie thought for a moment. "How would you get into town?"

"When we were getting supplies, I saw mountain bikes in storage. With one of them I could sneak in."

"The idea has merit, and I don't like not knowing what Reverend has planned." She said "Reverend" as more of a curse than a title of respect. "I get the feeling you've done these kinds of things before."

"Yes ma'am. Before I came to the USA, as a young man I was pressed into the service of militants in my home country." He looked embarrassed. "They made me do terrible things, but I ran away as soon as I could."

"What's past is past, Eli, what's important is what we do now. Are you sure you can get into town and back without getting noticed?"

She checked the coffee. Steam was starting to rise from the spout.

"I am still ashamed of things I did, but you are right. Now I may make amends by helping you and Mr. Frank, and your friends. I have delivered packages all over Fort Payne and surroundings; I know the roads, alleys, and paths. I am the only one who has a chance."

Katie took the coffee off the burner and closed it. She poured two cups—the pot's total capacity—and took the cups to the table, where she opened a packet of diet sweetener. Eli took his black.

"I can't argue with your logic. But don't be a hero. Be discreet, and if it looks like trouble, get out and get back. Take a radio; I don't know if it'll reach that far, but you never know."

"Yes ma'am, I will be careful."

They sat in silence, waiting for the coffee to cool. "Care for breakfast? I can make some eggs," Katie offered.

"No, I ate before I came up. Go ahead and make for you, though."

Eli blew on the hot coffee, then took a careful sip.

"I'll wait for the others. Eli, do you know anything about modifying a Mosin's trigger to make the pull a little smoother?"

"Yes ma'am. It is easy with the correct tools. If you have some spring or piano wire, I can fix the trigger take-up as well."

"I figured you could."

She smiled at him. "We are blessed to have you with us, Eli."

"I hope so, ma'am, I really hope so."

They soon finished the coffee. The rat-tat of woodpeckers and other forest birds filled the air—animals starting their day. Katie rinsed cups and dumped grounds into compost, and Eli retrieved a mountain bike from storage, and tools to adjust its seat height. Katie fetched a GRS radio from the charger and gave it to Eli. They synchronized their watches and agreed that Eli would check in every two hours. Katie made him take a pistol.

As Eli disappeared down the driveway and into the trees, Katie hoped she wasn't sending him off to his death.

Outside Henderson, North Carolina, 07:55 Zulu

The fuel gauge was on empty, and Willie had emptied the last jerry can into the tank the other side of Emporia, Virginia, before they got on I-85. Willie looked at Nick sleeping peacefully in the Jeep's passenger seat. "Nick, wake up."

It was annoying how Nick could come instantly awake.

"What's up?" Nick asked. "Oh, fuel. I'm sure we can find some somewhere. What's the next town?"

"Henderson, North Carolina, according to the signs."

They exited I-85 on Satterwhite Point Road and pulled into a Petro Mark station. As with most gas stations, there were the usual abandoned cars, and here one of the storage tank fill-valve hatches had been pried open, but no one was around the pump islands. In the distance, towering clouds of smoke marked Raleigh, with firelight reflecting off the roiling mass of smoke and fumes.

"Looks like Raleigh is out," Nick said cheerfully as he got out of the Jeep. "I'm going to check out the restroom; time to walk the lizard."

Willie was starting to resent Nick's disappearing act when work was at hand. Reaching into the back seat for the bucket containing the siphon equipment, he opened the driver's-side door, went to the back of the Jeep, and grabbed the two empty jerry cans. He had learned it was better to do the first pumping into the jerries, in case the hose went in too deep and reached the tank bottom. On the previous fill, at a rundown station, he had nearly put water into the Jeep's tank. Willie started with the valve with the missing cover.

After a few cranks on the hand pump, gasoline started gushing from the outlet hose, giving it a sniff, he determined it was uncontaminated, so he filled both jerry cans. Laying the pump beside the access hatch, he hauled the jerries to the jeep, strapped them in, got in the vehicle, started it and drove to the access hatch. As he started to crank, he heard the ominous sound of a 12-gauge pump-action shotgun being racked directly behind him.

"Ya'll care to tell me why you a'stealing my gas?" said a thickly southern voice.

Willie knew that an attempt to reach the pistol on the duty belt he'd stolen two days earlier from the dead policeman would result in being cut in half by a shotgun. He slowly set down the pump, raised his hands and turned around.

"Gee, Mister, I'm sorry. I didn't mean nothing by it, I'm just tryin' to get home." Willie tried his best little-boy-lost routine.

The man pointing the shotgun at Willie's midsection was a shade over six feet tall and tipped the scales at over three hundred pounds. He was wearing overalls, a white cotton shirt, and a Redman Chewing Tobacco hat. A chaw of Redman bulged out one cheek. "We don't take kindly to thieves in this area, boy." He lowered the shotgun, but Willie could tell he didn't lower his alertness. Redman punctuated his grammar by spitting a mass of brown fluid onto the pavement. "Where you headin'? Don't soun' like you'h from around here."

Hearing the suspicion in the voice, Willie did his best to sound harmless, while he plotted how to get the better of him. Damn, where the hell was Nick? "My dad's a US senator from Alabama—Senator Wright. I'm headin' to Bummin'ham now, to meet up with him."

"Ain't he that the piece of shit who moved to Alabama from up north so's he could get elected?" His voice was still unfriendly, but the shotgun lowered another notch.

"Yep. And I never forgave him for it, either." Willie decided to play the outraged offspring, which actually wasn't far from the facts. Willie had resented being moved from everything he knew and understood in New Jersey merely to further his father's political ambitions.

"From what I hear"—Redman paused to spit more nasty juice onto the abused sidewalk—"neither did the people of Alabama." He laughed at his own joke and dropped the shotgun barrel further.

Moving fast, Willie pulled the pistol from its holster and put two rounds pointblank into the big man's potbelly.

Backpeddling, Redman tried with suddenly lifeless hands to bring the shotgun to bear. The last sight the man saw was Willie leveling the pistol and firing directly into his face.

"Damn, I can't leave you for a second." It was Nick's voice behind him.

"Nick, just shut up," Willie said in disgust, holstering the pistol. "You always seem to disappear when I need you most."

Willie picked up the gas pump and finished topping off the Jeep's tank.

"Look, I had to pee. I'm sorry." Nick didn't look sorry.

"You better start being more useful, that's all I'm saying," Willie groused, pumping extra gas in a trail around and on the now dead gas station owner. When he finished drenching the corpse, he pulled the hose from the tank, coiled and stowed it in the bucket along with the pump.

"Or what?" asked Nick with a sneer.

"Or I'll leave your ass in Podunk Town." Willie voice was deadly serious.

Nick laughed.

For a second, Willie grasped the pistol grip at his belt and contemplated ending the friendship, but without Nick who would he have? Willie pulled the Jeep off about ten yards, stepped out, pulled a roadside flare from the emergency kit and lit it by jerking the cap. After letting the phosphorous burn for a few seconds, he tossed the flare toward the body.

Even at 3:00 a.m., the pavement was hot enough to drive the gas fumes up to meet the descending flare with a whoomp sufficient to concuss Willie as it raced by. The spilled gas caught and flamed yellow and blue.

Willie gunned the Jeep back on the road; he and Nick were a few hundred yards away when the underground tank blew, followed by the others, turning early-morning darkness into midday.

It was almost enough to make Willie smile.

Interstate 77 at the North Carolina border, 13:30 Zulu

"Eh . . . this omelet tastes like rubber."

Frank made a face as he swallowed. "Any hot sauce?"

He grabbed a condiment pack, removed the hot sauce and liberally doused the supposed omelet.

"I should'a warned ya. The omelet may keep soul and body together but it tastes like crap," Tex said.

Everyone shared an MRE breakfast with Tex. When they finished, they packed what little gear they had into the sleeper section of the cab. Delicia and Jane squeezed in the sleeper with the gear, and George, Tex and Frank took the bench seat in the cab—Frank shotgun by the window, George assuming backup with the .45 and his .38 Special.

"I shore am glad I ran into you folks," Tex said happily.

"How so, Tex?" asked George.

"Well, we've had a couple reports of supply trucks getting hit. I was the last one out before they started running 'em with guards and escorts." He peered in the rearview for a moment after answering. "Seems there are renegade survivalists out there whose method is take what they can."

Frank thought about the crazies he had run into on Internet

survivalist boards and their focus on guns instead of beans and water.

"Gives the lot a bad name, that's for sure," Frank offered. "I consider myself a prepper, I guess a survivalist to some degree, but I'd never take someone else's supplies or rob trucks."

"Well, those that do are lower'n snake's bellies. I'm jus' glad to have ya'll riding shotgun." Tex flashed an innocent grin.

Frank was pleased as punch that Tex had found them and trusted his instincts to let them tag along. No more side roads to avoid roadblocks, no worry about a vehicle on its last legs. If things played out he could be back in Atlanta before midnight. He glanced at the rearview beside him — in the distance, something reflected the early morning sun.

"Uh, Tex . . ."

"I see it pardner. Keep your eyes on't."

"What?" asked George, lacking a rearview.

"Sompin' coming up a'hind us; too far back t' say wha' tis." Tex shifted the truck into a higher gear and accelerated.

"And things were starting to fall our way." Frank racked a shell into the shotgun and watched his mirror.

"It may be nothing. Jus' keep your eyes peeled," Tex said grimly.

"What's going on?" Delicia's voice called from the sleeper.

The men looked at each other, silently debating what to tell the women. Frank spoke first. "Someone may be chasing us. We don't know yet."

"Great, and us stuck up here in the attic," Jane said.

"Brace yourselves; may've a rough ride in a few minutes," Tex answered.

In the rearviews, Frank and Tex could see the point riders for a group of motorcycles. Tex shifted again and the truck accelerated more, shaking the cab and starting the trailer to swerve side to side.

"That's it, folks. I don't dare push us any faster. We're over ninety and the trailer's unstablin'."

"What now?" asked George.

"We wait. Maybe they jus' out for a ride." His voice showed that was not the first thought in his mind.

"Delivering toys to the nearest hospital," said Frank cynically. In the mirror he could clearly see the point riders advance, one on either side. Bungeed to their handlebar cross braces were large teddy bears.

The riders waved as they roared by the cab and gave a show-off spurt of Harley high-power. The other bikes also had toys strapped on, not only the handlebars, but also to any available surface.

Tex and George goggle-eyed Frank, and the three burst into laughter.

Outskirts of Fort Payne, Alabama, 12:45 Zulu

Eli had taken County Road 114 to County Road 35, then cut over to County Road 153 and up Deans Rd to eventually reach Beason Gap Road, where he wanted to be. On the outskirts of the residences was the county water tank, where he hid the mountain bike. It was 7:45 a.m. Eastern Standard Time and usually the streets would be alive with people going to work or school, and pursuing normal lives. But since the EMP, things had hardly been normal. After the initial frenzy and panic shopping, which left local stores stripped of anything of value, people were now huddling in homes and shelters, wondering what would come next. Many had gotten out of town using any transportation they could find. Occasional groups of young men wandered the streets free of civilized constraints, looking for trouble; luckily they weren't early risers after a typical night of drugs, drink and mayhem.

Keeping to backyards, alleys and shadows, Eli showed his training in military scouting. He flashed back to being barely out of his teens and joining the Eritrea People's Liberation Front to fight for independence from Ethiopia and its communist dictator Mengistu Haile Mariam. By 1993 when Eritrea became independent, Eli had difficulty telling Eritrea's freedom fighters from the communist troops they'd defeated. He still had nightmares of the atrocities he'd seen and been forced to commit, still got sweats handling a machete. As soon as he could, he fled to Europe and then America, hoping the terror was behind him. But now his beloved America was sliding into the same darkness.

Six blocks from Godfrey Avenue and the church, Eli, hidden by the backyard shed of a house, paused and tried the radio; it was near the two-hour mark. Eli got nothing but static on the small handset — the hills between Fort Payne and Lake Weiss were too much interference. Feeling alone, he crept toward the church using every trick he had learned as a freedom-fighter scout.

All the church windows were open to catch the cool morning breezes before Alabama summer heat and humidity made non-air-conditioned buildings unbearable. Several older model cars and trucks were parked at the church for a meeting in the main chapel. Eli hid beneath a chapel window and listened to the stentorian tones of Reverend Sanders:

"I tell you all we need to purge the sons of Ishmael from among us! These heathens have attacked us in a cowardly and godless manner! One even killed my own son!"

Eli cringed — another soul to weigh him down — even as he knew he'd been defending himself. He knew the Koran gave no penalty for killing enemies and non-Muslims, but still he felt remorse. Reverend went on:

"The heathen that killed my boy is right over in Gaylesburg. We need to go there and make an example, isn't that right, Brother Ricky?"

A young, nasal voice: "Yep. I followed him jus' like you said, Reverend. That lady at the property jus' let him stay."

Brother Ricky's implications were clear. Eli felt the old anger rise, anger from when he'd seen atrocities committed on innocents by both sides. "But I heard lots of shooting the other day when I snuck up to spy on 'em. I think they got lots of guns, big ones."

"The righteous need fear no guns! Besides, Brother Daniels can provide us all the guns and ammunition we need, isn't that right, Brother Daniel?"

Brother Daniel Richards owned Dan's Rod and Gun, a local hunting and fishing store. "I . . . I guess so, Reverend." He didn't sound too sure to Eli.

"Good!" Reverend steamrolled. "I say time's a' wasting! We need to get that Black bastard what killed my boy. An unforgettable lesson must be made."

"Reverend, we better plan careful and not go off half-cocked. If they have guns, they may be better prepared than we think," an anonymous voice called out. It sounded to Eli like Lyle Haygood from the Feed Store.

"Brother Haygood, you are correct. Ricky, you feel up to more scoutin'?"

"It'd be an honor, Reverend. Need more fuel for the bike, though."

Eli looked quickly around the lot; near the church doors was an area reserved for motorcycles. A solitary bike was parked there. Eli dashed to the bike, pulled out his pocketknife, and stabbed both tires.

Inside the church, the sound of air rushing from slashed motorbike tires silenced the discussion. "What's that? Ricky, go see what's happening."

Ricky pulled a .38 Smith & Wesson from his pants pocket and headed out. As the door creaked open, Eli had ducked around the side of the church and was stealthily retreating toward the water tank. "Damn it, Reverend! Someone slashed my bike tires!" Ricky shouted.

Eli knew it wouldn't take long for the churchmen to fix tires, or find other transport, but he hoped he'd delayed any attempt to scout the BOL until they could prepare.

OUTSIDE GREENVILLE, NORTH CAROLINA, 14:10 ZULU

Willie and Nick delighted at the chaos and disaster visible from I-85 as they passed through North Carolina. Towns burning from either accidental or deliberate fires were frequent. With no water pressure and many fire trucks out of commission, minor incidents grew into block-consuming conflagrations. In subdivisions of California-style densities of seven units to the acre, a single house fire from a poorly tended fireplace, grill or camp stove quickly spread, reducing large urban zones to smoke and ash. More and more, they saw ragged, soot-stained stragglers — at times, entire families — with nothing more than what they could carry.

With their gas tank once again nearing empty and the jerry cans depleted, Willie and Nick needed to stop again, soon, but it was nearly impossible to find a gas station that didn't harbor refugees.

"We should just stop and take what we need," Nick said with casual menace. "Shoot a few and the rest will scatter."

"What if they have guns? I don't fancy being shot."

Willie looked warily at Nick, who shot back, "Unless you want to walk, we have to get fuel."

"Tell me something I don't know!" Frustration was clear in Willie's voice.

At the Greer exit, Willie spotted a truck-and-trailer rental company. On a hunch, he drove into the empty parking lot, assuming that the facility, lacking the food-and-drink temptations of a convenience store, would be deserted.

"Why we stopping here?" asked Nick.

"They rent gas-fueled trucks. I'll bet they have a fueling station," Willie said as he parked the Jeep. "I'm gonna look around." He checked his pistol, found the magazine nearly empty, reloaded and re-holstered, and walked around the back of the building, noticing Nick was right behind him. At the back lot, surrounded by anti-collision bollards, were diesel and gasoline pumps, with aboveground tanks nearby.

"Wait here," Willie instructed Nick. "I'll get the Jeep." He quickly pulled the car around to the gasoline pump station.

The simple lock protecting the gasoline fill valve was easily wrenched open with a tire iron. Using the hand pump, Willie quickly filled the Jeep's tank and the two jerry cans.

"Hey, give a girl a ride?"

The contralto voice startled Willie. He wheeled around with drawn pistol.

"Whoa, no need for that, I just want a ride!"

She stood a few feet away, a slim woman with coppery complexion that showed Native American genes, and hair made almost blue-black by the morning sun, looking challengingly at Willie. "I can pay however you like."

Her look and tone told Willie she meant it.

"Where you wanna go?"

Willie kept the pistol out; she might be a distraction for an ambush.

"I'm alone," she said, as if reading his mind. Her brazenness intrigued Willie. "I want to get away from here."

"Pay in advance?"

She nodded, led him to the repair bay, and began disrobing. Willie wondered where Nick had gone. Glancing at the girl, he decided he didn't care.

Willie found some clean shop blankets—normally used to protect truck bodies from scratches during engine work—and after she had finished paying, he sat up and studied her. "My name's Bill. What's yours?"

"Clara," she answered simply.

"Just 'Clara'?"

"Do I need anything more?"

"I guess not."

As long as she kept paying, Willie didn't care if her name was George. She had shown a capacity for depravity that had pleased and almost repelled him—in short, a perfect match.

"What have you found now?"

Willie turned at the sound of Nick's voice.

"Nick, meet Clara; she'll be riding with us. Clara, this is

Nick."
   Clara looked at Nick with puzzlement.

Bank of America Stadium, Charlotte, North Carolina, 17:12 Zulu

Tex enjoyed a stress-free drive through the North Carolina countryside. Other than out-of-control fires, abandoned vehicles pushed to the shoulder, apparently by National Guard work crews, and refugees heading for Charlotte, it could have been any day in the modern American south.

"So Tex, where do you think they'll send you after Charlotte?" Frank hoped it would be Atlanta.

"Don't rightly know." Tex moved his toothpick from one side of his mouth to the other. "It was supposed to be Atlanta, then Birmingham, but could be Florida or even Mississippi. They'll tell me at dispatch, I reckon."

"Hope it's Atlanta. Make our journey much easier."

"Well, drivers be headin' all over. I'll put in a good word for ya'll."

"Thanks Tex, we appreciate it," George said sincerely.

"What about us?" Jane chimed in from the sleeper.

"Shoot, we'll take care of you, ma'am! Don't worry none."

They caught up to the bikers at Bank of America Stadium. As Tex pulled into the lot they could see two dozen or so Harleys parked near the north entrance. National Guardsmen directed Tex to park next to several other big rigs in various stages of unloading.

"Ya'll wait here. I'll check with dispatch; chances are I can get ya some work unloading, and a ride." He jumped down from the rig. "Be right back."

They watched Tex walk to the dispatcher's tent, which was festooned with communication antennas and hurrying people, and talk to a Guardsman for a minute or so. After showing paperwork, he was allowed inside.

"Now what," asked Delicia, who, along with Jane, had squeezed into the main cab with George and Frank as soon as Tex got out.

"We wait, I guess," answered Frank.

Tex and his long-legged stride soon reappeared. "Ya'll hungry? They've a mess tent over there, and outhouses, too."

"Hot damn," George answered, climbing down. The others followed. "What'd you hear about destinations?"

"Well, I'm supposed to rest a few hours, then off to Florida," Tex answered. They could hear the apology in his voice. "But I've put the word out for rides to Spartanburg for Delicia, and to Atlanta for you gentlemen."

"What about me," asked Jane. "I live near Charlotte-Douglas Airport."

"Don't rightly know, ma'am. A lot of planes went down over there and one took out the tank farm. Hundreds of thousands of gallons of aviation fuel went up like a fuel-air bomb."

Jane turned white, nearly stumbled, and would've fallen if Frank hadn't caught her. "Jane, we'll find out," Frank assured her as the others looked on with concern. "We won't leave you here alone."

"It's just that I hoped for something normal, my apartment, my cat . . ." She broke into tears.

"Darn it, ma'am, I am sorry I'm such a twit. I should'a told you easier than that. If my Ma was here she'd dust my butt good for making a lady cry."

Tex was so contrite Jane had to smile in spite of her pain.

"It isn't your fault, Tex. It was silly of me to expect anything to be normal. Heck, I used to complain all the time about airplanes flying overhead; I never thought about them falling on my apartment."

"The blast may have missed your place altogether," Frank said with a confidence he didn't feel. "Let's get some hot food. Then we'll see what we see."

The chow line was a mix of bikers, National Guard, and refugees from the surrounding areas whose homes had burned in the fires or were otherwise uninhabitable. Tex made easy friendships with the bikers and they shared a good laugh over the fright thrown into the five of them when they'd roared past. It turned out they'd gathered the toys strapped on their bikes for a Charlotte hospital, but when the EMP happened they decided the kids in the stadium refugee center needed the love.

"Miss Jane?"

Jane turned to see a huge, dark-haired biker with a bushy black beard and mustache—and the twinkliest blue eyes she'd ever seen. His black leather vest and wife-beater showed off tanned, muscled arms covered with tattoos.

"Yes...," she answered tentatively.

"Tex tells me you need to see your apartment. If it's alright, a couple of the gang and me could escort you to have a look-see, after we eat."

"Only if I go along as well," Frank interjected.

The biker looked at Frank and then laughed.

"Of course. No need to worry, though. When I'm not dressed for biking I'm an OB/GYN." He laughed louder and handed a business card to Frank. "JoJo over there is a lawyer and Sid is an accountant."

Wordlessly, Frank passed the card to Jane, who read the name aloud. "Ira Lowenstein, MD, OB/GYN, Charlotte Obstetrics."

"A Jewish OB/GYN tattooed biker—isn't that a sign of the Apocalypse?"

Frank shook Ira's hand.

OUTSIDE FORT PAYNE, ALABAMA, 13:30 ZULU

Eli was literally running for his life. If he was going to evade Reverend and his followers, he had to get the mountain bike and make the woods around Little River Canyon State Park. He could hear car and truck doors slamming and muffled conversations as the church emptied in pursuit. By the time he reached the water tower and the hidden bike, he was nearly winded.

Climbing aboard, he felt a stitch in his side, reminding him he wasn't twenty years old anymore. Ignoring pain, he stood on the pedals and pushed the bike at top speed out of town. Unfortunately, to reach Little River Canyon, he had to climb a mountain. Electing to proceed on foot through woods rather than inch up a mountain road, he abandoned the bike under a windfall pine on the roadside. He hoped he could recover it later.

Eli crouched behind a large hackberry as two old cars and a pickup roared past. Knowing the pursuers would soon realize they'd missed him and double back, he bounded to his feet as the last vehicle passed and clambered up the steep hillside. He planned to run parallel to the road as soon as he reached the ridge. Nearing the top, he paused for breath and to allow the stitch, which had reappeared, to subside. He checked Katie's pistol and made sure his extra magazines were easily available.

At the ridge he turned and after only a few hundred yards cautiously crossed Skyline Boulevard, across the road from the Fairfield place. A fervent hunter and knife collector, Kevin Fairfield was always getting packages; while he'd never been unfriendly, he also hadn't gone out of his way to befriend Eli, either. Eli worried, too, because several months earlier he'd reported a group of young men who'd apparently been trashing the Fairfield residence; instead their son was throwing a party. Eli had just left the Fairfield property when behind him came the unmistakable sound of a pump-action shotgun being cocked.

"Eli, if I were you I'd put that pistol on the ground and turn around." The voice was Kevin's.

Eli considered running or trying to get a shot off, but did neither. He put the gun down and turned around.

"Mr. Fairfield, I have no argument with you. I just want to get away from town." Eli looked Kevin straight in the eye.

"You know Reverend's son died—choked to death on his own blood," Kevin said evenly, holding the shotgun at waist level, muzzle pointed at Eli. Kevin indicated a spot away from the pistol on the ground. "Move over there." Eli complied. Keeping Eli covered, Kevin picked up the pistol.

"Mr. Fairfield, sir, I was defending myself. They'd just strung-up my friend Achmed, saying we were all terrorists and deserved to die."

Eli kept his hands up and maintained eye contact. "Achmed was a Coptic, not even a Muslim. They would have done the same to me."

With the shotgun, Kevin gestured toward the house.

"You better come with me until we get this sorted."

Eli walked slowly toward the Fairfield residence, fear and anger playing with his mind. He hadn't a clue whether Kevin was going to hold him for the churchmen who sought his death, call the police—if any remained—or kill him outright. But then, if Kevin had wanted him dead, he'd have shot him straightaway.

"Hold up! I'll get the door. Better yet, you open it." Kevin tossed him the keys, taking care not to get within arm's reach.

Eli fumbled with the keys, finally finding the one to the deadbolt. With a snick, it unlatched; Eli pushed open the door and entered the dimly lit interior.

"OK. No one can see us, now. Put down your hands, Eli."

Kevin broke the shotgun and smiled.

"You did me a big favor, you know. That brush with the law straightened Joey out." Kevin stuck out his hand. "Thanks, Eli."

Puzzled, Eli shook Kevin's hand.

"What was all that about?" Eli looked to the shotgun.

"It ain't loaded. I was down by the road when I saw Reverend and followers, then I saw you cross the road. In case they doubled back, I figured I'd better get you out of sight." He smiled again. "If anyone saw me marching you in at gunpoint, they might not rush in right away."

"Now it is my turn to say thanks. May Allah bless you and

yours."

Eli bowed to Kevin, who acted embarrassed.

"No need for all that. I figure we're even now. You have a place to go?"

"Yes sir, but I would rather not say where; if Reverend learns you helped me he can't get information you do not have."

"Want some water? Maybe a sandwich?" Kevin walked to the kitchen.

"Yes, that would be good." As Kevin made the sandwich, Eli tried to reach Katie on the GRS.

"Base this is Black Rover, over." Eli used the assigned codes to maintain operational security.

"Black Rover, this is base. Where've you been? We're worried, over."

"Base, had some issues with Holy Roller; he may be inbound, over."

"Black Rover, roger that, we'll keep a watch. What is your 10-77? Over."

"Base, unsure. May need to wait until nightfall, over."

"Roger that, be careful. Report in two hours if possible."

"10-4, Black Rover out."

Kevin was quizzical. "A man of hidden talents. Here, eat." Kevin was handed him a chicken sandwich and a glass of water when they heard a car pull up the driveway.

"Help me with this table!"

Kevin grabbed one side of the kitchen table and Eli grabbed the other, moving it aside. Kevin moved the rug to reveal a trapdoor, which, with a grunt, he raised. Eli needed no encouragement as a banging came from the front of the house, he rushed down the ladder into blackness below.

North of Lake Weiss, Alabama, 11:00 Zulu

Katie was worried. Not just for Eli advancing on danger for them all, but also for their general safety. Whether they had to face Reverend and his flock as a consequence of helping Eli, or face unknown raiders after food, ammo, water, or whatever, the property must be made more secure. Recalling something about non-fatal traps and mines—if she could only find the reference—she began leafing through their survival notebook.

She sipped cold coffee and grimaced, wishing for a microwave to reheat the brew, but it would use more power than they could spare, even if one had been in the shielded container during the EMP. Taking a long, unsatisfying gulp, she returned to the notebook.

"Aha!"

She popped the binder rings, pulled out a couple pages and spun the crank on the surplus sound-powered phone connecting the two trailers.

In the trailer where David and Marlene were still sleeping, the sudden squawk of sound-powered phone brought them both awake.

"What the bloody hell is that racket?" Marlene sat up quickly.

"It's that phone," David said, pointing at the black receiver mounted on a box on the wall near Marlene.

"Hello? Hello . . . ?"

"Mum, I think you have to press that little button to talk."

"Hello?" Marlene said again, this time pressing a small brass button on the receiver. She knew enough to release it when she finished.

"Good morning, Marlene! As soon as you get dressed, come over to the main trailer. We have a project."

Marlene pressed the button and answered. "OK. But it'll be a wee bit. We just got woken by this bloody contraption." She hung up to Katie's laughter.

Katie went to the storage shed and grabbed a six-foot length of three-inch PVC pipe and caps; a length of three-quarter-inch PVC pipe, caps, and threaded adapters; primer and dope; a roll of half-inch Tygon tubing; a three-quarter-inch dowel; a box of inch-and-a-half wire nails; a box of number ten by three-quarter wood screws; silicon sealer; a spool of floral wire, and a box of C02 cartridges like those for air-powered BB guns. By the time she had it all on the picnic table, Marlene and David had arrived.

After a quick breakfast, Katie explained the project.

"David, get the chop saw from the shop and bring it here along with the drill and that box of hole-saw bits. Marlene, take this Sharpie. Help me measure."

Following the instructions from Katie's notebook, they had everything marked by the time David had the saw and drill ready. Katie provided safety glasses and work gloves, and supervised the initial cuts, then left them to the work while she started assembling the first set.

"Cool," David said as she finished the first device. "What is it?"

Katie smiled. "A non-fatal land mine, at least the way we'll use them."

"You're kidding! Show us." Marlene wiped sweat from her face.

"OK, watch."

Katie used the well spigot to fill the mine with water via the Tygon hoses protruding from its top. She removed the three-quarter-inch pipe cap, placed a CO2 cartridge nozzle-end-down in the inside tube and then eased the cap back on. Using the floral wire, she snugged the cap tight and tied it off to the side-mounted screws. She placed the mine on the ground.

"Who wants to be the guinea pig?"

Hesitantly, David volunteered. Katie and Marlene stood

back several yards as he gingerly depressed the pipe cap with his shoe.

With a whoosh, the CO_2 cartridge discharged into the mine interior, driving the contents through the two Tygon tubes to create an enveloping cloud of water and vapor, drenching David to the bone with cold well water.

"Wow, that's cold! Feels good." He grinned as water lined his face.

"Now imagine it with capsaicin dissolved in it," Katie said ominously.

"What's capsaicin?"

"It's the active component in chili peppers," Katie explained.

"Ouch! A pepper-spray mine," Marlene said.

"Exactly. We can rig them with different lengths of tubing so they spray a large area."

David looked thoughtfully at the supplies. "How many do we need?"

"I figure thirty or so, for the main trails and the driveway. We can put tire disablers along the fence to keep invaders channeled in the drive, and also put a few around the garden." Katie, too, looked thoughtful. "We may need more."

Marlene donned her safety gear and, with a vengeance, started drilling.

Outside Greenville, North Carolina, 15:00 Zulu

Thinking fast, Clara said cheerfully: "Hi Nick, nice to meet you. Bill didn't tell me about you."

Now Nick looked puzzled.

"Well," Willie said, "We were kind of busy. Nick helped me out of a mess in New York and we've been traveling together ever since."

"I 'magine y'have," Clara mumbled as she turned to straighten her blouse and tuck it into her jeans, wondering what she'd gotten herself into.

"What?" asked Willie.

"Oh, nothing. Shotgun, I claim shotgun!" She ran to the Jeep.

"She's going to be trouble," Nick said testily.

"If she is, we dump her," Willie answered, unconvincingly.

With tank and jerry cans full of gas, they returned to I-85 with Willie driving and Clara shotgun. Nick took the backseat without verbal complaint, but with a dark expression.

Willie looked in the mirror at Nick. "Don't sulk."

"I'm not," answered Clara.

"I meant Nick. He's sulking in the back seat."

"I'm sorry, Nick. Next stop, you're shotgun," Clara said.

Willie hoped they'd get along. It'd be nice to have someone to share the driving—with Nick's crippled leg he couldn't handle the Jeep's clutch.

"Clara, can you drive a stick?"

With a wicked grin, she stared at Willie's crotch. "Do you have to ask?"

"I meant the Jeep!" Willie, unused to such direct flirting, got flustered.

"I've driven stick since I was sixteen," she said. "And used a stick shift."

"Get a room, you two!"

Clara went on as if she hadn't heard Nick. "Nick can't drive a stick?"

"His leg won't let him use the clutch properly. At least that's his excuse." Willie looked in the mirror at Nick, who glowered back.

"So where are we heading?"

"Alabama. Birmingham first, to see my father, then up around Lake Weiss," Willie answered.

"Miss your dad?"

"Not if I can help it."

"What do you mean? That's a curious answer."

"My dad didn't know what to do with me after my mom died. He's a career politician with no room for a son. It was off to boarding school, then off to college, as far away as he could make it."

"Tough. Sorry about that. I think my dad loved me, at least that's what he said when he'd have 'special time' with me." Her face darkened.

" 'Special time'?"

"Rather not talk about it. Once I was old enough to realize what he was doing, I split."

"Oh, sorry." Willie felt embarrassed and oddly excited.

"Cry me a river, you two. My father cast me out but you don't hear me complaining."

"Nick," Willie said, "is that sour grapes I hear?"

"What'd he say? I'm having trouble hearing him up here." She smiled.

"Nothing important. You ever handle a gun?"

"What? Oh, not really." The change in topic took her by surprise.

"Open the glove box and get the pistol."

Clara retrieved the 9mm XD Sub-Compact. "What now?"

"First, press that button and let the magazine out."

Willie was glad the road was clear. He'd be able to split his attention between driving and teaching Clara the basics.

Clara pushed the button near the trigger guard with her thumb. The magazine dropped into her lap.

"Now feel on top of the receiver; find a bump?" Willie had examined the pistol before hiding it in the glove box, discovering that when it was loaded a small lever rose up on top, and if it was cocked, a small nub appeared on the back of the receiver as well.

"Yes."

"That means it still has a round in the chamber. Rack the slide."

"Do what?"

"Hold it in your right hand—finger off the trigger! Grip the top where you see those grooves and pull back as hard as you can."

Clara studied the pistol; her second try managed to rack the slide all the way. The round in the chamber dropped from the magazine well into her lap.

"Point the gun out the window and pull the trigger."

With a click, Clara successfully dry-fired the XD. "Now what?"

"Now we reload." Willie glanced at the back seat; Nick appeared to be asleep. "Put the gun down and pick up the magazine."

Placing the pistol on the front-seat tray, Clara picked up the magazine.

"Grab the bullet you ejected and push it into the magazine. Lay it flat against the others and push down."

Clara succeeded in pushing the round into the magazine.

"Good. Now take the pistol and with the bullets facing forward, push the magazine into it. You may have to smack it to get it to seat."

Clara easily got the magazine back into the pistol.

"Now rack the slide again—finger off the trigger!"

This time it was easier for her to rack the slide.

"OK. You've just reloaded a pistol."

Seeing a rest stop sign, Willie pulled the Jeep in. "Time for target practice." Willie parked the car and took Clara to find something, or someone, to shoot, leaving Nick asleep in the back seat.

Bank of America Stadium, Charlotte, North Carolina, 18:00 Zulu

Frank cleaned the macaroni and cheese from his plate. It was the box kind he remembered buying for four-for-a-dollar when Katie and he first married and they had mixed in canned ham and peas to make a "complete" meal.

Cornbread muffins were overdone but served as an excellent vehicle for the margarine. Frank polished off his weak sweet tea and stood. Jane, almost finished, was talking animatedly with Doc Ira and his motorcycle buddies.

"I'm going to the restroom," Frank said.

"Hurry back," Ira said. "We leave soon's we finish here."

"Will do." Frank turned to a National Guardsman by the door. "Which way the restroom?"

"Porta Potties thataway, behind the admin tent."

"Thanks."

As Frank drew near the admin tent, he saw rows of Porta Potties lined up behind it. There seemed to be a line so he joined it.

"I tell you it'll be a milk run," a man in line said to another. Frank couldn't help but overhear.

"Then why they need so many guards?" asked the man's companion.

"The Atlanta perimeter is a little dicey, but other than that the run should be easy."

"You guys heading for Atlanta?" Frank asked, butting in.

"The Feds are making a fuel run to Hartsfield-Jackson," the first man said. "They need volunteers to guard the trucks; the Guard is stretched too thin."

"Why Hartsfield? Didn't they get hammered by crashing planes, like the other airports?" Frank remembered he had been scheduled to fly into Hartsfield.

"They had a weather hold, no planes in or out, so everyone was detoured to other airports, and they got off with little damage."

"When they heading out? I might volunteer; I need to get to Atlanta."

"Around 3:00 p.m. you can sign up at the admin tent."

"Thanks, I will."

With a new sense of purpose, Frank made short work of the bathroom break and hurried to the admin tent. Inside, a long table displayed various volunteer signup sheets. It didn't take long to find the sheet for the avgas run to Atlanta; few had signed up. Frank added his and George's names. A tired Guardsman looked up from a tattered paperback. "Any military experience?"

"Navy; qualified on the service .45 and M1." Frank showed his veteran's ID card. "I've shot AKs, .38s and 9mm, as well as shotguns."

"Be back here 3:30 p.m. for truck assignment; what about this 'George' fellow?" The Guardsman put a star next to Frank's name.

"I'll vouch for him. He can handle a shotgun."

"I need to vouch for him; send him over."

"Will do. See you at 3:30."

Frank hurried to the mess tent and found George finishing a second plate. "George, I have us a ride to Atlanta. Go over to the admin tent and talk to the Guard at the volunteer table."

"Great!" George said around a cornbread mouthful. "I'll head right over."

"I need to go with Jane to her apartment, then we'll come right back. We leave at 2:00."

"I'll wait for ya at the admin tent." George gathered their bags as well as the spare weapons. "And I'll watch these."

"Great. See you at 3:30."

Frank shook George's hand, then went to find Jane and the bikers, who were getting ready to leave.

"Frank," Ira said, "we were just coming to look for you."

"No need. I was signing up for a ride to Atlanta."

"Frank, that's wonderful news," Jane said, happy for his good fortune.

"I have to be back by 3:30."

"Not a problem. Here, you ride with me." A skinny biker in jeans, black leather chaps, a Harley tee shirt and a black-leather concealment vest handed him a black half helmet, which Frank strapped on and then swung his leg over the indicated bike to take the queen seat. "I'm Frank," he said.

"Call me JoJo," the skinny guy said. They shook hands.

JoJo put on his own helmet — a black full-face painted with

a leering skull on the front and flames reaching to the back. He climbed aboard his Harley and, after kicking it into roaring life, they balanced, waiting for the others. Jane sat behind Ira in a bright-red full-face. At a signal from Ira they roared off toward the Interstate and Jane's apartment.

Marietta, Georgia, 12:00 Zulu

After a fitful night's sleep and a Coleman-stove breakfast, Fred and Earl started packing Fred's early-model Blazer. Earl carried a mug of coffee — he had taken to the American beverage soon after coming over, even though Marlene still insisted on tea — and was dreading the arrival of evening and his decision: should he leave with Fred, or wait and hope someone showed who knew where Marlene, David and Katie had gone?

"Fred, I appreciate your offer, but I'll probably stay and wait for word on Marlene," Earl said, loading a 7.62 ammo box into the old Chevy, rapidly filling with crates of MREs, duffle bags of miscellaneous supplies and a pair of wicked-looking black rifles.

"Well, I understand. I can't take all this, so when you do split, take what you need. Hell, take all of it. Better you than Hank's cronies."

"I appreciate that, Fred, but I don't know how to use most of this stuff. Maybe a little food and a better pistol and ammo."

"Well, whatever you want, mi casa, su casa."

After finishing the Blazer load-out, Fred showed Earl how to operate, field strip and reassemble the AR-15. Once Earl was fairly proficient, they moved on to the Mossberg 500 shotgun. By lunchtime, Earl's head was spinning with springs, hammers, cocking bolts, sears, receivers, barrels and ejectors. They ate potato chips and canned Spam sandwiches off of fine china in Fred's dining room.

"Sure you'll be OK by yourself?" Earl asked between sips of warm beer.

"Well, I have a couple of different routes to get where I'm going, plus a scanner and a CB that I kept in a Faraday cage."

" 'Faraday cage'?" Earl was vaguely aware of these grounded metal enclosures.

"I keep essential electronics in a Faraday cage. Good thing, because otherwise the EMP would have fried them."

"Brilliant! Wish I'd thought of that."

"Another CB and scanner in there; when you leave, take 'em."

"I'll do that. You be careful."

"I've got a battery rig in the basement. We'll hook up the CB, and we can talk until I get ten to fifteen miles away, maybe more."

"That'd be great," Earl said, finishing his sandwich and chips.

"Alright, let's strap the spare gas to the carrier, tie the last supplies on the roof, and I'll head out. I want to reach my retreat before dark."

"Let's do it."

Earl felt sad as he watched the Blazer pull out of the driveway; he waved as Fred disappeared toward the subdivision entrance. Earl went back inside and opened windows and sliding doors. Unfortunately it was a still day; the humid Georgia air hung hot. Earl grabbed another warm beer from the dead refrigerator, went to the CB on the kitchen table, flipped the power switch and set the channel to 14, the one he and Fred had agreed to try.

Earl keyed the mic. "Fred, this is Earl, over." He released the key.

"Fred here, over!" Fred's voice boomed over the squelch setting.

"Bloody hell!" Earl choked the volume and then said, "Fred, just doing a radio check."

"Roger that. I see a few people in the CVS drugstore; they appear to be ransacking the place. No police or other authorities."

The CVS was less than a mile away. Earl wondered how long before looting spread to houses. Of course, looking at his and Frank's homes, he guessed it already had. "Roger that. Maybe you should take Jones Road and skirt the mall, over."

"Good idea. Might be quite a mob there, over"

"Keep me posted."

Earl put down the mic and sipped his beer. In a few minutes, the radio squawked to life.

"Earl, I see a roadblock up ahead. Looks like ruffians, I'm going to try going through yards."

"Roger, stay safe." Earl gripped the mic, waiting.

"I'm past, but a couple of punks on a motorbike following me—shit!"

Before the squelch cut in, Earl heard the sound of a shot, or maybe Fred had released the mic button. "Fred, you OK? Fred...?"

When Earl released the key, there was only silence.

OUTSIDE LITTLE RIVER CANYON STATE PARK, ALABAMA, 17:00 ZULU

Eli stood quietly in the darkness of the musty root cellar. He could hear in the kitchen above the pacing of several sets of hunting boots and the occasional garble of what seemed to be amiable conversation. It seemed an eternity, but eventually came the sound of men leaving, and a closing door. After another eternity, he heard the scrape of table leg and a slice of light appeared around the trapdoor at top of the ladder.

"Eli, come on up, they're gone for now."

Kevin's voice was the best thing Eli had heard in a long while.

Eli climbed the ladder into the day-bright kitchen,

squinting as his eyes adjusted from the darkness. "What did you tell them?" he asked, helping Kevin replace the table.

"They asked if I'd seen you. I said what with you reportin' my son to the police and all, I would know what to do if I did." He smiled. "I figure we wait til dark and I'll guide you out the escape tunnel off the root cellar."

"You have an escape tunnel?"

"Part of the Underground Railroad. You familiar with that?"

"Not really. I know about the Constitution and some American history, but only enough to pass the citizenship test."

"The Underground Railroad was a group of people and places to help escaped slaves get north. My escape tunnel was a part of it."

"It is sad we still have a use for such things."

"You are right, there, Eli."

"I don't know how to thank you, Mr. Fairfield."

Eli reached out his hand. Without hesitation Kevin shook it.

"Call me Kevin, Eli. I don't agree with what Reverend is doing; never liked him much. I'll choose for myself who I like and who I don't." Kevin opened the refrigerator and handed Eli his unfinished sandwich and tea.

"You are a good man, Kevin. I am staying at Katie and Frank's. Seems we good folks need to stick together. You need us, you call us. I'll leave the radio. I don't suppose you have a way to recharge it?"

"I've an old generator out back; it's keeping the fridge cold. I can rig something up."

"Excellent. Will you let us know if Reverend is on the move?"

Kevin looked pensive, then smiled. "Sure, of course I might be right ahead of him; I'd like to show him a thing or two, myself."

"I am sure you would be welcome."

"Well, we've lots of time. How 'bout you telling me about yourself, eh?" Kevin turned a kitchen chair around, sat spread-legged and leaned on the back.

"I don't like to talk about my past, Mr. Kevin, but seeing as you saved my life, I owe you that much." Eli finished his sandwich and relaxed. "I was born in 1966 in the country of Eritrea in North Africa. I had a normal childhood in my village. There were rumors of conflicts and stories of battles and occasional raiders of cattle, but otherwise it was boring. I dreamed of leaving the village and seeing over the horizon. I look back and curse the child that wished that."

Eli looked sad as he took a drink of sweet tea.

"I was fourteen when the Eritrea Army conscripted every able-bodied 'man' in our village. 'To fight for Eritrea's freedom from Ethiopia,' they said, and told tales of great atrocities, of men with machetes killing other men, and women and children; of whole villages burnt, no one alive, cattle and other livestock left to rot in the sun."

Eli took another drink.

"Many of us young men and teenagers, excited and enraged by these stories, went willingly. I guess they, too, wanted to know what was over the horizon. We marched for several days with little food and water, and we were glad when we reached the training camp. We were grouped by age and moved into tent cities. We trained with sticks and then given AK-47 or old Mosin-Nagant rifles. Some got shotguns, and everyone uniforms, and packs with basic kit including machetes. I grew to hate machetes."

Kevin refilled Eli's tea.

"In a few weeks we moved to the front, and as guerilla fighters we raided across the border, and even in our own country with villages that were friendly to Ethiopia." Eli's face darkened. "One day when I was twenty-three, I found myself standing over a mother protecting her baby, my machete upraised to end her life, and I realized I had become the monster from the stories the recruiters had told in my village when I was a child. I looked to left and to right and when it was safe, I sent her and her baby to safety. Shortly after, I went AWOL—north into the Sudan. It took weeks, but I made Port

Sudan and boarded a container ship. It was easy to get a passport. I worked container ships until I could look at mothers with children and not see the frighten eyes—a few years. I learned to read and write in ship libraries. I thank you for this tea."

He paused to drink.

"On board ships you do as you are told, sleep when told, and eat when told. I saw that the only place I would be more than a slave would be America. I transferred to any ship coming to America, and eventually I jumped in California and worked my way to here. In California I convinced them to give me political asylum and I became a citizen. I went to work at UPS and you know the rest."

Eli rocked in his chair. Kevin was quiet.

Eli could tell he was weighing words.

"What a story, Eli. Wow, I never would've thought. I am proud to know you. It took guts to walk away from that bunch of killers."

"I vowed to be a man of peace. Circumstances have made me break my vow."

"Many of us have had to re-evaluate where we stand. I'm sorry you have had to go back on your vow."

"I am glad I have honorable people to help, like Katie and Frank."

"I see them now and then, or did; they seem to be good folk."

Kevin took Eli's plate and glass. "Nap. I'll wake you at dark."

"Thank you Mr. Kevin. You do me honor."

As Eli settled on Kevin's couch, he sensed that for the first time in years he might peacefully sleep.

Rest Stop, Interstate 85, North Carolina, 15:30 Zulu

The pistol's sharp crack excited Clara almost as much as having Bill's arms around her, showing how to hold and shoot the 9mm. "This is fun," she shouted, because of the pistol's numbingly loud reports.

"Time for you to shoot solo. Let me set up some more targets." Willie unwrapped his arms; he felt oddly incomplete once they were apart.

He grabbed the bag of scavenged soda cans, walked to the backstop hillside, arrayed a dozen targets and turned to face Clara. Color drained from his face — she was aiming directly for his head.

Laughing, she dropped her weapon hand. "Bang! I got you!"

"Never, never point that thing at me again!" Willie yelled.

Clara, wide-eyed, looked confused. "It's not loaded."

"Really?" He grabbed the pistol, turned, aimed at a Pepsi can and pulled the trigger . . . the can leapt into the air as a 9mm slug rent the soil beneath it.

"Oh god, I am so sorry!" Clara's hand flew to her mouth. "I counted rounds. I thought we shot them all."

"Did you count the one in the chamber as well as those in the magazine?"

She looked at the ground. "No, I didn't."

"Always treat a gun as if it's loaded, especially around me!" Willie quivered with post-adrenaline shock. "Reload. Let's see you hit shit without help." He sat at the picnic table, put his palms on it to hide the trembles and watched as Clara reloaded the magazine, shoved it in the grip and racked the slide. As she lined up the first target, Willie heard Nick behind him.

"Pissed you off a bit, did she?" He smiled as he sat beside Willie.

"She just pointed a gun at me, without thinking."

"Are you sure?" Nick asked slyly, watching as Clara shot cans, hitting a surprising number on first try.

"Yes, damn sure. You should've seen her reaction when she realized it was still loaded."

"Or maybe when she realized she missed her chance."

Willie looked directly at Nick, whose eyes flashed with anger.

"Don't go there," Willie said coldly.

Nick smiled, said, "I'll see you back at the Jeep," and walked away as Clara exhausted the sixteen-round magazine.

"Good shooting, Babe!"

Willie walked to Clara's side as she dropped the magazine into her hand. Willie took it, and smiled when she handed him the pistol with the slide still locked open. "You are learning!"

"Why didn't you tell me the slide locks back when it's empty?" she admonished playfully. "I'd've known it wasn't empty."

"You should've remembered," he said lightly, anger forgotten. "Both the chamber indicator and cocking indicator would tell you."

"I love it when you say cock."

She kissed him and slid her tongue in his mouth. Letting the pistol drop, he wrapped his arms around her and they sank to the warm grass.

"What about Nick," she asked as he unbuttoned her blouse, freeing her breasts. She wore no bra. She nuzzled his neck; his dick started to harden.

"He's back at the Jeep. I think I pissed him off," Willie said breathlessly as she nipped at his neck.

"Poor Nick."

She reached for his zipper.

Charlotte, North Carolina, 18:45 Zulu

Harley rides are exhilarating. The deep throb of the engine and the bass notes from the exhaust, as well as the wind of other passing motorcycles, reminded Frank of his youth, when he'd ridden for a few short months. Of course his was a Yamaha 650, a "rice burner," as the Harley crowd referred to them in polite moments. Frank had loved the freedom of a bike, until the morning he wrecked it on the way to work. Waking in an emergency room with no memory of any wreck was not a good start to your day. His family was young then, and he'd promised not to ride until the kids had grown.

As they neared the airport the air thickened with acrid fuel smoke. They stopped and donned goggles and N95 particulate masks that Ira provided from his saddlebags. The last few blocks to Jane's apartment were worst— burnt shells of buildings, wrecked cars and occasional charred bodies reminded Frank of a war zone and didn't bode well for Jane's place.

JoJo followed Ira into a relatively intact apartment complex, where they parked in front of a partly destroyed building. The bike hardly stopped when Jane jumped off and ran into the smoking structure.

"Damn. Stay here, I'll go after her," Frank said, pulling off the helmet but keeping the goggles and mask. He rushed into the smoke-filled building and saw Jane disappear into an apartment in the most damaged section. Concerned she'd hurt herself, he followed. She was frantically searching the wreckage.

"Oh, Frank, it's all gone," she lamented.

"I am so sorry, Jane," was all he could say. He watched her search; for what he wasn't sure. She cleared fallen wallboard from a bookcase; he moved it away. Underneath, she grabbed a photo album and a small lockbox.

"Let's search the bedroom," she said, clutching her recovered treasures.

Once a cheerful light blue, the bedroom walls were now waterlogged and soot-stained. A jagged hole over the bed went up to daylight, or rather to a smoke-filled sky. A chunk of airplane had crushed her bed.

"Good thing you weren't home," Frank said lamely.

She looked at him with pain in her eyes.

"My cat—Mother was supposed to bring him back so he'd be here when I got home. His name is Rex." She looked around forlornly.

"Where did you feed him?" Frank asked, wracking his brain for feline instincts. He was a dog person, whom cats usually ignored.

"In the kitchen," she said, and rushed out. Frank again followed.

The kitchen was basically intact. A metal cat bowl sat near the trashcan. Frank asked, "Dry or wet food?"

"Dry mostly. In the pantry." She pointed beside the refrigerator to a small door, which Frank opened and peered into. As his eyes adjusted, he saw on the lower shelf a sack of cat food and handed it to Jane.

"Try filling his bowl. Most dogs would come running, soon's they hear food hit bowl. If Rex hasn't eaten for a day or two, he'll show up."

"If my mother dropped him off before it all happened."

She opened the sack and started pouring. The first pellets of reconstituted chicken protein clattering into the bowl brought forth a pitiable meeow-w and the scritch of small claws as Rex bounded into the kitchen from a hiding place.

Frank hadn't seen a more desolate cat. Rex was wet and sooty with singed tail hair. With a cry of relief Jane tried to hug the bedraggled cat, but Rex had his priorities and dashed for the bowl of chow. After a few bites he gave another plaintiff me-eow, as if asking for water. For Frank, it was almost comical.

Shuffling off his backpack, Frank handed a bottle to Jane, who twisted the cap and filled a second bowl. With an intensity that made Frank smile, Rex lapped up half the water before turning back to feed.

Because smoke was minimal inside the apartment, Jane removed her goggles. She was smiling and crying at once, watching Rex eat.

"Do you have a cat carrier?"

"In the storage shed out back."

Leaving Jane and Rex to get reacquainted, Frank searched for the cat carrier. Before he opened the sliding-glass doors to the tiny back yard—smaller than the bedroom—he replaced his goggles and mask. The door wouldn't budge. Glancing down, he saw a sawed-off section of anti-burglar broomstick. He set it aside and the door slid smoothly open. Frank stepped out and shut the door to lessen the entry of toxic smoke.

Someone had forced the storage door and scavenged its interior. Lamps had been smashed; clothes littered the floor. Combing the debris, Frank found the corner of a soft-sided cat carrier, the kind for airplane travel.

Returning, Frank pulled off his mask and goggles. Jane had found a towel and dried and cleaned Rex. Other than being skinny from a few days of living off mice and birds, Frank could tell he was well cared for and a handsome animal. For a cat, that is.

"Room in your backpack for the food?" Jane asked as she rubbed Rex dry.

"Sure." He took the bag, folded the top, then stored it in the backpack. "Here's the cat carrier. Someone broke into the storage room."

Jane looked up from the purring cat; she was smiling.

"Garage-sale and charity crap. Only thing I need is that cat carrier."

"Anything else?"

"Hold Rex. I'll check the bedroom; my grandmother gave me some jewelry and other odds and ends."

Rex put up with Frank as long as Frank scratched his chin.

Jane soon returned carrying a small, cloth jewelry case.

"The plane wreck was a blessing; they didn't search the bedroom closet."

"Great," Frank said, giving Rex a last scratch and returning the animal to Jane, who, with only minor protest from Rex, stuffed him into the carrier. With a last tearful glance at the apartment, Jane said, "Let's get out of here."

Outside by the bikes, Ira and JoJo watched for looters and thieves.

"All clear?" Frank asked.

"Still as a tomb," Ira answered. "You guys ready to head back?"

"Could we go by Mom's place? It isn't far," Jane pleaded, hugging the carrier, drawing comfort from the cat purring inside.

"Frank's departure is soon," Ira said, looking at his old windup watch, his voice oddly muffled by the mask.

"It's a couple miles." Jane pointed away from the destruction.

"OK, but hurry." Ira swung his leg over the hog and kicked it into life. JoJo did the same. With a little gentle squeezing — and more protest from Rex — they nestled the carrier into a saddlebag with Jane's other meager belongings.

Tires squealing, the big bikes fled Jane's wrecked apartment.

North of Lake Weiss, Alabama, 20:15 Zulu

Removing her safety glasses, Marlene wiped a hand across her sweaty brow; the final land mine was assembled. Looking like thirty-two toy tops — each with two octopus-like plastic tubes — the mines littered the table and surroundings.

"Wheeew. I'm glad that's over." She put down the drill. "Now what?"

"Well, Eli's overdue for check-in." Katie was worried.

"Want me to take a four-wheeler and go looking?" David asked.

"Not yet. Give him a bit more time. Let's get out the topos and aerials and decide where to place these little bad boys. Be right back." She put her glasses on the table, went into the trailer and came back out a few minutes later with a file folder. "Clear off the table and have a look."

Katie extracted several plastic-coated topo-maps and aerial photographs showing the property. One photo was from summer, the other dead of winter, leaves off the trees. The winter photo showed main ATV trails in black marker, along with Frank's permanent hunting stands.

"We need to cover the trail entrance points, and put a couple on the main gate. We'll mark each one on this map so we don't nuke ourselves." She smiled devilishly. "Next time, they won't be loaded with cold water."

"Looks like a good plan, but what about Eli? If he comes back after we do the placement, he could get nuked, and if people are chasing him . . ."

"He could get captured before we can help him," finished Marlene.

"That's why I wish he'd check in."

Just then the GRS radio chirped on Katie's belt. With a hopeful look at David and Marlene, she answered. "This is Base, over."

"Base, this is Black Rover. Sorry about the delay, over."

"As long as you're safe, Black Rover. Over."

"I am fine, thanks to Good Neighbor. Returning on foot to base, over."

"Roger that, Black Rover. We are putting out welcomes for visitors, over."

"Welcomes, eh? I was going to leave the radio with Good Neighbor, but I guess I had better carry it, over."

"Roger that. Can you return by the northwest corner? It is

closest, over."

There was a pause. Katie hoped Eli would decode her simple attempt to obscure. She actually wanted him to return by the southeast because it was closest to his location, which he should realize.

"Roger that, Base, I wouldn't want to be contrary, over."

"He got it!" Katie said to her companions.

"Roger that, Black Rover. Time estimate? Over."

"Negative, I will be walking. Over."

"Roger that, Black Rover, we will leave the light on. Over."

"Black Rover, out."

The radio went silent.

"OK," Katie said, pointing in the aerial photo of the southeast corner where a trail snaked toward the pond. "We cover all the trails but this one."

"I thought you told him the northwest corner?" Marlene was confused.

"I did. But I also said 'the corner nearest his location,' and that is what I said last." Katie smiled. "Being Muslim, he would understand that what I said last takes precedence."

Marlene still looked confused.

"The Koran is written such that contradiction in later verses supersedes previous verses," Katie explained.

"Kaitie, you are such a clever girl."

"Enough of this. We have mines to charge and place."

With that she fetched from the trailer the large cookpot and a vacuum-sealed pouch of concentrated capsaicin powder. She filled the pot from the well, placed it on the Coleman stove, pumped up the tank pressure and turned on the burner. As the water heated, she passed out N95 particulate masks to Frank and Marlene, as well as swimming goggles.

"What are these for?" Marlene asked, putting on the mask.

"If I drop this bag of finely ground capsaicin, it'll act like pepper spray."

"Brilliant!" Marlene said, hurriedly pulling on the goggles.

"You don't have to worry until the water heats up a bit."

They gathered mines while Katie fetched a funnel and a

cheesecloth filter. When the pot was steaming, she carefully opened the bag of capsaicin and nursed the reddish powder into the hot water. Gently, she set the empty bag aside and stirred the mixture to eliminate lumps. At last, satisfied the capsaicin was fully dissolved, she turned off the burner and let the mixture cool.

"Alcohol would be better, with a little oil, but I was afraid the alcohol would evaporate too quickly."

"We could block the tube ends to prevent evaporation," David offered.

"Good idea, any other suggestions? I am plumb out of tiny corks."

"How about cutting small sections off those wood dowels in storage?"

"That might work. Go get a few of them David," Katie said.

David returned shortly, holding several dowels that looked to be the correct diameter. Using pruning shears, he cut a couple of half-inch sections and handed them to Katie, who took one of the mines and placed the plugs into the tube ends. The plugs stayed put. Removing one plug, she blew into the opened tube; the other plug popped out.

"Excellent. Start cutting and Marlene and I will start filling."

The women used a ladle and funnel, with a thrice-folded section of cheesecloth to filter any remnant powder. Two ladlefuls of pink liquid filled each mine. As they finished each, they put wooden plugs in the spray lines, sealing in the homemade pepper spray. Soon, all were filled.

"Marlene, we need to wash our hands thoroughly."

Looking over at Marlene, Katie carefully removed her mask.

"What? Why?" Marlene was puzzled but followed suit.

"A couple years ago, I was cooking with red pepper and I didn't wash my hands before I used the restroom, and let's just say that the rest of the evening wasn't exactly pleasant. And this stuff is several times stronger than red pepper."

Katie smiled rascally.

"I see." Marlene looked at her hands as though they belonged to a pariah. "Where's the soap!"

"David, how about going to the shed. There are some solar driveway lights there, with little plastic tabs on their bases. Pull the tabs, will you please? then set them along the back fence while Marlene and I wash up."

"Not a problem."

David removed his safety gear. He'd enjoy a walk in the woods.

After completely washing hands and faces, the women returned to join David at the waiting mines. "David," Katie said with a smile, "Get the ATV with the attached trailer. We have some mines to lay."

DEEP WOODS NORTH OF LAKE WEISS, ALABAMA, 23:00 ZULU

It was only thirty minutes since Eli had followed the old, partly blocked tunnel leading from Kevin's root cellar into the woods. Kevin had scouted his property line, seen no one watching the house, and gave Eli the all clear. With a handshake, Eli had vanished into the Underground Railroad.

Through tall oak trees, the sun was nearing the horizon. Holding up his hand Eli counted fingers between horizon and the blinding orb—three barely fit. "Forty-five minutes," he said aloud, figuring he could make the edge of the Lowman property in about three hours if he didn't run into trouble.

Trying to stay in woods and off roads was proving difficult. Brambles, blackberry bushes and vine tangles— including poison ivy, oak and sumac—made going slow. With no flashlight, the hollows were dark enough Eli could misstep and break a bone, or at the least be cut or bruised.

Eli was glad it wasn't weeks into the emergency. He

remembered running into packs of feral dogs with his platoon—if a group of poorly trained kids toting machetes and old Russian rifles could be called a platoon. A smaller boy had fallen behind and been badly mauled before the others had killed or driven off the vicious erstwhile pets. The boy nearly lost his face in the attack; luckily the dogs had missed vital arteries. But infection claimed him before he could get medical treatment.

Eli had heard of feral hogs in south Alabama and knew that for a man alone they could be as dangerous as dogs. Supposedly the feral hog plague didn't yet reach this far into north Alabama. He prayed to Allah that it was so. According to the Koran, to be killed by such an animal would defile him, preventing entrance into heaven. He listened diligently for any noise, and used his best scout-craft not to make any noise. Twice as the light faded he scared up a deer that then bounded away. He was terrified at first, but then became enamored of the graceful creatures, wishing he could move as fast through tight cover.

Eli knew he needed to find the road before light gave out. Without a flashlight he would soon be hopelessly lost. But as twilight faded into night, he stumbled onto an old logging road. Thanking Allah for his good fortune, he fell to his knees in the red clay, removed his shoes, faced east and prayed.

Finishing his worship, Eli followed the nearly overgrown road as it wound fortuitously in his general direction. Several times he nearly tripped on vines snaking the path, or had to muscle through blackberry tangles, but even with these obstacles, traveling the old road was many times faster than through second-growth forest. When he heard water flowing he diverted to a stream. Other streams he'd crossed had been mud-stained and in the peak of summer, but this was cold and clear, which told Eli it was spring-fed. He filled his cupped hands and drank, once again thanking God for favor.

Near midnight he saw lights through the woods in front of him. He approached and as he neared he recognized solar lights, like those he'd seen beside driveways when he made deliveries, placed alongside an old barbwire fence paralleling the road. He hoped he was reading this signal correctly. If not, he was about to surprise strangers—something not smart to do these days.

Crossing the fence, he was even more circumspect, penetrating the enclosure as carefully as anything he'd scouted in Eritrea. As he rounded a storage shed, a female voice barked.

"About time Eli, we were getting worried."

Katie stood at her lawn chair and tilted up a night-vision monocle from in front of her face; a special head-brace designed for that purpose supported it.

"I've been watching you for the last ten minutes. Very instructive."

Eli smiled widely.

"It is good to be home, Miss Katiee, you are full of surprises!"

CHARLOTTE, NORTH CAROLINA, 19:45 ZULU

At Jane's mother's house they found a note saying she'd gone to the arena in accordance with emergency radio instructions. What transportation she'd used wasn't clear, but several neighbors who were near her age had old cars, which they delighted in driving to classic car meets. Jane assumed her mother traveled with a neighbor. The ride back was enjoyable and uneventful.

"Thanks for the ride, JoJo. I have to find George and get to the convoy. Jane," Frank asked with obvious concern, "will you be OK, here?"

"I'll check with the admin tent and see if my mother is checked in." Jane cobbled a brave smile. "I'll be fine."

"Don't worry. Me and the boys will watch out for her," Ira said, putting his arm around Jane. She smiled at him at little more convincingly than she'd smiled at Frank, who could tell something was happening between Ira and Jane. Staring into each other's eyes, they looked like teenagers.

"Looks like you'll be well taken care of, Jane. Goodbye; I have to run."

Jane gave Frank a big hug and a kiss on the cheek. "Thanks for getting me home, Frank! I'd still be stuck in some camp in New York if it weren't for you." She hugged him again before letting go.

"Be careful, and I hope you find your mom."

"I will. I think I saw her neighbor's '56 Chevy over in the lot as we pulled in. I'm sure she's fine." Jane stood beside Ira, who again put his arm around her.

"Go on Frank, take care of yourself, and find your wife," Ira said.

Frank shook the big biker's hand and headed for the fuel-convoy muster station, arriving as a young lieutenant dressed in desert digital camouflage BDUs sharply called his name.

"Frank Lowman!"

"Here!" Frank answered, stepping beside George.

"Just in time," George muttered, handing Frank his shotgun.

"Looks like," Frank answered, taking the weapon and checking the chamber for a shell. There was; he flipped the safety and held the gun with the butt under his arm and the muzzle pointed safely at the ground.

The lieutenant went through a list of about a dozen names; all were present. He looked up from the clipboard at the last Here and said, "I am Lieutenant Jackson. You are all volunteers, helping guard a fuel convoy from here to the Atlanta airport and back. How many have weapons?"

Both George and Frank raised their hands, as did most of the others. To those who didn't have a weapon, Lt. Jackson issued Beretta M9 pistols with web belt and standard military holster, two-place magazine pouch, three magazines and a brown box of military 9mm ammunition. He had each demonstrate proper chamber checks, and loading and unloading, then covered malfunction clearance and other procedures. Since the men—and one woman—all had prior military experience, they easily performed the drills. Once Lt. Jackson finished, he turned to those that had brought their own weapons.

Each person had to demonstrate the same basic set of safe checks and malfunction clearance drills that Lt. Jackson had shown the others. Frank was grateful he had been trained in both military and civilian classes, demonstrating the required skills with his XD. He said a prayer of thanks for his routine of thirty minutes dry practice daily. The lieutenant handed him a box of military 9mm ball ammo and a box of 12-gauge double-ought buckshot for the Saiga, and issued George an M9 9mm pistol to go with his shotgun, plus boxes of shotgun and pistol ammunition.

"Listen up! Those with both shotgun and pistol will ride shotgun seat in the fuel trucks. The rest will ride shotgun seat in the convoy vehicles." He looked at the semi-circle of men and one woman surrounding him. "You may only shoot if we are shot at, and then, if possible, only on command. You are all hereby considered to be in the militia of the State of North Carolina until the conclusion of this assignment. Any questions?"

"Lieutenant Jackson!" Frank called out.

"Yes, Mister Lowman?"

"George, here, and I, wish to remain in Atlanta, will that be OK?"

"Remain in Atlanta? We hoped you'd do a round trip."

The lieutenant paused and looked thoughtful. "Tell you what, Mr. Lowman, it'll depend on what we find on the way. Scout expeditions report the I-85 direct route has numerous blockages due to stalled cars and wrecks, but the southern route through Columbia and Augusta is clear, no problems. If we reach the airport and get the trucks filled, we'll determine at that point if you can be released from further duty. Will that do?" He looked at Frank and George.

"Yes, sir, I guess it'll have to." Frank looked with worry at

George.

Once the weapons were sorted out and skill levels assessed, the vehicle assignments went quickly. The convoy was soon heading down I-77 toward Atlanta. A single, solid-rubber-tired APV with a driver and two armed National Guardsmen led, followed by a Humvee and the four fuel trucks. Frank was in the first truck, and George the last. Another Humvee completed the convoy, again with a driver and two well-armed National Guard personnel.

The first part of the trip was boring until after the Columbia bypass and connection to I-20. Heading into Augusta, they took sniper fire near the Georgia state line. The 7.62mm medium machine gun on the APV made short work of the sniper, and a quick recon by the National Guard showed no additional hostiles.

"That was exciting," Frank said, flipping the shotgun safety back on.

"At least we aren't dealing with IEDs," the youngish driver said as he restarted the fuel truck. "In Iraq, we'd send out the disposal units and the sand bunnies would hop in right behind and replant. Lost a buddy to one of those damn things."

"Sorry to hear that. You'd think these yahoos'd wait until we were on the way back. We'd have fuel, then."

"How do they know? You can't tell if these things are loaded or not."

"Good point." Frank thought for a moment. "How many tours you do?"

"Just the one before we pulled out."

"Happy to be home?"

"I wish we could've prevented the subsequent collapse of the democratic government. They're back to worse than when we went over."

"True, but that happens just about anytime you let the politicians run a war. Look at Vietnam."

"Right. I don't really remember 'Nam, it was all over before I was born, but my Dad has told me a lot."

Feeling old, Frank sat back in the seat and watched the

road. Unless someone set up roadblocks, they probably wouldn't realize they were being attacked until a vehicle took a hit. As they topped a blind hill, the driver slammed on brakes and narrowly avoided rear-ending the front Humvee. Frank could see some vehicles ahead, blocking the road — an apparent collision. The writhing body of a young girl lay between wrecked vehicles.

Something looked fishy to Frank. How did the girl wind up on the ground between the cars? All vehicular glass was intact, as far as he could see, and other than the girl, he could make out no injured. "Looks like a trap!" Frank said. Automatic weapons fire suddenly raked the APV crew, who'd gotten out to check on the wreck.

"Damn it!" The drive swore as he shifted the fuel truck into reverse, but he was trapped in front by the Humvee and behind by the rest of the convoy.

Frank lowered the fuel truck window and raised the Saiga to his shoulder, thumbing off the safety. He scanned the woods on the passenger side. The automatic fire slackened as the APV crew dropped to the ground, wounded or dying. Apparently the attackers were targeting only the APV and the Humvees, sparing the fuel trucks. It was clear what they were after. From the corner of his eye he caught sight of the supposedly injured woman bounding into the woods like a deer.

"You in the fuel trucks, throw out your weapons!" snarled a magnified voice from the woods.

"Well, what now?" Frank asked nervously, eyeing the woods for a target.

The dash radio crackled to life. "This is Bravo-2, Bravo-1 is down, repeat, Bravo-1 is down."

"Lieutenant Jackson has been hit, that's Staff Sergeant Rogers talking." The driver translated the message for Frank.

"The APV crew and their weapons have been neutralized," the radio reported. "We are going to surrender."

"Like hell," Frank said, setting aside the shotgun. "Cover me!"

Frank pulled the Colt from his holster and, flinging the

door open, jumped from the cab, tucking into a roll as he landed. He bounded to his feet and sprinted toward the APV. It took a moment for the attackers to realize what he was doing, but then automatic fire resumed, tracking the running Frank. Guardsmen and civilians fired toward the source of the automatic fire.

Frank reached the open door of the APV and tumbled inside, closing the light-armored door behind him; he heard thuds of automatic rounds slamming the door immediately after he'd shut it. He was thankful they appeared to be from a 9mm such as an Uzi rather than steel-cored rounds such as surplus 7.62x39mm AK-47s might shoot. Still, he was desperate, and reached for the access hatch to the light machine gun. Hoping it was an easy weapon to use, he pulled up to the gun access area and studied the weapon as 9mm rounds pinged off the skin of the vehicle and the shield for the gun.

Frank could see the 7.62 ammo belt was already fed into the breach of the mounted M240 machine gun. Grabbing the pistol grip and placing his shoulder to the butt, he racked back the charging handle and pointed the weapon toward the majority of fire. When he saw muzzle flashes from the handheld weapon, he aimed and pulled the trigger. The resulting spray of bullets silenced the automatic fire. Frank moved the weapon back and forth like a garden hose spraying lead. The sound of the M240 was deafening and Frank wished whoever was screaming would shut up until he realized it was he. Seeing no more enemy fire from the passenger side, he took his finger off the trigger and pivoted to the driver's side. It appeared the activation of the M240 to deadly effect on the right-hand attackers had induced a case of reduced valor in the left-hand attackers, because it was quiet as a churchyard following the ravening storm of destruction caused by the machine gun. Frank started as someone touched his leg.

He turned to see a Guardsman, clutching his leg where a round had grazed him. A last look revealed Guardsmen from the Humvees fanning into the woods on both sides, but Frank couldn't hear a thing; machine gun reports had temporarily deafened him. He climbed down from the gun. The Guardsman mouthed words at Frank, but he couldn't hear over the ringing in his ears. Finally the Guardsman wrote on a clipboard and handed it to Frank.

Good shooting, sir, I'll take it from here.

The Guardsman saluted and smiled; Frank gestured for the pen. He wrote: *How bad is your leg?* and returned the clipboard.

Just a graze, was the answer.

Frank stood aside and the Guardsman took over the gun position.

The two patrols returned after half an hour. By then, Frank had regained some hearing in his left ear, but the right was still church bells at noon.

"Looks like they hi-tailed it when the machine gun kicked in," Sergeant Rogers told the group. "Good job, Corporal Havers."

The soldier who had relieved Frank on the weapon looked uncomfortable. "Sir, it wasn't me on the weapon, sir. It was him." Havers pointed at Frank.

"You're Lowman, right?" asked Sgt. Rogers.

Frank nodded. "Yes, Sir," he said, a little too loud.

The sergeant smiled.

"Next time you need to shoot an M240, use ear protectors."

MARIETTA, GEORGIA, 21:00 ZULU

Earl slung the AR-15 across his chest using the three-point sling that Fred had showed him. He slid a paddle holster onto his belt on the right side and inserted a cocked and locked .45 Colt Commander. With the worn TT-33 Tokarev automatic pistol and its leather shoulder holster as backup, he felt ready to help Fred. He placed an NRA ball cap on his head and a pair of yellow-tinted shooting glasses over his eyes.

On the way out the door, Earl caught a glimpse of himself in a hallway mirror. "Shit, a bleeding English Rambo," he said aloud. Inside, he thought he looked ridiculous and was probably going to get himself killed.

A few neighbors on their decks or front porches started to wave as he went by, but thought better of it when they got a good look at his armaments. Fred had traveled only about a mile before the trouble. Earl was thankful for the time he'd spent at the gym as he broke into a jog in the Georgia heat.

As Earl neared the CVS, where Fred had radioed about twenty minutes ago, he saw smoke rising over the tops of houses lining the cross streets ahead. Leaving the road, Earl maneuvered surreptitiously through back yards until he could view the smoke source.

What Earl saw as he peeked around the corner of a French provincial brick house wasn't encouraging. Fred's truck appeared to be the smoke source. Fire licked from under the vehicle's hood, and black, oily smoke billowed. Earl ducked as a loud pop sent the hood cartwheeling into the sky. It crunched to earth a few yards away from Earl, and now the cab and engine compartment were aflame. Earl couldn't see well enough through the smoke to learn if Fred was still inside the burning vehicle. The passenger-side door appeared to be open, so maybe he'd bailed out.

Down the block, Earl could see the roadblock Fred had radioed about. It appeared to be inactive; Earl saw no one around the vehicles partially blocking the street. A dirt bike lay at the curb in front of Fred's Blazer, and a body wearing a Nixon mask, now askew, lay near it. Earl saw a hand and arm poke from behind the rear of the burning vehicle; the fire hadn't reached there, yet.

Making a split-second decision, Earl ran from cover and, with the AR-15 pointed toward whomever it was, rushed the vehicle.

"Took you long enough," Fred said hoarsely. "I'm hit in the shoulder and the leg. Get me away from here before we both fry."

Earl slung the rifle across his back and helped Fred to his feet. They made it back the shelter of the French provincial when the truck's fuel tanks blew.

"Where are the bad guys," Earl asked, easing Fred to the hot ground.

"I shot the guy on the motorcycle, but he got a couple slugs into the engine; must've hit a fuel line because it caught fire. As I bailed out, two of the dead guy's buddies attacked. I shot one dead, I'm sure, and wounded the other. The wounded lit out, maybe to find more thugs. We need to scram."

Earl examined Fred's wounds. The shoulder was a through-and-through and while it was bleeding a bit, it didn't appear to Earl to be fatal, at least with his limited medical knowledge. The leg wound was outer left thigh, no exit wound so the slug was a problem, and the entry was seeping blood. Removing the AR- and shoulder rig, Earl cobbled a makeshift sling to immobilize the arm. He tore long strips from their shirts for a makeshift shoulder compress.

Earl felt a little silly with the shoulder holster and AR-slung across his naked chest, especially since any claim to a sculpted body had fled with his twenties. He helped Fred to his feet and they hobbled toward Fred's house. Two blocks distant, they heard shooting and the whine of motorcycles as the roadblock gang returned and vented their anger on the remains of Fred's Blazer.

Earl and Fred stuck to cover on their slow retreat, not making the relative safety of Fred's kitchen until nearly 6:00 p.m., local time. Earl swept the dirty china off the table and helped Fred on to it. Fred's shoulder had begun to bleed.

"Have you got a first aid kit?"

"In the storage room; looks like a backpack."

Earl found the large, surprisingly heavy kit and dashed back upstairs.

"What the bloody hell is in this thing?"

"A full medical kit. In the front compartment should be disinfectant and QuikClot," Fred said through clenched teeth. He looked pale and sweaty.

Earl found EMT shears, snipped cloth away from Fred's wounds, doused each with disinfectant, and cleaned. He read instructions and dumped QuikClot into the tears. When the bleeding stopped, Earl dressed the wounds, roused his semi-conscious patient and feed him two wide-spectrum antibiotics. After a drink of water, Fred passed out again.

Earl carried Fred into the master bedroom, used the shears to remove his outer clothing, and covered him with a clean sheet. Temperature was mid-eighties, so Earl not only spared the blankets, he opened the windows to circulate any breeze the humid Georgia summer cared to offer his friend. Using the waterBOB in Fred's tub, he soaked a washcloth and mopped Fred's forehead.

"What the hell do I do now?" Earl asked the darkened interior.

Fort Payne, Alabama, 23:00 Zulu

Reverend Sanders was in a foul mood; that heathen bastard had escaped again. He was sure the spy had been the deliveryman Eli, and vowed that when he caught up with him, he'd give that nigger a strong dose of God's wrath.

"Alright, Brothers! We missed the heathen today, but we know where he'll be tomorrow—that den of unbelief they call the Lowman property. Why, anybody who'd take in a Moslem would truck with the Devil!"

A muted chorus of "Amen" echoed from the men in the stuffy church, even as most wished they were home with their families. In fact, the desertion rate from Reverend Sander's Christian soldiers had been high. Reverend had sworn retribution against the deserters, but few were buying into it.

"Tomorrow, we will burrow into that den and retrieve the heathen, who shall face the wrath of God for killing my son!

And God's wrath will rain down a deluge on anyone that stands in our way!"

Spittle flew from the mouth of the almost apoplectic Reverend.

"Tomorrow we meet here for a planning session. Bring your weapons for blessing and with God's will we will rid ourselves of this plague."

It wasn't lost on most of the churchmen that one scared black man, Moslem or not, and three white people could scarcely be considered a plague, especially when they minded their own business. However, there were many who enjoyed mayhem and looked for any reason to go shooting. Some were as fanatical as Reverend; a handful were feral-hog crazy.

Reverend continued until he ran down, or ran out, of spit. Eventually he called for a closing prayer. Little did he realize that for a long time to come this would be his last appearance in the pulpit.

Interstate 20 near the border of Georgia and South Carolina, 22:00 Zulu

"Attention! As you all are aware, Lieutenant Jackson and two other men have been wounded. Luckily no one is dead; we'll be returning wounded to Charlotte in one of the Humvees. You should be ashamed! I ought to write up all of you in the lead vehicles. You let your guard down because a woman was involved, and we nearly all got killed. Rescue helicopters in Charlotte are depending on us to secure the avgas. If it hadn't been for Mr. Lowman risking life to re-man the M240," Sergeant Rogers said, pointing to Frank, "we would have lost the convoy."

He let his words sink in.

"All Guardsmen, form up on me. We will redistribute to

the vehicles and continue. We have radioed a sit-rep to HQ; they're send a replacement Humvee that will catch up to us on route."

"Sergeant!" Corporal Havers called out.

"Yes, Corporal?"

"Request permission to remain. My wound is minor, and bandaged."

Rogers glared. "Not going to leave your post again to rescue a damsel?"

The corporal looked embarrassed. "No, Sergeant. I've learnt my lesson."

"Man your post, Corporal." He returned the corporal's salute and turned to assign the remaining troops and volunteers.

"Mr. Lowman, a word, please," Sgt. Rogers called to Frank, who approached the larger-than-life Guardsman.

"Lowman," he admonished, "I've done several tours in the sandbox, and never have I seen such a boneheaded brave stunt as that. I'm glad you're with us, but from now on, I promise not to need my butt saved if you will let the soldiers do the dirty work." He stuck out his hand.

"Deal. Don't know why, but I just did it."

Frank took Roger's hand—his grip was firm but not crushing. The sergeant eyed him for several beats of the heart, then released his grip.

"Hate say it, but you and George cut loose in Atlanta after we get fuel."

"Thanks, Sergeant."

"You've earned it, Frank. Now excuse me; I've got to kick butt. See you in Atlanta." Rogers turned and yelled at the APV gunner to verify reload and check. Frank went to tell George the good news.

As the convoy neared Augusta, smoke and fire thickened and spread to woods and fields lining the rural section of highway, threatening to block the road. The convoy inched ahead, keeping a sharp eye for hijackers taking advantage of the smoke screen and the convoy's low speed. Finally, near

Social Circle, fires cleared and visibility returned.

"By the way, my name's Sam." Frank's driver held out his hand.

"Brave damn thing you did back there, Mr. Lowman. Thanks."

"Call me Frank, Sam. You'd have done the same."

"I'd like to think so, but I froze. You acted." Sam paused. "Under the seat should be some MREs if you're hungry."

Frank came up with a couple of pouches. "Any warmers?"

"Nope. We eat 'em cold. What we got?"

"Looks like an omelet and some spaghetti."

Sam was quiet for a moment. "I'll take the omelet, you take the spaghetti."

"You sure? You don't look too enthused."

Frank could tell Sam wanted the spaghetti.

"Omelet's easier to eat while I'm driving. Just open it and douse it with hot sauce from the condiment package—make that a lot of hot sauce."

Frank did as Sam asked, and watched as he choked down the cold concoction. "Eat, Frank, it won't get any warmer."

Sam ate crackers to rid his mouth of omelet taste, followed by a large drink from his canteen. Frank opened one corner of the spaghetti and squeezed a bit into his mouth, wondering if this was how astronauts felt. The spaghetti wasn't too bad, and if the omelet was as bad as Sam's expression indicated, Sam deserved a purple heart.

By dark they saw signs for I-285. Sergeant Rogers called a halt to determine the best route to the airport—straight on to I-85 or swing south around the Perimeter. After discussion, Rogers chose I-285 to avoid the heart of Atlanta and the high trouble potential inherent in a dense urban zone.

On the west horizon, burning structures lit the sky with flames, and smoke fed a blood-red sunset. Intermittent gunfire and distant explosions also marred the evening, but I-285's southeastern leg was nearly deserted. On overpasses, they sometimes saw vehicles and gangs, but the sight of Army trucks made them want to be elsewhere. Once, a bottle broke on the hood of Sam and Frank's fuel truck, but otherwise the trip was uneventful.

However, it wasn't until Sam took the airport exit that Frank released his death grip on the shotgun.

Fort Payne, Alabama, 23:30 Zulu

Bubba—Franklin Thomas Downey—was getting hot and irritated waiting for Reverend to shut up. He had joined Reverend's cadre for a chance to shoot and partake in mayhem. He made sure to chime in on the Amen's, but anyone who listened could tell his heart was far away.

Bubba had whistled through high school on football skills. No one in town would have dared to fail a star quarterback bringing in championship after championship. He had ruled the school; what came afterward hadn't been nearly the fun. His Auburn scholarship hadn't worked out; seemed they expected athletes to maintain a nonnegative GPA. How rude. He joined the Marines.

Bubba had done well in boot camp, and until his first assignment it appeared he and the Marines had been made for each other. How was he to know non-combatants from combatants when they all dressed the same? The court-martial had nailed him and his sergeant. His "Discharge at the Convenience of the Service" hadn't set well with most employers. Gone was his fit, lean body, and his teeth weren't far behind, aided on their deteriorating path by the slug of chew he kept between his gum and lip. Yep, he had to admit, life had peaked in his senior year of high school.

As Reverend droned, Bubba's mind wandered to Maxine, the Lowman bitch. He'd met Max a couple times when she came to town for groceries, and tried to be friendly but she'd rebuffed him. Or worse, ignored him; once in front of his friends. Well, not exactly friends, rather the other lay-abouts at the feed store, who'd found great humor in her putdown, the frigid witch. He bet she batted for the other side. Payback time was coming. He'd show her.

As Reverend finished his last prayer, Bubba chimed in an overloud "Amen!" and grinned as Reverend looked his way. Outside the stifling church, he went to his Kawasaki dirt bike— his only working vehicle—mounted the bike and kicked it alive. In a cloud of oily two-stroke smoke, he spun his rear tires and sprayed gravel at Reverend's other raiders. Oblivious to their angry shouts and raised fists, Bubba rode into the sunset.

Roswell, Georgia, 23:45 Zulu

Earl desperately rifled Fred's large medical backpack. Finally, in a small side pocket he found what he was looking for: a US Army Medical Field Manual. Most of the information dealt with food poisoning, dysentery, and allergic reactions to various plants, animals and foods, some with NBC—Nuclear, Biological and Chemical. He turned to the gunshot wounds section, which was brief, but stressed the removal of foreign material and the criticality of prophylactic treatment for infection.

Earl searched a packet and found antibiotic powders, a vial of morphine, and a couple vials of injection antibiotics, marked veterinary. He also found muscular-injection syringes and a sealed Field Surgical Pack. The manual said any wound closed with the various clotting products should remain untouched until proper medical personal could safely remove the clotting material, unless it was the new, "sponge" type. Earl knew one bullet was still in Fred and if it weren't removed it would probably cause serious if not fatal infection.

The manual listed morphine and antibiotic dosing

suggestions by body weight. According to a chart, the antibiotic was a Keflex generic; Earl did a quick estimate of Fred's weight and calculated a dose. He removed the thin metal seal on the vial and exposed a rubber seal. Taking care not to contaminate the needle, he removed the protective plastic tube, pulled out the plunger to a hair beyond the proper number of cc's, stuck the needle into the vial and injected air, producing an overpressure in the sealed vial.

"Fred?" Earl called lightly, shaking Fred's shoulder.

"Fred!" He called louder.

"Wha— What— Oh, shit—" Fred moaned in pain.

"Sorry to wake you, Fred, but I have to go in for that bullet or it might kill you. I'm giving you an injection of morphine to reduce the pain."

"Go ahead," Fred mumbled through tight lips. "Hurry!"

Fred winced as pain flared in his wounds.

Earl swabbed Fred's shoulder and, praying silently, he pulled the correct dose and gave the first shot he'd ever done. In only a few moments, Fred relaxed and smiled. "No wonder people get addicted."

"Let's hope it keeps working. Do you have any local anesthetic?"

"There should be lidocaine in there, somewhere."

Fred sat and immediately threw up.

"Aw shit," he said, wiping his face.

"Side effect of the morphine, I'm afraid." Earl handed Fred a wet wipe, helped clean, then helped Fred lay down. "Can you roll onto your side?"

"Will it make me throw up again?"

"It shouldn't if we take it slow," Earl said unconvincingly, helping Fred onto his non-wounded side. Earl studied the thigh wound; on the back below the butt cheek, Earl found a lump.

"Ow! What the hell are you doing?" Fred felt it through the morphine.

"Found the bullet. Looks like I don't need to probe for it. If I leave you a moment, you won't have any problem staying like you are?"

"Don't think so."

"OK, I am letting go." Earl made sure Fred wouldn't flop over, then searched the medic pack for lidocaine.

Earl folded a cotton sheet to several thicknesses and placed it to protect the bed behind Fred. He then opened a sterile bandage and laid it on the clean sheet. Repeating the steps he'd done with the morphine, he loaded a second syringe with lidocaine and laid it on the sterile dressing. Using Betadine, he sterilized his hands, donned a pair of nitrile gloves from the medical kit, and a second pair over the first. He swabbed Betadine over large area around the swelling where he hoped the bullet was located.

Earl opened the surgical pack, laid it next to the bandage with the syringe, injected Lidocaine in several places near the swelling, under and around where he estimated the bullet to be, and waited several minutes for the Lidocaine to bite. Next he took the scalpel and made an incision top-dead-center over the bullet. His first cut was too shallow; luckily it didn't bleed much. Tracing the cut, he felt the blade scrape along the bullet surface. He put the scalpel on the sterile dressing, opened the incision with two fingers of his left hand and grabbed the exposed bullet with the forceps in his right.

It was surprisingly difficult to pull the bullet free.

Trapped fluid squirted from behind the projectile, and Earl rushed to tear open another QuikClot package, but the flow rapidly faded to seepage. The manual said bullet wounds should drain for hours, if not days, to prevent infection. As the seepage slowed to a trickle, he opened a sterile pack labeled Drain, Surgical—foot-long lengths of sterile tubing and a plastic drain bag— and rinsed both the incision and the entrance wound with sterile water. He placed a tube-end into the incision, closed around it firmly with steri-strips, and attached the other end to the drain bag. With a 4x4-inch sterile dressing, he covered and taped the area. The lidocaine and morphine must have been effective; Fred's only sound was a wet snore. Earl taped the drain to Fred's hip and gently rolled him to his back. Fred muttered but stayed asleep.

After cleaning spilt blood and fluid, and sanitizing, Earl put all the used gear—except the surgical pack—in the trash, stripped off the gloves and washed with anti-bacterial soap.

Nausea hit him with a power not unlike that with which he imagined Fred had been smacked by the bullets. He barely made the waste can.

Afterward, Earl Tolliday sat in the kitchen, hands shaking uncontrollably, trying his damndest to drink a glass of water. He'd have to put a drain in Fred's shoulder wound as well, but right now didn't have the strength.

"Bloody hell. What can possibly happen next?"

Day Four

Hartsfield-Jackson Airport, Atlanta, Georgia, 01:30 Zulu

The drive north along Riverdale Road to Airport Boulevard was surreal. Abandoned cars littered the roadside; and big jets sat like prehistoric fossils on runways. Hatchways protruded above mobile stairs and emergency slides; luggage ports gaped above boxes and packages peppering the runways, but nowhere were the living in evidence. In the distance, a sun low and red in the western sky highlighted the spires marking the Atlanta skyline, obscured by smoke drifting from several fires. The IBM building's upper floors were fire blackened, and many lower-floor windows had blown out. Other buildings also showed damage, whether from fire or mayhem was unclear.

Frank gripped the Saiga 12-gauge not knowing what to expect. As the convoy pulled up to South Terminal, a ragged group waving a white napkin tied to a broom handle greeted the lead Humvee. Sensing no threat, Frank stashed the Saiga, but made sure his XD was loose in the holster as he climbed out of the tanker and walked to the knot of people talking to Sergeant Rogers.

"The damn airport folks left the first night! Nicked a transport bus and lit out!" The group's spokesman was practically yelling.

"Calm down," Rogers said sternly. "We're here for avgas, not personnel rescue. We'll contact headquarters and get a relief convoy on the way."

The spokesman grabbed Rogers arm, which was a mistake. When his friends lifted him from the concrete he sported a bloody nose and a better attitude. Rogers apologized. "I'm sorry, sir. We're all on edge. I'll leave one of the Humvees here for message relay and security, but we have to get avgas and return to Charlotte. We have rescue helicopters sitting idle."

"But we have to get home," The spokesman whined through a bloody handkerchief.

"Sir. We're dealing with a total breakdown of infrastructure." Rogers looked at Frank. "Mr. Lowman, tell these people what it's like out there." The sergeant turned to the stranded citizens. "Lowman has just traveled from New York city, post-event."

With everyone staring, some with hostility, Frank was uncomfortable but knew he must speak.

"At first it was OK. The EMP was late at night; few people were out and about. But people are getting more aggressive. This convoy was ambushed on the way here. I suggest that unless you're going only a few hundred miles, you wait here until the military can arrange transport."

"What are you going to do?" The spokesman asked pointblank.

"I live in Roswell. If Sergeant Rogers allows me to leave the convoy, I'm going to try and get home. I've spent three days getting here from New York." Frank answered honestly.

Rogers turned to the spokesman. "How many in the terminal?"

"About three hundred. Some took whatever working cars they could find and took off. Others left with airport workers."

"Food and water?"

"Food—Well, we pulled all we could from the restaurants, and scavenged a bunch of warmers and propane stoves for omelets and such. We have maybe another day or two's worth of food and water."

"We can help with that. I'll arrange for a mobile kitchen and mess to be delivered in a couple hours. I'll also send additional men to assist with security. I want two volunteers, preferably with military experience, to ride back with us as guards. Mr. Lowman, you and George are released. Thanks for your help." Rogers again shook Frank's hand, and then saluted.

"Thank you, Sergeant Rogers. I wish we could help further

but . . ."

"I understand. If I had a family I'd want to be with them now myself. Good work with that M240." With that, Rogers turned to the crowd, growing as more came out from the terminal.

Frank retrieved his backpack and the Saiga from the tanker cab. He wished Sam luck and met up with George.

"Well Frank, what now?" George studied the agitated crowd surrounding Sergeant Rogers.

"Let's stick around a bit and see if Rogers needs a hand, but then it's off to the north parking garage and see if my Montero will start."

The discussion around Rogers got heated but he eventually prevailed. As things seemed to quiet, the replacement Humvee arrived, and Frank and George decided to book.

Keeping their weapons discrete, they made their way through the scared crowd, which had had three days of no news. Frank and George answered what questions they could, but didn't stop moving. When anyone tried to detain them, showing the shotguns had an ameliorating effect in their favor. The once-omnipresent TSA had vanished. Being local, they had left as soon as they could, leaving stranded passengers to fend for themselves.

Frank gave a sigh of relief as he forced the glass doors leading to the lower parking deck. Before Frank had known about EMPs and other disasters, he preferred to park on level three of North Parking; it was closest to terminal check-in. But since he'd learned an EMP's effects on a car's electronics, he started parking far down and close to the center of parking structures. He didn't know if it would help, but figured a few layers of rebar-filled concrete and hundreds of metal cars would help dissipate an EMP or a CME.

With the sun beginning to set, the lower garage was dark. Frank dug out the Zaplight and maneuvered through the outer layers of cars, many with doors and trunks ajar and hoods up. As he neared the center, more spaces were empty, which was encouraging.

Soon the Zap's beam caught his red Mitsubishi Montero SUV, sitting by itself. The rear window had been smashed, and the front driver's-side door hung open, but other than that, it appeared intact.

"Well, well, here at last." Frank felt cheerful for the first time in days. Placing shotgun against fender and backpack on concrete, he used the light to check the gas tank and tires for punctures. He opened the rear hatch and unlocked a series of hidden compartments. "Thank god they weren't really searching," he said aloud. His emergency supplies were undisturbed.

"Let's see if she starts."

George looked doubtful. "Wouldn't they have taken it if it started?"

Frank smiled, reached inside the open driver's-side door and pulled off a panel below the dash, revealing fuses and an unobtrusive switch that he flipped to up. Looking at wires someone had yanked from the dash, he twisted several together, matching colors. Climbing in, he smiled wide, put key to ignition and turned — the engine caught.

"George, load up. Let's get the hell out of here."

INTERSTATES 85 AND 285, A.K.A. SPAGHETTI JUNCTION
ATLANTA, GEORGIA, 02:00 ZULU

"Gettin' low on gas, Bill," Clara said matter of factly to Willie.

"Watch for a station. I have a pump in the back," Willie answered, glancing in the rearview. " — Damn!"

He slammed on the brakes, screeching to a halt in the middle of the southbound lane. "Where's Nick?"

"Huh?" Clara was confused.

Willie looked at her, then back in mirror.

"Fooled ya," Nick said, grinning at Willie through the

mirror.

Willie turned around and looked straight at Nick. "Whatever you did, don't do it again. This shit is screwed up enough."

"There may be a gas station off the Chamblee-Tucker Road exit," Nick said, settling back into his seat.

"What's the matter, Bill?"

"Nothing. Watch for the Chamblee-Tucker Road exit. I didn't see Nick, that's all. Thought we might've left him back there."

"No such luck," Clara whispered.

"What?" Willie didn't hear her clearly.

"Nothing," Clara said, looking out the window. "Let's get moving. We need a place to sleep and it's getting late."

"Good idea. Gas first, then a place to crash." Willie answered, shifting into gear and accelerating toward a roller-coaster tangle of ramps and flyovers.

Pedestrians strung along four levels of overpasses watched the lone Jeep pass through what normally was one the planet's busiest highway interchanges. In the distance, buildings smoked; Atlanta resembled a third-world nation.

The first exit after Spaghetti Junction was Chamblee-Tucker. Willie exited and immediately focused on a Motel 6 and a QuikTrip.

"One-stop shopping," Nick said from the back.

"How much food we got left?" Willie asked.

"I don't know," Clara answered. "It's in the back seat."

Willie was perturbed. "I was asking Nick."

"Not much," Nick offered, enjoying the front-seat stress. "We need more."

Willie pulled into the QuikTrip.

At one of the pumps sat a heavily laden pickup truck, its Hispanic owner staring dumfounded at the non-functioning pumps. Willie pulled in next to the man and asked, in his best helpful voice, "Need gas?"

"That would be a neat trick, amigo. The pumps they don't work." The man wiped sweat from his brow with a red-and-white checkered handkerchief.

"I have a hand pump. Check the office for fill-valve keys while I get it."

"Thank you. My name is Jorge. I am trying to get back to Mexico, this is loco!" He shoved his hand out for a handshake.

"Bill." He shook Jorge's hand. "Hurry along and get those keys." Willie nodded toward the darkened store.

While Jorge hunted keys, Willie cased the pickup. It was loaded with furniture, electronics . . . and several boxes of dry goods, fresh fruit and MREs.

Suddenly, a shotgun discharged inside the QuikTrip.

"Guess Jorge found the keys," Willie said, pulling out his 9mm. Clara had the other pistol in the car. He lined up the sights on the building's broken-glass doors as an Asian man stepped through carrying a shotgun. Willie didn't hesitate; he squeezed the trigger and smiled as the shot took the man in the gut, doubling him over. For insurance, Willie put one in the top of the man's head and watched him tumble, drop the shotgun and twitch as his nerves shut down.

"Stay here," Willie ordered Clara. "I'll get the keys."

He noticed that, as usual, Nick was nowhere to be seen.

Willie walked across the asphalt bleeding off the day's heat, pausing to kick at the man, make sure he was dead. Half the man's head was gone. Willie studied the store's dim interior, guessing the owner hadn't arrived in time to save much; it looked pretty picked over. By the counter, Jorge lay in a pool of blood; he'd taken a load of double-ought buck to the throat and head.

Willie grabbed a small flashlight from an overturned rack and searched behind the counter, finding not only the keys but also a couple boxes of shotgun shells. He holstered his pistol and returned with the shells to the Jeep, stopping to pick up the Asian's pump action short-barrel shotgun.

"Stow these in the back," he told Clara. "While I fill the tank and the jerries, load as much food as you can into the Jeep."

By the time Willie finished, Clara had moved most of the

food and found a stash of silver coins and a .380 Bursa pistol with ammo.

"Would you really have helped that man get gas?" Clara asked, stowing the last MREs wherever they'd fit.

"Maybe," Willie answered honestly. He hadn't felt the desire to destroy so much since he'd met Clara. "Where's that Nick? He always wanders off when there's work."

"I wonder why," Clara stage-whispered.

"Great haul," said Nick, startling Willie from behind.

"Shit, Nick! You want to get shot?" Willie lowered the gun he'd raised in panic; Nick gave another of his patented annoying smiles.

"Climb in; let's check out Motel 6."

"There's a Marriott over there," Nick gestured across the road.

"Too many people."

"Huh?" Clara said, confused again.

Willie cleared things up: "Motel 6 will have less people to worry about than that Marriott Nick's so hot for."

"Just so long as there is a clean bed, and separate rooms." Clara looked forward to being shorn of Nick.

Motel 6, surprisingly, was intact; a generator chugged in back. Willie sent Clara in with the newfound silver to ask for rooms. She was back out soon.

"He took four silver dollars for two rooms, 121 and 123, down there."

Actually, it had been four silver dollars for one room, but she figured Nick wouldn't care. "The manager says the AC is off to save power, but hot water's on and lights work." Willie parked in front of the rooms and cut the engine.

"The electronic locks don't work either, so we're supposed to block the doors with chairs for security." She smiled in anticipation: "Showers still work but the pressure's only going to last as long as the county tank."

"We'll need to watch the Jeep. Or unload it."

"Let's unload it so we can 'rest'." The way she said rest showed that was the last thing on her mind. "Well, grab a load," Willie said. "I'll get the door. Nick, we'll keep the stuff in our room, where two can watch it."

"Sounds like a plan." Nick watched Willie enter 123.

Willie and Clara unloaded and then he disabled the ignition, pulling the main fuse under the hood. Leering, Willie led Clara to the room.

"Let's get a shower and then rest."

Hartsfield-Jackson Airport, Atlanta, Georgia, 02:00 Zulu

"Damn," Frank swore as he looked at the Montero's gas gauge.

"Forgot to fill it." The needle hovered between a quarter-tank and empty.

"Well," George offered, "we can siphon out of one of these other cars."

"It's funny, on the road I didn't think about it, taking gas from abandoned cars, but it hits home in my own vehicle. What if someone had taken my gas?"

"Well, them cars we gassed from were dead and useless — going nowhere. Taking from some EMP-fried thing out in the open should be OK."

"Probably. I can make it to a gas station, but all I have is a shaker siphon. It won't work on an underground tank."

"Can a car run on avgas?"

Frank thanked the stars he'd met this simple man. "You are a genius! Let's find Rogers." Frank reached to shift into gear, then stopped. "Geesh, I almost forgot." Frank turned off the car and removed the key. "George, reach under the seat and fish out the gun safe."

" 'Gun safe'?"

George fumbled under the passenger-side seat and found a rectangular metal box attached by a plasticized steel cable to the seat's braces. Someone had hacked at the cable—its plastic coating was cut and chewed. The lock edges were dinged and gouged, signs of attempted forced entry.

"Whoever they were, I'm glad they didn't have bigger tools," Frank said, handing George a small silver key. Inside the gun safe was a Springfield XD9 Sub-Compact with one extended magazine inserted and two spares. From under his seat, Frank pulled out a Cross Breed SuperTuck inside-the-waistband holster that had been undetectably snugged against the seat springs.

Frank removed the Colt .45 Commander and holster from his belt, handed it to George, fastened his belt, slid the concealed-carry holster into place on his right side and inserted the XD9. The spare magazines went into his left pants pocket. "That feels like home!"

George was skeptical. "Not as much punch as this .45."

"Maybe, but I have sixteen rounds per magazine and one in the pipe. Plus my spare ammo fits this weapon, not the .45." Frank put the Montero in gear and backed out of the parking spot.

They navigated the stalled cars and once out of the parking structure Frank made good time to the tank farm and the fuel truck convoy, which they approached slowly. A hundred yards distant, they parked the Montero, got out and showed their hands until they were recognized.

"Frank, George, I thought you'd be halfway home by now," Sergeant Rogers said as they were escorted to him.

"We would be but we're riding on fumes. Could we get some gas?"

"This high-octane stuff will really ping, but I don't see why not." Sergeant Rogers pointed a crewman to the SUV. "Private Smith, fill up that Montero."

"Sergeant," Frank said as they watched the private fill jerry cans and haul them toward the vehicle. "I had one question I forgot to ask."

"Ask away. I'll answer if I can."

"Where's the Georgia National Guard? I mean, wouldn't it

have been easier for them to get the avgas and bring it to you?"

Rogers gestured for them to follow, but he went only far enough to get out of earshot of the troops. "I figure you deserve the truth, but this is on the super-QT. Raul Castro sent two battalions to Florida in an attack coordinated with Chavez, who sent the EMP. The Georgia, Mississippi and Alabama National Guards were called to contain until the Army can counterattack. The Deep South is basically lawless." He looked grim. "You're heading to Roswell—take the Perimeter. Reports say I-85 North and Campcreek Parkway are big trouble."

"Damn hell of a thing," George muttered.

"You can say that again. Lock and load. You need more ammo, see Corporal Juarez in the last Humvee."

"Thanks, Sarge, but I got plenty at the house and enough to get me there. Did you keep any of the hijacker's weapons?"

"A couple of AKs and an M15, why?"

"I got some spare 7.62x39 in the SUV, but nothing to shoot it with."

"Tell Juarez to give you both the AKs; we don't need them." He shook their hands, said, "Good luck out there," and returned to the other National Guardsmen. Soon, he was ragging on them about not being worth ticks off a dog's butt. Frank and George found the corporal and headed back to the Montero, each carrying an AK-47 and a few spare twenty-round magazines.

They thanked Private Smith as he poured the second five-gallon jerry in the tank, and then carried him back to the tankers. Sergeant Rogers, before he let them leave, made sure they had two spare jerries secured in the vehicle.

"That was sure nice," George said, lowering the passenger-side window.

Frank did the same with the driver's side. With the stowed jerry cans and the broken rear window, they needed to keep air flowing or exhaust fumes would be drawn into the car by negative air pressure as the SUV moved.

They were soon heading north on I-85 toward Atlanta. Frank had decided to ignore Rogers and the long route around

I-285, preferring his chances with a high-speed run through the center of town.

Everything went smoothly until they neared Georgia State University, where broad, low overpasses made dark tunnels of the expressway underneath. A lone motorcyclist gestured for them to stop; not seeing a threat, they did.

"Looks like an enterprising gang of thugs has pushed stalled cars into a roadblock near the tunnel midpoint, then take whatever you have as a toll. I wouldn't go through there."

"Thanks, need anything?" Frank asked.

"No, I have an apartment nearby. I was checking things out."

"A piece of advice: get out of town. Things are going to get a lot worse before they get better."

"No place to go. Lived here my whole life." He shrugged.

Frank took paper and a pen from the center console and sketched a map to the BOL. "Here. We have a place, and you'd be welcome."

"Thanks, I'll think about it. Be safe." He waved, put the bike in gear and drove off.

Frank and George didn't want to know what the thugs were extracting as tolls, so Frank took to the streets. "Glad we got warned in time," Frank said, coasting the exit ramp. "Let's hope they don't have something up here, too."

Frank would wish he hadn't said that out loud, soon enough.

A few blocks up the street paralleling I-85, the same gang had another roadblock, but this one, a single car perpendicular to the street, wasn't well manned.

"Seatbelt on," Frank said, gunning the engine. The SUV leaped toward the car. George grabbed his shoulder belt and snapped it in place as Frank jerked the wheel to the right and bounced onto the sidewalk, shooting past the roadblock as the thugs dove for safety. Beyond the obstruction, Frank swerved back onto the road with the thump-thump of tires hitting asphalt.

"Guess they didn't plan on that," he said, laughing.

In the rearview he watched the thugs struggle to recover and get off a shot; he jerked the vehicle back and forth to lessen their luck, none of the shots hit. A few blocks more was an entrance to I-85.

As they passed the Chamblee-Tucker Road exit and took the long graceful spaghetti loop onto I-285, Roswell and home, Frank would have been startled to know that not more than 500 yards away, Willie and Clara had just finished wild sex and were settling down to a good night's sleep.

Chamblee-Tucker Road and Interstate 85, Atlanta, Georgia, 02:30 Zulu

After helping Frank and George, motorcyclist Larry Handy had done a little more scouting along I-85. Inattentive to his fuel gauge, he'd been surprised when the bike's engine began stuttering from an empty tank, and switched the fuel petcock to reserve, giving him a few more miles before he had to refuel. He'd skirted the roadblock and was now nearing the Chamblee-Tucker exit.

Seeing the QuikTrip sign for the store a friend of his managed, he pulled off the Interstate and into the QuikTrip lot, parking beside the picked-clean carcass of a truck near the gas pumps. He saw the dead body of what appeared to be his friend Ravi lying near the door of the deserted store. His bike backfired and stalled; he put it on the stand and looked around for Ravi's killer. Hearing nothing more ominous than birdsong and wind-rustled papers, he recalled the end-of-the-world Twilight Zone shows he had watched as a child. He walked to the QuikTrip and ducked inside.

In the Motel 6, the motorcycle backfire woke Willie, who looked over at Clara, innocent in sleep, the setting sunlight from the shaded window playing across her face and naked body. The contradiction of her innocent appearance and the carnal nature he knew possessed her made him hard, but he had more important matters—what was this noise that had woken him from a sound sleep? Going commando, he pulled on black jeans, a tee shirt and shoes. He stuffed his XD 9mm into his back waistband and crept from the room.

Larry examined the store, noting the wreckage of what had once been well maintained. By the counter, he noted a second body in a widening pool of blood and realized the killer was probably still nearby. After a quick search for keys he left the store.

Willie watched from shrubbery cover as Larry returned to the motorcycle and rolled it to the fill-valve hatches. Willie advanced on him, hugging shadows, hiding behind the building, wanting to see how Larry got fuel out of the tank.

Larry found the hatches open and the keys nearby. He returned to his motorcycle and removed a squeeze-bulb suction hose from a saddlebag. Larry closed the fuel cock and unlatched and removed the fuel tank. He carried both hose and tank to the fuel fill hatch, uncoiled the hose, inserted one end into the fill valve and one end into his tank and commenced squeezing the bulb.

Larry appeared to be unarmed, so Willie decided to see if Larry had anything worth taking. Pulling the 9mm from his waistband, he stepped from behind the corner of the QuikTrip.

"Don't move," Willie said, loud enough for Larry to hear.

Startled, Larry stood and turned toward the sound. The last thing Larry heard was the crack of the 9mm as Willie's first shot missed. The second caught him in the chest and the third in the stomach. Falling, Larry dropped the hose and pulled the end from the half-full tank, spewing fuel over the ground where he gasped his last, smelling hot asphalt and strong gasoline.

"I said, don't move."

Willie put the pistol in his waistband, walked to Larry, crouched and rifled his pockets, finding the motorcycle keys, which he kept, and a folded piece of paper, which he almost discarded. Instead, he unfolded and studied it, at first with an idle curiosity that, as he realized what he held, turned to amazement.

It was time for a little payback.

ROSWELL, GEORGIA, 03:45 ZULU

Earl suddenly sat up, and then groaned as pain in his neck and shoulders reminded him that falling asleep hunched in a chair wasn't a good idea. He glanced at Fred, sleeping peacefully. He stood, stretched to get the kinks out, then examined the two surgical drains, one on Fred's shoulder wound, installed before he fell asleep in the chair, one on Fred's thigh, installed after bullet removal—no sign in either drain of puss indicating infection. He emptied the shoulder drain bag of blood and plasma. Fred's temperature, although slightly elevated, seemed reasonable, so Earl decided a warm beer and a sandwich might settle him in for a night of watching Fred. He made his way through the darkening house to the kitchen.

Earl used a strike-anywhere match to light a decorative candle, which gave enough light for Earl to see what was in the refrigerator that probably wouldn't kill him after three days without electricity. Avoiding the obviously fuzzy stuff, he made a sandwich on stale bread with some stiffening American cheese and ham that didn't smell too far gone. Taking a pull of warm beer, he was starting to feel sorry for himself when he heard an automobile engine.

Grabbing the AR-15 he had carried on Fred's rescue, he snuck to the front window and peeked through closed blinds.

"Damn, Frank. Looks like you've been plundered," George said as he got out of the Montero and stared at the gaping garage door and wreckage.

Frank, too, stared at what had been a beautifully organized

garage. Anything useful was gone; the rest spread over the floor. "Crap. Get your shotgun, George; we need to see if Katie is alright." Not waiting for George, Frank pulled his XD and entered the dark garage. From his fanny pack, he pulled out his Zap flashlight, switched it on and, using the Harris technique, braced his pistol hand by locking together both wrists.

George hurried to catch up; Frank had already entered the basement. George could hear Frank swearing as he encountered the destruction leveled on each room, looking for some sign of his wife as he cleared each. Frank noted the partly full waterBOB in the basement bathroom tub. Based on the upstairs ransacking, he didn't understand why it hadn't been slashed or otherwise abused, but he was grateful. The search ended on the main floor in the wreckage of the master suite, Frank facing the empty gun safe. He got down on his knees and felt under the bed, then stood, facing away from George.

"I'm sorry we didn't find her, Frank," George said, heartsick.

Frank was quiet, motionless, but when he turned to face George, George thought he'd gone mad, because Frank was grinning. "I'm not. If we'd found her, it would mean she was here when this happened." He gestured toward the bed. "Her defense weapon, a .38 Smith and Wesson Bodyguard we keep in a hidden holster under the bed, is also gone."

"I hadn't thought of that."

"No blood or signs of a struggle. Just vandalism."

Frank holstered the XD. "Help me clear the closet."

Frank and George cleared underneath an attic pull-down hatch. Frank pulled the stairs into place and handed the Zapper to George.

"Follow me and keep the light so I can see."

George followed Frank into the hot, humid attic. At the top of the stairway, Frank told George how to hold the light so he could see as he crawled over insulation and rafters to an area over the master bathroom.

"Hold the light so it projects in front of me," Frank called to George, who corrected the beam.

Clearing away insulation, Frank exposed a flat four-by-four-foot piece of three-quarter-inch plywood with a rope handle. With an upward tug, the plywood came up, revealing a dark hole.

"When they built the house, they didn't vault the kitchen or bathroom ceilings, so there are voids; I decided to make hidden storage compartments."

Frank reached inside the cubbyhole and began pulling out five-gallon buckets and ammo boxes. He finished with a couple of long rifle cases.

With George's assistance they emptied the other two storage areas and carried the contents of all three into the bedroom. Both were sweaty and itchy from fiberglass insulation. All told, they had ten five-gallon buckets of freeze-dried food packets, MREs and various survival supplies; a wooden crate with two spam cans each holding 440 rounds of 7.62x54R ammo and two surplus Mosin-Nagant rifles, a case of 7.62x39 ammo for the AKs in the Montero, as well as two 640-ounce cases of bottled water; a folding camping stove that used military-surplus fuel tablets, an emergency tent and space-blanket sleeping bags, a fry pan and an aluminum soup pot.

George whistled. "Damn. Prepared for Armageddon."

"Not prepared enough. I should have been here."

Frank sat heavily on the bed, the weariness from the long trip catching up to him. "Hopefully Katie somehow escaped all this and made it to the BOL."

"The what?"

"B-O-L—Bug-out location," Frank explained. "Property we have across the Alabama border."

Heavy footfalls began pounding rapidly up the basement stairs.

Frank had the 9mm drawn and pointing toward the door onto the basement stair landing. George's view was blocked, but was shocked again when Frank lowered the pistol and grinned broader than he had before.

"Alabama, did you say? Brilliant," Earl said, smiling as he clomped to the top of the stairs, the AR-15 at the ready. "When do we leave?"

North of Lake Weiss, Alabama, 12:00 Zulu

Max was feeling the effects of her mid-watch. Unless she stood and stretched and walked around, she would suddenly realize she had been asleep for an unknown amount of time, not smart when hoards of bible-thumping rednecks might attack at any minute. She sighed and eyed the now empty thermos of hot tea that had run out at 5:00 a.m. and it was now 7:00 a.m. She knew her relief, David, wouldn't arrive until 8:00. At least the sun was high enough she could read if she wanted, but she was terrified of falling asleep.

A twig snap brought her full awake.

She had drifted into a pseudo-sleep, but now adrenalin tingled her belly. She caught movement from the corner of her eye, slowly turned her head, and brought her Mosin-Nagant to ready. She relaxed as a doe ambled in front of the observation post, nibbling white mushrooms. Eli and David had done such a good job of camouflaging the plywood construct that the deer hadn't realized anything was out of the natural order.

The doe suddenly looked up, ears twitching and nostrils flared, all senses alert. Max didn't think she'd startled the animal; she was right. The doe looked toward the road and with a flash of her white tail bounded into the woods.

Gripping the Mosin, Max peered intently in the direction the doe had looked in before she fled. Morning mist hadn't yet burned off, so Max had limited visibility beyond fifty yards. She donned headphones. The digital earmuffs had a dial to increase their sensitivity, giving Max nearly the audile acuity of the fleeing doe.

Max tensed as she heard muffled conversation, indistinguishable but definitely the sound of humans, two or more. Max put her hand on the crank of the sound-powered phone unit; the agreed danger signal was three cranks, which would generate three whoops in the main trailer, but she didn't want to alarm everyone if it were only a neighbor getting water from a stream.

In a minute or so, she could make out some words, and relaxed. The across-the-road neighbors, the early-rising Rothbergs, soon came walking down the road, fishing gear in hand.

"I tell you, Lynn, Reverend's gone around the bend if what Lyle says is true." Carl Rothberg's voice was clear to her digitally enhanced hearing.

"Now Carl, you know how Lyle exaggerates," Lynn told her husband.

"I heard it from Katie, too. He and his army of believers hung some Muslims. Almost hung Eli, too, that nice delivery man, but he got away."

"So what does that have to do with Katie?"

"Eli killed Reverend's son when he fled, and now he's holed up with her, according to Lyle. Reverend's gonna attack — today — and finish the job."

"I can't believe Eli would do such a thing. Maybe we should warn them."

"We warn them and Reverend finds out, we could be next."

Max thought that Carl, in his seventies and not exactly up for a fight, sounded scared, but she knew that Lynn had spine enough for them both.

"Carl, if the Messingers had felt that way, your family would've died in Treblinka."

"As usual, Lynn, you are correct. Let us go and warn them."

The Rothbergs were approaching the bend in the road closest to the observation post. Putting her Mosin down, Max opened the door and went to meet them. Lynn clutched at her chest when Max appeared from seemingly nowhere, standing suddenly in front of them.

"My God, child, you startled me!"

"It's OK, Mrs. Rothberg. It's only me, Max."
"Where on earth did you come from?" Carl asked.
"I was scoutin' game and heard you coming."
Max gestured to the digital earmuffs.
"That electrical stuff still works?" Carl was not a prepper.
"We store stuff in a shipping container; it protects from EMP."
"Well," Lynn said excitedly, "we need to tell you something."
"I heard. Reverend's planning on attacking, today. Any details? Numbers? Time? Anything?" Max asked, probing for details.
"No, Max, I'm sorry. That's all Lyle told me."
"Well, thanks for the tip. You all need anything?"
"No honey, we're fine," Lynn said brightly. "Thank you for offering."
"OK, well, I'll be going, good luck fishing," Max said, waving as they continued toward the creek. Once they were out of sight, she ducked into the observation post and gave the squawk box handle a fast turn.
"Yes Max?" Katie answered almost immediately; she had been starting the stove for breakfast.
"Just talked to the Rothbergs. Lyle told them Reverend will be attacking us today."
"It figures. Well, we're as ready as we can be. David's getting dressed and will be down to relieve you as soon as he gets some food in him."
"No rush. Have something hot ready for me."
"Will do honey, be careful."
"Always am, Mom. Over."
Distracted by the conversation, Max was taken by surprise when Bubba Downey seized her from behind, a grimy hand over her mouth.
"Well, well. Lookie what I found," he hissed in her ear.

Roswell, Georgia, 10:00 Zulu

Frank looked out the airplane window at all the lights; he was glad to be getting home. A part of his mind told him he had been gone longer than the day or two he remembered . . . as he gazed on the night sky and panorama of lights the plane suddenly lurched and bucked; oxygen masks popped from concealment like dozens of tentacles reaching for him, and he was surrounded by screams as the plane banked sharply right and began to stall . . .

Frank almost fell out of bed from the jerk produced by the falling sensation in his nightmare. He was disoriented for a spell, and then it all came back. Because Frank's home had been wrecked, he and George had joined Earl and Fred at Fred's house. Over the last of the warm beer, Earl told his story and Frank and George told theirs and, after changing Fred's dressings, Frank had climbed into a soft bed and slept like the dead.

But today was the day. He was going to the BOL, Katie and Maxine, and perhaps news of Lizzie, her husband and children.

Frank got out of bed and stretched more sore muscles than he'd ever had before. On the way to the back deck, where they'd set up a camp kitchen with Frank's emergency supplies, he knocked on the other bedroom doors and waked George and Earl. Fred he let sleep, or so he thought.

As he slid the glass door, the pungent aroma of fresh coffee struck him, followed by the sight of Fred, sitting on a folding chair and eating bacon and reconstituted scrambled eggs.

"Well good morning, Fred!" Frank said, looking over his wounds — no seepage or surgical drains.

"I thought I heard you come in last night, Frank. Sorry I was out of it."

Fred creaked to his feet and shook Frank's hand.

"Yep, my new friend George and I made it back from New York."

Frank poured hot coffee into a mug.

"That must be quite a tale," Fred said.

"You've had quite a week, too," Frank replied, and began fixing a similar meal.

"My stupidity. I lost supplies and a perfectly good vehicle." Fred was mad at himself.

"None of us expected things to go to hell so fast." Frank stirred eggs over the Coleman burner, adding bacon when they were nearly done. Fred passed his empty mug for Frank to fill. "Wish I could see what supplies are left."

Frank had little hope of finding anything. "We'll scout the scene and see."

George and Earl came out the sliding glass door, searching for the coffee. After introducing George and appointing Earl as cook, they planned out the day: George would pack the Montero, and Earl and Frank would check the ambush site for salvage. Fred said, "Check the garage for any supplies you need."

Frank went in to the kitchen and down the basement steps to the garage, where he saw the hidden door left open by Earl in his rush to rescue Fred.

"Holy crap," Frank exclaimed, finding the cache of rifles, ammunition and supplies. "I never imagined." Securing the door, he pondered how to carry in one Montero their combined supplies, three healthy adults and one wounded.

Upstairs, he cornered Earl. "You didn't tell me Fred had Napoleon's arsenal and the storerooms of Egypt."

"Slipped my mind, I guess." Earl knew how to keep a secret.

Frank eyed Earl. "Slipped your mind, huh? Well, we have to find something to haul it all. A trailer or something."

Outside was calm and clear, and smelled of wood smoke — someone cooking in their fireplace since it didn't have the acrid smell of a house fire. Frank and George took a stealthy half hour to reach the ambush site. Other than empty shell casings and a scorch where the truck had burned, the area was clear. Even the wreckage had been hauled away.

"Must've used a car carrier," Frank said, scanning the scene. He spotted a small trailer in a driveway a few blocks down. "Let's go do some haggling."

Nearing the house, Frank said, "Don't let on we have a working vehicle. I'll say we want to pull this by hand." He handed Earl his rifle and concealed pistol. "No need to frighten them any more than they already are."

Leaving Earl hidden across the street, Frank held up his hands and walked toward the front door. Louvered blinds shut as he knocked.

"Hello! May I talk to you?" Frank called out. "I want to ask about your trailer. I'm unarmed."

Footsteps approached. Frank hoped he looked respectable; he'd cleaned and shaved last night. The door cracked to the limit of a guard chain. "What you want with the trailer?" a youngish voice asked. "You got a working car?"

"No." Frank tried to maintain an honest face. "My friend and I are walking to Alabama and we want to use it for supplies."

"You got supplies? What can you trade?"

The door closed, the chain rattled undone and the door opened. Frank confronted a scared young man, maybe not yet in his twenties.

"I can give you a two-week supply bucket for two of freeze-dried food."

"Two two-week buckets." The scared young man was also stubborn.

"Done. We'll fetch the buckets and come back for the trailer." Frank paused. "You got water?"

"Not much."

"If you got means to haul it, I can show you a couple gallons fresh water."

"Where?"

"Got a pencil?" Frank wrote down his address and how to

find the WaterBOB in the downstairs bathroom.

"Thanks, mister." The young man looked less scared.

Looking into the house, Frank saw the shadowy outline of a young woman. "You got a way to defend yourself?"

"That's none of your business," the man blustered. Frank was sure that meant no.

"Well, we can't carry everything, so I'll tell you what, under the pile of clothes in the master bedroom I'll leave something to help you out, OK?"

"You'd do that for us, mister?" A very pregnant woman came forward.

"We aren't savages. You two have a place to go if things get bad here?"

"Her folks live over off Lake Lanier. We'd planned to go there, but with no working cars . . ."

"I hear you. Can you be ready in two hours? And at that address?" Frank asked, indicating the slip of paper.

"You said you don't have a vehicle."

"We might be able to arrange something."

"We don't know how to thank you, mister."

"Call me Frank." He held out his hand.

"Martin Williams, this is my wife, Greta."

"Two hours. We'll arrange something."

Frank left the happy couple. He hated to delay getting to the BOL and Katie, but thinking of what could happen to this young couple made him queasy.

"Well?" Earl asked as Frank returned.

"They were good negotiators, but I got it."

"What'd it cost us?"

"Four weeks of food for two, all the water they can carry, and a ride to Lake Lanier."

Chamblee-Tucker Road and Interstate 85, Atlanta, Georgia, 11:30 Zulu

Clara was exasperated with Willie. "You want me," she complained, "to drive the Jeep with Nick, while you scout ahead on the motorbike? How do you relay what you learn? And if you get creamed, I . . . uh, we, have no chance—"

"Look, I'll ease back periodically and give you the ok sign." Willie sounded reasonable. "I want to make sure the road ahead is safe."

"What if you don't ease back? What do I do then?" Clara asked, forgetting to include Nick.

"Nick will know. Do what he says," Willie answered.

"Right." Clara sighed.

"I know where to go." He brandished the paper from Larry's corpse. "And I know this guy; he'll have shelter, food, weapons. Besides, he owes me."

Clara studied the crude map. "How far is this?"

"Well, in the old days—you know, last week—it would've been two hours. Now, who the hell knows."

"OK, but you better make sure I know what the hell is going on."

She grabbed Willie and roughly kissed him.

"You got it!"

"Don't you two look lovey-dovey."

Willie turned toward the resonant sound of Nick's voice in the open door, and spoke with a crafty politician's innocence: "I was just telling Clara I found out where that guy I told you about is heading. I think we can really get ahead by a little visit."

"I think you are right, my friend. Where'd you get the rice-burner?" Nick gestured at the 650 Yamaha beside the Jeep.

"Liberated it from a prior owner. I'll ride scout; Clara will drive the Jeep."

"Who do I ride with?"

"You'll be more comfortable with Clara."

Nick narrowed his eyes and stared at Willie. "I'd rather ride outside with you; I can see more."

"Suit yourself. Ride with me then," It was Willie's turn to be exasperated.

"Bill, it's OK. He can ride with you." Clara was accommodating.

As Nick turned to head outside, Willie noticed his limp had worsened. "Something more than usual wrong with your leg?"

Nick rubbed the calf of his bad leg. "Sometimes before a storm it acts up."

Willie peered at the clear sky, but he, too, wanted to be accommodating. "Clara and I can load. See what else we need at the QuikTrip.

"I can do that," Nick smiled and waved as he limped out.

"Figures," Clara grumbled.

"Huh?" Willie asked, picking up a box of food.

"Nothing. Let's get this stuff loaded."

Clara grabbed a second box and followed him out to the Jeep.

Reloading took only a few minutes, and after a breakfast of granola bars, bottled water and beef jerky they hit the road, following Frank's map. Willie and Nick sped ahead on the Yamaha and Clara, a couple miles behind, followed.

Without a radio or Willie's presence, Clara's fear returned, fear of being alone, of being helpless. She felt the pistol she now wore at her belt — perhaps she didn't feel as helpless. Willie and Nick doubled back every few miles and gave the all clear, then continued scouting. Other than some improvised and easily avoided roadblocks, no hazards presented themselves along the top arc of Atlanta's Perimeter.

Trouble came on the long entry-ramp curve from I-285 onto I-75.

What had spilled didn't matter. Diesel? Oil from a

shattered engine? No matter, the result was the same: one second Willie and Nick were kings of all they surveyed; the next the powerful bike was out from under, and each was rolling and skidding on coarse asphalt to end in a trash-strewn grassy zone separating the exit and 75. A few minutes later, Clara skidded to a stop at the fallen Yamaha.

"Oh baby, Willie—wake up!"

She shook Willie gently, afraid to worsen any injuries. She saw no broken bones, but road rash and lacerations covered any and all exposed skin.

"Nick? Nick—Where's Nick?" Willie winced as muscles bruised and torn by the accident protested.

"I don't see him; he must be OK." Clara tried to reassure. "Anything broken?"

Willie moved each limb and stretched; his left-hand index finger bent at an odd angle. Other than that, and maybe a broken rib, he seemed fine. With a yank and a scream, Willie pulled the disjointed finger back into place.

"How's the bike?" he asked through gritted teeth.

"I don't know. I ran to you first."

"Help me up."

With only a few curses, and Clara's help, Willie got unsteadily to his feet and used Clara for support to hobble to the bike. The front fork was bent and the oil feed pipe from the engine to the overhead cams had sheared off.

"So much for scouting," Willie said with resignation.

"Partner, I don't think you could ride, now," Nick said from behind them.

Willie turned, wincing again from pain, towards Nick's voice. Other than a scrape on his chin, Nick looked unscathed.

"I agree. Looks like we're all back in the Jeep."

"Yep. That rice-burner is toast." Nick climbed into the back seat.

"Looks like I drive," Clara said, "until we see how seriously you're injured." She helped Willie into the passenger side.

Leaving the now useless bike leaking oil on the roadside,

the Jeep sped north on I-75 toward Rome and the road to Alabama.

NORTH OF LAKE WEISS, ALABAMA, 12:10 ZULU

Bubba dragged Max into the woods, keeping her off balance. Max struggled and fought for leverage, but Bubba dragged her, and swung her side-to-side, which prevented her from gaining balance and purchase to strike back. Looking for any advantage, she saw the disturbed earth of a mine.

"Stop your damn struggling. You know you want it," Bubba whispered in her ear, which incensed her, and drove her to struggle more. She found an opening when Bubba tripped on a vine. Planting her feet, Max grabbed his arm and, using his unbalanced state, smashed her booted foot into his instep, then bent forward, shoving her butt into his stomach. With a yell, Bubba sailed over her huddled form and landed full on a hidden mine. Max dove to the side, praying to escape the range of the pepper spray.

Landing heavily on his back, Bubba felt something give beneath him and was suddenly engulfed in a burning, suffocating cloud. Screaming, he clawed at his eyes, which made the burning worse. With each breath, his mouth, nasal passages and throat burned hotter.

Max, avoiding the fumes, lay with her back toward the thrashing man until the mine's hissing stopped, whereupon she jumped to her feet and ran to the observation post. Her glancing exposure to the capsaicin cloud was causing her eyes to tear, and her throat and nose to burn. Grabbing a water bottle she washed her hands and face, and listened to Bubba curse. He seemed to be on his feet and coming toward her. She grabbed her Moisin-Nagant and pointed it at the charging Bubba.

"You bitch!" he yelled. "What'd you do to me?" He held a large-bore revolver that he waved wildly, and screamed, "I'll kill you!"

"Stop! And drop the gun, Bubba," Max yelled, fixing her bead.

Still mostly blind, Bubba targeted the sound of her voice and pulled the trigger. The revolver, a .357 magnum, belched fire and noise, but missed Max by several feet. With a jerk, she returned fire. While her shot wasn't a textbook center-of-mass hit, the 7.62mm slug slammed into his right shoulder joint, the bullet nearly ripping away his arm and spinning him like a bloody top. Despite the massive wound, he still held the revolver in his left hand and tried to bring it once again to bear. Max cycled the bolt, aimed and squeezed the trigger, shooting Bubba dead center in the chest and toppling him backward.

Bubba didn't get up this time.

Gasping, Max let the rifle drop to her side and then to the ground. She felt her throat engorge as she took in the carnage created by two bullets, and vomited what little was in her stomach. Behind her came the buzz of an ATV crashing through the bush, making its own trail.

David pulled up and jumped off the ATV.

"Holy crap, Max. We heard shots. You OK?" He was so concerned for Max he hadn't seen Bubba's body, and now recoiled at the sight.

"Damn! What happened?"

Max looked up with red, tear-filled eyes and wiped her mouth on her sleeve. "Bubba wanted more than I could give," she said simply.

It took David only a moment to understand.

Roswell, Georgia, 12:00 Zulu

Frank and Earl, pulling the trailer, made a beeline for Fred's house, taking turns pulling while the other kept watch. Other than a few swishing window shades as fearful people spied, and a friendly stray dog, the streets were empty. They heard a two-stroke motorcycle over in the power-line right-of-way, but it didn't come near. By the time they reached Fred's, they were sweaty and tired.

"Hey, a trailer! No sign of the truck, eh?" Fred met them, leaning on a makeshift cane.

"Nope. Either the hijackers came back for it, or someone else nipped it. But we did get a trailer, after some horse-trading."

"So," George chimed in. "What'd we give up?"

"Four weeks of food for two, an AK-47 with ammo, the water in my WaterBOB, and a ride to Lake Lanier."

"That's a two-hour detour!" Fred was mad. "I want to get out of here."

"I couldn't leave a pregnant couple stranded. Her folks are up on the lake." They were silent; each had children. Fred finally broke the quiet. "Well, I'm hoping someone is helping out my Jamie. What's done is done."

Frank looked with concern at the nearly loaded Montero. "I hate to risk our main vehicle and the supplies."

"Here's a thought," Fred offered. "The Emersons summer in Florida, and they left last week to beat the crowds. Henry has that old Studebaker he takes to car shows, and it should still be in his garage."

"I hate to steal their car," Frank said.

"He told me to watch over it. The way I see it, if you get to the lake and back, no harm; if you die in the attempt, you'll be beyond caring." Fred turned and began to hobble up the driveway. "They gave me a key to look in on the place; I'll go get it."

"Nice of you to put a positive spin on it, Fred. I see your point. I'll go see if I can borrow their car. Turn the Montero, hook up the trailer and start loading."

George looked at the Montero's rear. "Hey Frank, where's the hitch ball?"

"In the first compartment . . ." He too looked at the nearly loaded SUV. "Son of a gun. You'll have to unload the back a little to get to it." He tossed his keys to George, who snagged them out of the air. "Sorry. I should've thought of that before I had you start loading."

Slinging the AK-47 around his back, Frank walked down four houses to the Emerson's, watchful for nosy neighbors. He felt like he had as a teenager when he "borrowed" his dad's car; he'd gotten grounded for two weeks for that stunt. The key fit the front door; inside was dark because the shades were drawn. Using one of the small flashlights from his emergency supplies, Frank headed for the kitchen, where he found a pegboard with several sets of keys, one obviously the Studebaker's. He grabbed it and headed for the garage, which was even darker than the house. Frank disengaged the overhead door from the automatic opener and pulled on the service handle. With a squeal that made Frank cringe, the door opened, flooding the garage with daylight and revealing a gleaming, robins-egg blue 1937 Studebaker Coupe Express.

Frank felt the pang of regret, but rationalized it was for the greater good. Getting in, he located the starter, pulled the choke, pumped the gas twice and turned the key. After grinding a bit, the engine caught and, with a belch of white exhaust, started. Frank let the engine warm, then slowly pushed in the choke.

He released the emergency brake and depressed the clutch, shifted into reverse and eased up on the clutch, giving the car a little gas as he did so. With a slight lurch the classic car backed out. Once clear of the doorway, Frank shifted into neutral, applied the emergency brake, let the car idle in the driveway, re-entered the garage, closed the door and re-engaged the automatic opener. Frank retraced his steps through the house and locked the front door on his way out.

"Where do you think you're going with Mr. Emerson's car?"

Frank turned to find Karl Jones, one of Hank Petrod's lackeys.

"Hi Karl, how are ya? Emerson left it in Fred's care, if you must know. Fred has authorized me to use it for an errand. I'll bring it back."

"Sure you will. Just like that bitch wife of yours shared your supplies."

Frank felt his temper rise. "Out of my way, Karl."

"Or what? You'll shoot me?"

"Nope. No need to waste a bullet," Frank answered. "Now get out of my way." His voice was cold and even.

"Sorry. This is now neighborhood property. I can't let you take it."

Karl stood blocking Frank's path to the car.

Frank pushed Karl out of the way. Foolishly, Karl swung a roundhouse punch at Frank's head, which Frank trapped before it could reach his head. Frank turned, pulled Karl's arm rigid and, with his other hand, used his open palm to disjoint Karl's elbow, which made a sickening crack as Karl folded to the ground clutching his disabled arm.

"Word to the wise, Karl: don't let your alligator mouth write checks your hummin'bird ass can't cash." Frank walked to the Studebaker and, with a moderate clash of gears, drove off, leaving Karl moaning on the Emerson's lawn.

NORTH OF LAKE WEISS, ALABAMA, 12:45 ZULU

David Robert Alexander—Jimmy Bob to his friends—was worried; Bubba Downey hadn't returned from his scouting mission and Reverend was depending on his report to plan today's attack. Then he heard Bubba screaming like a demon possessed, followed by the distinctive boom of Bubba's .357, the crack of a high-powered rifle, and then a second rifle shot. Discretion being the better part of valor, at least in Jimmy Bob's mind, he gave it another five minutes, until he heard the sound of an ATV, then beat a strategic retreat to the advance camp at

Little River Canyon park.

"You left Bubba behind!" Reverend stormed at Jimmy Bob, making him cringe.

"Yes sir, but I heard more people comin' so I figured it best to bring ya'll the report rather'n get myself kilt too." Jimmy Bob was nearly crying.

"Well, what information do you have?" Reverend's glare seemed to pin Jimmy Bob to the floor.

"Uh . . . they have a forward lookout post, manned by that girl Max. That's where Bubba was headin' to when I heared the shots. Before that, he started a'yelling and screaming like they's torturing him. Then an ATV came and I figured I was outnumbered."

"So this important information is 'they have a lookout post,' and no idea if they have or have not any automatic or advanced weapons?"

"No sir." Jimmy Bob looked down at the floor.

Reverend considered the situation, then smiled. "I'm sorry, Jimmy Bob; you did right, go get some breakfast." He reached out and Jimmy Bob flinched, but Reverend patted him on the shoulder. "Go on now."

Soon as Jimmy Bob was out of earshot, Reverend turned to Deacon Carl Edwards, a former Marine who was now his second in command. Carl had returned from Desert Storm not quite right, but with a burning faith for God and desire for vengeance against Moslems. "That damn Bubba was thinking with his dick instead of his head," Reverend spit out to Carl, and slammed his fist on the concrete picnic table. "We don't have a clue what we're facing."

"They've probably improvised booby traps; sounds like something nasty if it made Bubba scream like Jimmy Bob said." Carl stood, sliding his KA-BAR knife in and out of its scabbard.

"Any ideas where?" Reverend pointed to a topo map marked with the boundaries of the Lowman property, spread on the table and weighted down by rocks. "Where would you put them?"

"It'd depend. If it's trip wires and tangle feet, then all

through the woods where we'd enter from. If it's an improvised land mine, then I'd rig the trails and the road." He indicated on the map probable locations for each strategy.

"So we need to tell the men to watch for trip wires and disturbed earth."

"Yep. But if that dirty Moslem what killed your boy was helping, they may be well disguised. I get the feeling he knows a bit about killing, the neat way he did your boy." He seemed to respect Eli.

Reverend pondered, and from a worn-leather messenger bag pulled a roster. "Who're our least valued men?"

"Let's see the list." Carl marked it up. "Here. Poorest shots and least experienced."

"Tell me what you think: we send them in first, through the defended spots, then, after they trip the majority of the traps, follow up with a second wave of our best fighters. We'd also learn how they're armed." An idea sparked. "We could also flank them with a squad from the Parkenson's property."

Carl looked for holes in the plan. "When should we attack?"

"During lunch— precisely noon."

Worried, Carl checked his watch. "Four hours to brief and place the men."

"Shoot, Deacon, these boys are so raw, if'n we had a week to plan and train it'd not make a difference." Reverend laughed. "I figure with our lambs keeping the Lowmans busy, the flankers will take them out easily."

"I like that. Let's smooth it out a bit, but the basics sound great. You sure you were never in the military, Reverend?"

The big man declined to speak.

ROSWELL, GEORGIA, 14:00 ZULU

Frank pulled the Studebaker into Fred's driveway, put the car in neutral, yanked the handbrake and, for fun, turned on the radio. While the tubes warmed, he heard only static over the speaker. He cranked the volume and spun the dial across the AM frequency covered by the old radio. With a squawk, the dial reached the emergency broadcast channel.

"We repeat, President Paul has declared martial law for the entire country. All citizens should stay in their homes unless otherwise directed by emergency personnel. Combined armies of Cuba and Venezuela have invaded areas of southern Florida, Alabama, Mississippi and Texas. All National Guard members are called to active duty and are reporting to their muster locations for immediate deployment.

"Emergency food and water are being staged and you will be notified where and when to pick up supplies for your family. You will be required to provide identification proving citizenship such as a social security card, DD Form 214, or certified birth certificate plus a valid driver's license. Stay tuned for additional broadcasts on the hour." The station returned to static.

Frank turned off the car, got out and locked the door. Confirmation of what Sergeant Rogers had confided made it more real. Frank hoped the troops could assemble quickly enough to repel the invasion. In the back of his mind he knew the president would authorize limited use of nukes if things started going bad.

Frank told his three companions what he'd heard on the radio. Grimly, they loaded the promised supplies into the Studebaker, finishing as Martin and Greta arrived, lugging small backpacks. Martin was awed by the Studebaker.

"Do you know what this car is?" Slack-jawed, Martin circled the vehicle.

"A Studebaker?" offered Frank.

"Not just a Studebaker! This was one of a limited release offered to police departments. The windows are almost bulletproof, the steel is extra heavy—shoot, it'll stop a .38 Special or even a 9mm."

Frank regarded the Studebaker. "Looks like a good choice, then." He gestured to Martin. "Let's get some gas from the garage and top off her tanks; I'm sure Greta's folks are anxious for your safety."

The tanks were soon topped off from Fred's stash of jerry cans, and George, leaving Fred and Earl to finish the load out, offered to ride in back with the supplies. After a short lesson on the proper use of an AR-15, Martin sat shotgun, with Greta beside him.

Their armory could spare an AR-15, an AR-7 .22 survival rifle, and a handgun each for Martin and Greta, along with ammunition. Greta looked askance at the murderous .380 Automatic Colt Pistol, but after Frank told them about the emergency broadcast, she accepted it. After a quick meal of MREs, they hit the road for Lake Lanier.

Greta said that her folks lived in a retirement community on the lake's northeast side. Frank and George decided that backtracking to I-285 and then north on Ga. 400 was safest. Highways 20 and 120 through small towns would become dangerous as people realized that authority was nonexistent.

Frank was most concerned about the journey's last part, off Ga. 400 and across the top of the lake. They made good time, but many fires and burned-out buildings along I-285 were sobering; they traveled in silence. At the Concourse buildings—called the King and Queen due to their resemblance to chess pieces—Frank moved to the 19/400 exit and they were soon headed north. Passing Concourse, they saw the entire Perimeter Mall in flames, and the King gutted by fire from the twentieth story up.

"I used to work in that building," Frank said.

They made good time up Ga. 400. It was easy to see threats, and as they passed Exit 10 Old Milton Road, they hadn't had to stop or even slow. Nearing the Lake Lanier exits, they saw more pedestrians, most of whom looked up as they passed; some waved. Frank felt bad passing refugees, but knew that if they helped everyone, they'd never get back to Fred and Earl, much less reach Alabama and his family.

It was a short drive up Ga. 306 to the right turn on Ga. 369. A few miles further, they passed Cains Cove Road and came up on the first bridge over Lake Lanier's northern tributaries. As the road narrowed, Frank and George watched for roadblocks and ambushes, spotting one on their end of the bridge. Frank pulled over and parked the Studebaker in the dry grass on the roadside.

"I'll go up and see what's happening. If they start shooting, cover me and I'll try to run back. If I go down, get the hell out of here." He handed George the AK-47 he'd worn around his neck with a two-point sling. Martin and George stood anxiously near the car as Frank walked hands-up toward the roadblock.

"Hold there, stranger!"

A husky voice from behind the roadblock: "What's your business?"

Well, thought Frank, at least they didn't shoot first.

"My name's Frank Lowman. I'm delivering Martin and Greta Williams to her folks up at Cresswood."

He stood patiently while a hurried conference took place behind the roadblock. "Put that pistol on the ground and come forward."

Frank removed the XD, did as instructed, then walked to the barricade.

"Got any ID?" A burly man stepped out, holding a sawed-off shotgun.

"Let me get out my wallet."

The man gestured with the shotgun, so Frank pulled his wallet out, removed his driver's license and handed it over. The man studied it, returned it and lowered the shotgun; Frank saw several other weapons pointed at him from behind the barricade. "Mr. Lowman, why should we let you through?"

"I only want to drop these kids off and get back to Roswell."

"Have them step out."

"Martin, Greta, step out so they can see you," Frank called.

Martin and Greta did as asked, and stood while a decision was made.

"OK, but we'll have someone ride with you."

"Deal." Frank shook hands with the man.

As Frank picked up his pistol and returned to the car, the two blockading vehicles backed clear. Frank paused at the barricade and picked up their escort, a nervous young man named Kent Hill, armed with a Colt .45 Commander.

Waving to the men manning the roadblock, they continued across the top of Lake Lanier on Ga. 369 until a second barricade, past Wilkinson Road on the second bridge. With a wave from Kent, they cleared it without problem. Another mile and they reached the Cresswood entrance, blocked with picnic tables and guarded by two older gentlemen with sidearms and scoped deer rifles.

"Dad!" Greta yelled as they stopped at the makeshift barricade.

Greta climbed over her husband in her haste to get out. One of the guards hastily propped his rifle and was nearly knocked over by his daughter.

"Well, George, I guess they might let us in," Frank said.

After unloading the welcome supplies and swapping news—what little there was—Frank and George topped off the Studebaker's tank with gas siphoned from ruined cars in the complex, and were soon on their way. They dropped Kent off at the second barricade.

"Be careful, we're getting reports of ambushes. They stage a fake accident or have a woman 'flee a pursuer'; when you stop to help, they steal you blind. Couple folks been killed."

"We've seen some of that already. Everyone's on their own; with the National Guard fighting off the Cubans, it's the Wild West out here."

"You said it, champ. Be careful." The gruff guard shook hands with Frank. "That was a top notch thing you did for those kids."

"I hope someone would do the same for my girls if they got stranded."

"Unfortunately, folks just ain't wired that way so much anymore."

"I hope you're wrong, my friend."

Lowman property, north of Lake Weiss, Alabama, 13:00 Zulu

"We need to prepare for Reverend Sanders, and we don't know which direction. I propose we move the camera watching the house to the border at the rear of the property. We also have two more for the east and west borders."

Katie paused to take a drink of coffee. Eli smiled at her approval.

"We should also set tangle-foot snares and as many booby-traps as we can devise—trip wires and deadfalls—in the next few hours." She indicated spools of wire, trip signals and snare releases she'd pulled from storage.

"These are good ideas." Eli addressed the group and passed out drawings. "I have drawn some simple traps that can be set up quickly."

Katie checked the drawings and approved. "Marlene, you and David do the back; as many as you can. When you hear three shots, come back in. Max, you and I'll do the east, Eli the west."

They used ATVs to reach their assigned areas. With thin strong wire they set tangle-foot snares a few inches above ground between close-spaced trees. With snare releases they rigged whips of bent branches wire-tied to the releases. They strung noisemakers made of mousetraps and 12-gauge birdshot. When Katie felt they'd run out of time, she fired three shots in a safe direction and met the others at camp. "Let's grab some food, grab our Mosins and whatever other weapons we can carry, and wait."

They ate a cold lunch of hasty sandwiches, kettle chips and fruit. Katie manned the monitor and cycled between cameras, praying for a glimpse of Reverend's men before they attacked.

West of the Lowman property, Lake Weiss, Alabama, 15:30 Zulu

Reverend raised his head from the topographic map when he heard three distant shots, then returned to his cartographic studies. The men he'd chosen to lead the two groups waited impatiently. Finally he stood.

"All right. Deacon will lead the main attack, sweeping in on the main road after John"—he nodded to the other leader, chosen more for his brutality rather than his leadership ability—"distracts them by attacking their rear border. Once the Lowmans fully engage John's force, the main group will advance until discovered, and then attack. Our goal: capture or kill the Moslem Eli; the rest is collateral damage."

He paused as they considered the plan. "Let us pray."

Reverend bowed his head, as did Deacon and John.

"Dear Lord! Give us victory this day as we capture the heathen Eli and extract your revenge for the killing of my son. Spare us casualties and smite our enemies. Delivery them into our hands, Lord! In the name of Christ, Amen!"

With muttered Amens, Deacon and John went to gather their men.

Junction of Ga. 306 and 19/400, North of Lake Lanier, Georgia, 14:30 Zulu

"That went smoother than I expected," George said, rolling down the window in the Studebaker, then slid open the vent-flange. Classic the Studebaker might be, air-conditioned it wasn't.

"I wish you wouldn't say things like that; you'll put a hex on us."

"Frank, I didn't take you to be superstitious."

"I'm not. It never hurts to be careful." Frank turned onto Ga. 400 heading south toward Roswell and Fred's place.

The fat, old-fashioned tires hummed pleasantly on the asphalt, and combined with the soporific July heat, Frank had nearly been lulled into Highway Hypnosis when the sight of two rapidly approaching motorcycles in the rearview jerked him awake.

"George, wake up! Visitors coming up behind."

George opened his eyes and hawked over his shoulder. "Damn, they're coming fast. And I don't see no teddy bears this time." George racked the 12-gauge and checked his .45.

"Neither do I," Frank said grimly. "Hold on."

Frank floored the gas pedal; the old car topped out at ninety miles an hour. "We can't outrun 'em."

He backed off, afraid to damage the ancient engine.

As they slowed, the bikes closed. George reported two riders on each bike, each passenger armed with what appeared to be an AR-15.

"Let's hope the kid was right," Frank muttered.

"Huh?"

"That this thing is bulletproof. If those are .223s, they may not penetrate."

One bike pulled even; the other took the rear. The front bike, a flat-black Harley Softail, swung near as the passenger pointed an AR-15 at the car. Frank jerked the wheel to the left, smashing into the bike, spinning it onto the asphalt and slinging the riders into a bloody heap of black leather and torn flesh.

The crack-crack-crack of an AR-15 from the rear bike was nearly synchronous with the smack of bullets impacting the car's body and rear window, which did not shatter. Frank jerked the car evasively; the bike tried to pass. Frank swung right; the bike tried to squeeze through the left lane. With a quick turn of the wheel Frank swatted the bike into the center divider, with deadly results for its riders.

"Damn, didn't have to fire a shot." George was relieved.

"I had the superior weapon," Frank said, patting the Studebaker's dash.

The rest of the trip was uneventful; Frank gave silent thanks as they pulled into Fred's driveway. "What time is it?" Frank asked, turning off the car.

"Why?"

"I feel I'm missing something important."

Interstate 75 Exit 290: Georgia
20/Canton Highway, Georgia, 13:07 Zulu

"This burning is making me crazy; we have to fucking stop." Willie's road rash, sweat-wet from riding in the hot Jeep, had him mad with itching.

"OK love, there's a service station ahead. We'll find some cream or something." Clara could tell Willie was in agony; his complaints had increased with the heat in the Jeep.

"Bill, my boy, you need to learn how to roll with the crash. Look at me, barely a scratch."

As Willie turned painfully, several scabs cracked and began weeping clear serum. He scowled at Nick. "Shut up! For the last time, shut up!"

"Or what?" Nick asked calmly.

"We're there!" Clara interjected. "Hold on while I turn."

At the deserted gas station, a few abandoned cars occupied the non-working pumps; surprisingly, there were no bodies.

"Why is no one here?" Willie asked, gritting teeth, opening his door.

"With all the hotels we passed, no need to hang out here,"

Clara said.

"Probably picked clean," Nick offered.

Clara and Nick entered the store through broken glass doors; goods lay scattered on the floor. Clara found the First Aid area and scavenged some usable antibiotic ointments, gauze bandages and pads.

"Let's go outside so I can see." She led Willie by the hand to the Jeep.

It opened the fresh scabs, but Clara removed his shirt, applied ointment, and bandaged the worst abrasions. She removed his pants and did the same for the gouges and scratches on his legs. Using a pocketknife, she made shorts of the ruined trousers, then laid the shirt against the seatback. Shirtless, Willie got in.

"Better?"

"Much, but they still hurt."

"I found no pain killers—they were probably the first things taken."

"Wimp," was all Nick had to say.

"Clara, can you and Nick fill the jerries? Hate to waste a chance."

"Sure. I'll find the keys." Clara left Willie sitting, eyes closed, as the last morning coolness soothed his skin. She searched the counter and found a locked box affixed beneath the cash register. She pried it open with a cheap screwdriver too useless to steal. Inside were keys to the pumps and a .38 Special snubnose revolver with two speedloaders. She tucked the revolver in her waistband at the small of her back and covered it with the tail of her blouse; the keys and speedloaders she put in her pocket.

Clara returned to the jeep and grabbed the siphon bucket and a jerry can.

"Get Nick to help you," Willie called.

"Haven't seen him," she answered honestly.

Willie looked around and assumed Nick was scouting.

Clara unlocked the hatches, opened the unleaded fill valve and snaked the hose through. The hand pump soon filled one jerry, which she lugged to the Jeep and topped off the tank. She returned to the fill valve, refilled and racked the jerry, stowed the pump and hose in the bucket and stowed the bucket in the vehicle.

As she climbed behind the steering wheel, Willie looked asleep; he opened his eyes as she turned the key. "Don't forget Nick."

"I'm here," Nick said from the back seat. "You didn't wake when I got in."

"Nick! I didn't hear you. I was concentrating on anything but road rash."

Clara drove west on Ga. 20, wishing she could forget Nick.

ROSWELL, GEORGIA, 15:32, ZULU

"Guys, I'm sorry, but I have to get going. Here's a map; when you get to Gaylesville, use GMRS radio channel 5 with the security code I gave you." Frank was upset over leaving, but knew he'd travel faster without having to tend Fred's wounds.

"You sure you don't want me with ya, Frank?" George asked.

"Earl and Fred need you more than I do, George; someone has to help Fred while the other drives."

"But Frank—look what happened to me when I took off alone," Fred said. "Damn near got my ass shot off, lost supplies and my truck."

"I know it makes no sense, Fred, but I must. I hope the Emersons don't mind my taking the Studebaker."

"If they were going to make it back, they'd be here by now."

Frank was grim as he loaded the Studebaker with supplies—two five-gallon plastic cans of leaded gas he'd found in the Emerson's garage, food, an AK-47 and a spare tin of AK-

47 ammo and two AR-15s with ammo from Fred's stockpile. In front, he carried a few bottles of water and some energy bars.

"We'll be an hour behind you, so don't be a hero unless it's absolutely necessary," George admonished.

"I'll be careful, but I'm getting the overwhelming feeling that I should've been at the BOL yesterday." Frank shook George's hand. "Take care of Earl and Fred; we'll need all the good people we can get. I fear this is all just a prelude to coming darkness."

Frank backed the Studebaker out of Fred's driveway, oblivious to his friends' farewells. His mind was already in Alabama.

Georgia Hwy. 20 at Alabama Hwy. 9: the State Border, 16:00 Zulu

The drive through Rome, Georgia, had been fairly uneventful: one tense moment when a group of teenagers had blocked the road, but one look at Willie's weapon had moved them out of the way. The roadblock that Katie and Marlene had earlier avoided was now abandoned. The National Guard had been called to Florida to fight Cuban and Venezuelan invaders, and local and state police had long since bailed to protect their own families. Clara studied the deserted roadblock. "Where's the Guard?"

"I don't care," Willie said. "As long as they aren't stopping us."

"Maybe," Nick offered, "they're busy somewhere else."

"What?" Clara asked.

"Nick said maybe they're busy somewhere else." Willie wondered why Clara never seemed to hear Nick, even though he heard him just fine.

Nearing Centre, Alabama, two large trucks loomed ahead,

parked nose-to-nose, blocking the divided highway. Behind them, two more trucks pulled out from concealment and blocked their retreat.

"Damn. What now, Bill?" Clara sounded panicked.

"Just stop, and we'll see what they want." Willie concealed his handgun.

Clara pulled up to the obstruction and several men armed with deer rifles and shotguns stepped out. A tall, broad-shouldered man in overalls and white tee shirt, sunglasses and feed cap, spoke: "What's your business in Centre?"

"Just passing through. On our way to Gaylesville." Clara smiled.

"What happened to your husband?"

"Motorcycle accident."

"Here's where we're going." Willie showed the hand-drawn map he'd taken from Larry Handy. "Frank Lowman invited us to stay." Willie smiled his best smile.

"Frank Lowman? I did fence work for him. OK, you can proceed. Just make sure you don't stop. Go straight on the bypass." He returned the map. "Be careful; bad people out there."

Clara and Willie stifled laughter until they were well past the roadblock.

Outside Centre, they turned off Ala. 9 onto Ala. 35 and then County Road 114. They hadn't gone a mile when they hit another roadblock.

"Who are you?" Jimmy Bob pointed the shotgun directly at Clara's face.

"Clara Jenkins. This is my boyfriend, Bill." She stared at the barrel.

"We're jus' tryin' to get to the Lowman place," Willie said.

"The Lowmans! Out, assholes." Jimmy Bob menaced with the shotgun.

"What do you want?" Clara asked as she got out of the Jeep, hands high.

"Just get out and shut up."

Willie looked nervously for Nick. Nick got away! he

thought. And for once I'm glad he did. Willie winced; scabs broke open on his forearms when he raised his hands. "Is there a problem?"

"Why're you two going to the Lowmans?" Jimmy Bob gestured again with the shotgun.

It was clear to Willie that Jimmy Bob was no friend to the Lowmans. He decided to take a risk and tell the truth. "I want to kill Frank."

Jimmy Bob lowered the weapon. "Well, Bill, you need to talk to Reverend Sanders."

Centre, Alabama, 17:00 Zulu

When Frank pulled up to the Centre roadblock, the old Studebaker was blowing steam from under the hood. The temperature gauge on the dashboard had been pegging high for thirty miles and Frank feared a blown head gasket or a radiator hose before he could get to Katie. His sense of dread had strengthened with each mile. At the makeshift roadblock in Rome, he'd worried, but put pedal to metal and crashed through like a bulldozer, scattering the ragged teenagers. A few .22 caliber rounds had spattered the bullet-resistant glass, but nothing else had slowed him on his race to the BOL. Until this roadblock.

"Whoa, where you headin' so fast?"

As Frank lowered the window, the man in the feed cap looked into the car. "Frank, that you? What the heck you doin' with this old bucket o' bolts?"

"I need to get home, Harold. Please, let me through."

"Sure thing, Frank, but this ol' car ain't gonna make it. Way it's blowing steam, I'm s'prised it's made it this far."

"I need to get to Katie. Something's wrong."

"Hold up a second." The man called to the other

roadblockers, "Anybody got a car to loan Frank Lowman? I'll vouch for him."

"How 'bout a four-wheeler?" hollered Ted Silas, owner of a used-equipment lot. "We got a couple old ones what still run." Frank had bought his used tractor from Ted.

"That OK, Frank? Leave this to cool? Borrow Ted's four-wheeler?"

"Sure, anything. I'll even throw in ten gallons of leaded gas." Frank indicated the containers, handed over the keys, and gave thanks. He strapped the AK-47, an AR-15, ammo and a few supplies onto a 1988 Honda 300 4x4 FourTrax and nearly pulled a wheelie roaring out.

Southwestern border, Lowman property, Alabama, 17:00 Zulu

John Smit's radio crackled to life. "Group One, begin the attack."

John, as he'd been instructed, gave the two-click response. Slipping the radio in his pocket, he signaled his men to cross the Lowman property line. In preparation, John had already cut the barbwire fence in several locations, and, for the pleasure of it, tore down and tossed aside Frank's No Trespassing signs.

Using woodsman's skills learned hunting deer and turkey, the men of Group One advanced silently toward the heart of the Lowman land until the first mine went off with a roar of escaping CO_2 and the screams of a man doused with capsaicin-laced water, followed by the blast of a 12-gauge–birdshot tripwire. A deadfall trap wounded a third. Without firing a shot, the Lowmans had reduced Smit's squad by 25 percent and alerted themselves to the attack.

"Hell, boys, they know we're coming now. Charge!" John bellowed.

At the trailer, Katie watched the perimeter penetration and smiled as the traps triggered. As John shouted, she grabbed her Mosin-Nagant, stashed an open ammo tin in a carry bag and ran to reinforce the battle line.

Everyone converged on the southwest border. When Katie realized the rest of the perimeter was unguarded, she ordered Marlene and David to keep watch—David outside the trailer and Marlene on the monitors—and radio if anything else happened. Grim-faced, she shoved a stripper clip into the top of the Mosin, forced five rounds of 7.62x54 ammunition into its internal magazine, removed the empty clip and rammed the bolt home. With a fully loaded rifle she turned to face the invading rednecks.

Reverend heard the first shots—at least he thought he did. Actually, he'd heard the 12-gauge tripwire alarms scattering birdshot several yards. Unaware his shock force was down four men before the real shooting even started, Reverend told Willie, "God is with us!"

"I don't think so," Nick whispered to Willie, but Willie shushed him, which drew an odd look from Reverend.

"I want to be the one to kill Lowman," Willie repeated.

When Willie had learned what Reverend and his band were up to, he'd first made the request. And when Reverend heard Willie's tale of recent events— and getting assurances he and Clara were Christian—he readily accepted them.

"I told you, Bill, I don't think he's in there. But after we get the nigger Moslem, you can do what you want, with my blessing." Reverend smiled to hear distant screams, certain it was those heathens shielding his son's killer.

Katie drew a bead on the first invader, hiding behind a four-inch-diameter pine tree. Hating the long pull of the Mosin trigger, she held sight on the man's chest until the Mosin roared with smoke and fire. The 149-grain fully jacketed bullet, barely pausing in the pine, completely pierced the breastbone of the man behind it, the wound channel splitting the lungs where the trachea branched. Bone fragments from the shattered torso pierced spongy tissue. The man was dead without having fired a shot. Katie drew a bead on another, who seemed to be the leader, as his companions commenced firing.

Eli was racking his third kill and Max her second when Katie's next round killed John. Disheartened, the remnants of Smit's squad dropped their weapons and fled. They hadn't signed up for dying.

Reverend, mistaking the now silent battlefield as a positive sign, gave the order for his men to advance and mop up, and learn if the Moslem still lived. Willie, ordering Clara to stay behind, took a 12-gauge pump shotgun loaded with double-ought buck and followed Reverend and his men into battle.

"Keep on!" Reverend bellowed as tripwires, deadfalls, and tangle-foot traps injured or incapacitated man after man. At the monitors, Marlene watched wide-eyed as the main force advanced up the dirt driveway.

"Kaitie!" she yelled into the radio. "Attack at the main entrance. Hurry!"

"Roger that, Marlene, on our way," Katie gasped. She signaled Eli and Max to follow and ran toward the trailer. Marlene grabbed her Mosin and ran to the pole barn, where she hunkered behind a water catch-barrel and drew a bead on the first man coming up the driveway.

Willie was glad to see Nick beside him as he followed Reverend up the dusty driveway. Nick was armed with an old Mauser; where he'd gotten it, Willie didn't know or care. At least he was there.

When the point threw up his arms and keeled over, blood blossoming on his back, everyone dropped to ground almost before the rifle report reached them.

"Jimmy Bob—take five men, go up by the house and come around behind them," Reverend ordered.

Nervously, Jimmy complied, picking five at random. They crawled until they were out of sight of the trailer, then stood and ran toward the house, smack into more mines and tripwires. Three made the house, although two of those could barely see through their burning eyes.

"Bill, take five men over that way and come up that side.

We'll put 'em in a tong and hammer!"

Willie chose four others, counting Nick to make five, and led his assault party in the indicated direction.

"When the other groups start shooting, we'll advance. Deacon Carl, you lead the charge," Reverend ordered. Deacon smiled and cycled the bolt, running a round into his 300 Weatherby Magnum. On the far side of the house, Jimmy Bob and his three-man squad crept through long meadow grass to the trailer. Unknown to them, Eli had scrambled on top of the trailer and could clearly observe them. As Willie attacked their left flank, Katie and David joined Marlene at the water barrel.

Before they could react, David took a .223 round to the shoulder.

Screaming with fury after seeing her son wounded, Marlene became possessed. An automaton, she aimed, fired, cycled the bolt, aimed, fired, reloaded, and started again. Katie joined in, pinning down the attackers trying to flank them.

Methodically, Eli aimed and fired, killing two more of the squad before Jimmy Bob and his last man abandoned weapons and stood, hands up. Eli climbed down from the trailer roof, tie-wrapped the pair together, and ran to rejoin the battle.

The three angry women's withering fire drove Willie's squad back. Nothing seemed to stop the Mosin-Nagant rounds. Willie watched a man killed while standing behind an eight-inch-diameter oak. With only one other man and Nick remaining, he fell back to Reverend's position.

Reverend, nearly blind with rage, ordered Willie and the sole survivor of his squad to join Deacon's men, then ordered Deacon to attack.

Sending his weakest men in first, Deacon ordered them to draw fire so he could get a bead on the shooter. He put the scope of his 300 Weatherby Magnum to his eye and scanned around the trailer—the punctured water barrel would soon offer no protection. At the trailer, Katie noticed the same thing.

"Marlene, Max—we have to find better cover. The barrel is leaking like a sieve. Marlene, listen to me!" She had to shake Marlene to get her attention. "We'll cover you—run behind the tractor."

Marlene gazed skeptically at the tractor and then back at Katie and Max, still firing at the invaders. She looked at her wounded son, wishing she could drag him to safety. But until they ended the threats, there was no safety.

"OK. Then I'll cover you while you join me."

"Get ready," Katie aimed her Mosin at the cluster of prone men near the middle of the driveway. "Go!" she yelled, pumping out round after round, the metal butt-plate of the Mosin kicking painfully into her already raw shoulder. Between her and Max's fire they kept the invaders' heads down.

"Damn!" Deacon yelled, dropping prone as a round from Max's rifle passed so close he could hear it buzz. He brought the rifle to bear on the water barrel. Aiming dead center, he began squeezing off a round.

Dropping behind the tractor, using the front-end-loader blade as a shield, Marlene aimed at the prone men in time to see the Weatherby's muzzle flash and the water barrel erupt like a geyser. Katie screamed.

"No!" Marlene cried, afraid she had lost her son and her best friend. She aimed where the muzzle blast had been and squeezed off a reply.

Katie shook her numb hands. Max was frantic, certain she would find her mother mortally wounded. The .300 caliber round had mushroomed in the water barrel and then slammed into the receiver of the Katie's Mosin-Nagant, knocking the rifle into her chest and probably leaving a nasty bruise, but saving her life. As feeling in her hands returned, she examined the rifle. Other than a small crack in the stock below the impact point, she saw no damage, and smiled reassuringly at Max. She worked the action, ejecting a live round—everything worked.

"Marlene, I'm OK, they hit the rifle," she called out, unsure if Marlene could hear over the relentless shooting. Katie waited until Marlene was reloading and then called out again, "Marlene, I am OK. Cover me!" Still unsure if Marlene had heard, she braced, gathered the Mosin and the ammo bags, and ran to join her friend as soon as Marlene opened up again. With Marlene and Max providing cover, she was safe from return fire.

"Marlene, I'm OK," Katie said a third time, breathlessly, dropping beside her friend, safe behind the loader blade.

Marlene gaped: "But I saw the bloody barrel explode."

Katie showed her the spot on the receiver where the bullet had deflected, then there was no time as Reverend forced his men once more to the attack. With Marlene and Katie providing cover, Max joined them behind the blade.

Deacon winced as he pulled a two-inch sliver from his arm. Marlene's first shot after she'd thought that Katie was dead had shattered his rifle stock, driving splinters into his arm and face. He felt cold anger building as he tossed aside the ruined rifle; it had been his favorite. He pulled the accuritized Colt .45 Commander from his holster and again ordered his men forward.

Reverend grabbed Willie's arm as he started to go with Deacon. "Bill, you stay here and guard me; Deacon can handle this."

"Yeah," Nick spat. "He's done such a brilliant job so far."

Willie was glad the gunfire cacophony muffled Nick's snide remark.

About a mile from his property, Frank heard the unmistakable clang and clamor of a pitched battle—the boom of shotguns, the sharp crack of Mosins and the stutter-pops of lesser rifles and handguns. Knowing it was foolish to ride front-and-center into the middle of a gunfight, he parked the Honda at the property corner. Leaving the AK-47 but taking several extra magazines for the AR-15, he crept into the woods to get a closer view, hoping he wasn't too late. Passing the observation post he noted one dead body. Further in, he saw landmine remnants and smelled the sharp odor of capsaicin. "Katie you clever girl," he said softly, now doubly alert for the slightest sign of disturbed earth or tripwires.

Meanwhile Deacon, with ten rifles firing at Katie, Max and friends, moved relentlessly uphill toward the trailers. Even with Eli joining them, the defenders' four rifles were no match for the combined arms of Reverend's men firing as one.

"We have to fall back," Katie said. "If we can make the bluff behind the pond we'll have the advantage of high ground."

"You women go. I'll cover," Eli yelled, firing his rifle, its barrel so hot the residual cosmoline in the wooden hand guard was smoking. Katie and Marlene fell back, taking cover where possible and providing covering fire for Eli when he retreated. Katie's ammo sack was getting distressingly light and her shoulder was bruised raw. She wondered how much longer she could continue.

Frank made it to one of his deer stands. The platform, thirty feet up in a pine, would provide a perfect place to observe. Rifle slung over his shoulder and spare magazines stuffed in his pockets, he climbed the screwed-in pegs to the elevated stand. Strapping on a safety harness, Frank studied utter carnage: several bodies lay in driveway dirt, several wounded, crying out, were nevertheless ignored by their fellows, who were single-mindedly advancing up the hill and firing toward the trailers, which were blocked from his view by trees.

"Enough of this shit," he spit through clenched teeth, unslinging the rifle and pulling back the charging handle to cycle a .223 round into the battery. Putting rifle to shoulder, he methodically began to assassinate the attackers. As soon as one stopped moving—usually after a single shot—he moved on to another, and another, grimly destroying the rest of Reverend's forces. At first Reverend Sanders didn't realize what was happening. He'd been concentrating so much on the forward attack he failed to notice men falling until a fourth body hit dirt.

"Deacon, you are being flanked!" he blurted into the radio, but realized Deacon couldn't hear him over the gunfire. Raising binoculars, he scanned the trees, finally spotting Frank as he pumped round after round into his remaining men. He dropped the glasses, turned to Willie and pointed to Frank's sniper nest. "You wanted a chance to kill Lowman—you got it."

Smiling, Willie racked a round into his shotgun and snaked down the driveway, planning to come up behind Frank.

Reverend's men finally understood they'd been flanked and began searching for new attackers. But, unaware that the new threat was a lone man in a tree stand, they peppered the woods with wild shots, clearly starting to panic. Deacon sensed he'd lost the momentum; he had to do something or he'd lose his men—and the battle—to panic.

"Cease fire! Take cover!" he ordered, but few were paying attention; they were too busy shooting at shadows behind every tree.

Noting the confusion, Frank halted fire and stepped to place the tree between himself and Deacon's remaining force. But Willie, undetected, slowly advanced onto Frank's position. He knew the shotgun didn't have a rifle's range; he needed to close. Besides, he wanted to see the look on that bastard's face when he realized who it was that shot him.

Katie, Marlene, Max and Eli didn't know what had happened to ease the attack, but they were grateful for the respite. Max and Eli quickly dragged David to the trailer and Marlene bandaged his shoulder wound.

"Katie . . . ! Max . . . !" It was Reverend's voice.

Katie and Max looked at each other, wondering.

"We don't have to fight. Just give us Eli and we'll go."

Eli put down his rifle and started standing. "Ma'am, I will go to them. I don't want to see you die to help me." Katie pulled him down. "Eli, no! You'll do no such a thing."

"Tell you what, Reverend," Katie yelled, bringing a tired smile to her crew. "Pick up and leave and I promise I won't kill all your men."

"I still outnumber you," Reverend rejoined.

"Not for long," Frank muttered, taking a bead on Reverend.

Suddenly a 12-gauge boomed; Frank felt the scoring of pellets along his left arm and cheek, nearly dropping his AR-15 in shock.

"You asshole, Frank! You left me to die in New York. Now it's your turn," Willie cried, stepping wide around a tree to get a finishing shot, but his right heel snagged an active tripwire, which triggered a buried mine and an engulfing fog of Capsaicin-saturated water. His road-rash bandages acted like wicks, drawing the burning fluid deep into his gashes and lacerations.

Dropping his shotgun, Willie screamed as nearly every nerve in his damaged flesh protested at once. The vapor filling his eyes and mouth made him cry and choke and rub at his eyes, which only made things worse. As Willie passed out from pain he heard the sound of Nick's laughter.

When Frank heard the whish of the CO_2 cartridge releasing, he knew what was happening. Taking a bead on the body thrashing beneath his tree, he started to squeeze the trigger, but when Willie's body went limp, Frank lowered the rifle. Through the bandages he recognized the senator's son from the New York hotel and felt regret. Maybe if he'd been nicer...

From the driveway, Deacon watched what transpired at the deer stand. Grabbing a rifle from one of his men, he dialed the 3-by-9 scope to its maximum value and centered the crosshairs on Frank. As he was about to pull the trigger, his head exploded.

"Never cared for Deacon Carl," Katie said, lowering her Mosin.

After watching their leader collapse, the remaining assault force fled—a gun-dropping rush to escape these mad women and their man-eating rifles. No amount of cajoling or threat of damnation would return them to the fight. Grabbing an abandoned rifle, Reverend took aim at Katie watching the retreat, but before he could fire, a single pistol shot sang out and Reverend dropped, seemingly lifeless, to the ground.

"Asshole. You got my Billy killed," Clara said, dropping the .38 revolver in the dirt and running to where Willie lay semiconscious.

Frank sat on the deer stand as a wave of dizziness hit. Afraid he'd drop the AR-15, he laid it behind him. Blood freely flowed from the pellet wounds and his last thought before he passed was My Katie is OK.

By the time Eli and Katie reached Frank, Clara and Willie were gone.

As they puzzled how to safely lower Frank, George and Earl and Fred arrived in the Montero, followed by Kevin Fairfield and several men from Centre who'd heard the extended gunfire at the Lowman place. With their help, Frank was lowered down from the deer stand.

"Looks like we missed all the fun," Earl said, looking around at the carnage.

Marlene hit him.

Day Five

Ravine at the edge of the Lowman property, 02:00 Zulu

Eli moved the attackers' bodies to the ravine until townspeople could come for them. Reverend regained consciousness lying with his cheek pressed against the remains of Deacon's face. Clara's revolver shot had grazed Reverend's skull, knocking him nearly comatose.

Clutching his throbbing head, Reverend struggled to a sitting position, then became gradually aware of someone speaking...

"There's a creek down a bit where you can get some water."

The voice was pitched low and melodious.

"I'd come down to help you but I have a bum leg."

Reverend looked up at the ravine's crest toward the voice, but the night was dark and the moon inadequate.

"Who are you?" Reverend called out weakly from a parched throat. Grabbing the remains of Deacon's 300 Weatherby and using it as a crutch, he clambered to his feet.

"A friend. The creek is a dozen yards down. I'll join you there."

Reverend hobbled down the ravine, finally reaching a creek, where he fell gratefully to his knees and drank of the muddy water.

"Feel better? There's a working car down that path, at the road."

Turning to the voice, Reverend saw a man standing with his back to the moon, his face in shadow. Reverend held out his hand.

"My name is Reginald, Reverend Reginald Sanders."

"No offense, Reverend, but I have a thing about being touched. You can call me Nick."

—Finis—

Made in the USA
Coppell, TX
27 August 2024

36535017R00138